The Honeymoon

The Honeymoon

JUSTIN HAYTHE

PICADOR

For Muriel

First published 2004 by Picador

This edition published 2005 by Picador
an imprint of Pan Macmillan Ltd
Pan Macmillan, 20 New Wharf Road, London N1 9RR
Basingstoke and Oxford
Associated companies throughout the world
www.panmacmillan.com

ISBN 0 330 41989 7

1 3 5 7 9 8 6 4 2

A CIP catalogue record for this book is available from
the British Library.

Typeset by SetSystems Ltd, SaffronWalden, Essex
Printed and bound in Great Britain by
Mackays of Chatham plc, Chatham, Kent

All Pan Macmillan titles are available from www.panmacmillan.com
or from Bookpost by telephoning 01624 677 237

Part One

A word of encouragement for the travelers, the explorers,
the seekers – you can find what you're looking for in the world.
It's all out there, don't let anyone tell you different.

M. C. Garraty, *Turned Back at the Border:
An Art Guide to the Great Cities of Europe*

Life goes on and on after one's luck has run out.
Youthfulness persists, alas, long after one has ceased to be young.
Love-life goes on indefinitely, with less and less likelihood of
being loved, less and less ability to love, and the stomach
ache of love still as sharp as ever.

Glenway Wescott, *The Pilgrim Hawk*

One

On a nice day, we used to go out as if we were going out for a night on the town. I sat on the bed and watched her dress the way she thought a French woman would dress: a thin blue sweater, yellow linen trousers with a zip on the side, a hat for the sun. Light from the window fell at her feet. Her hair was folded up beneath her hat, a few loose strands dabbing at the nape of her neck as she leaned down to put on her shoes without bending her knees.

We spent our afternoons in the museums; our mornings in the park across the street. The leaves on the branches were swollen with sunlight. All across the park, the trees staggered with the weight. We walked around the empty pond, along the gravel path and through the flower beds until we found a bench in the shade of a tree. It was a wealthy part of the city. Most people had gone away to the beach or to the mountains and only tourists or those unfortunate enough to have to work all summer spent their mornings in the park. The tourists sat in outdoor cafes while the workers ate sandwiches and bathed their feet in the fountains. Maureen did not consider us tourists.

The only other children in the park were the children of wealthy Arabs, dressed in perfect miniature suits and dresses. They came with nannies and minders, and spoke English like royalty. I stood watching until they invited me to join in. We chased each other around the fountain and over the prohibited grass while Maureen sat aloof and reading, a shoe dangling from her foot.

When I grew tired of the game, she put away her book and took my head on her lap. 'To the museum?' she asked. She lifted her hands on either side of her, palms up, as if it was she who guided the airplanes on to their destination. 'Aren't we lucky?' she would ask, and I felt as if we were. But it was the breeze that answered, spinning the leaves above us with the sound of faint applause.

Maureen had wanted to live in Paris for a long time. She had aspired to it. As it happened, we stayed there only briefly, for just a few months, in an apartment she borrowed from a friend.

She had met Marcel somewhere else, in another European city I was too young to remember. That's what he told me when we met. We stood in the front hallway of his apartment and shook hands. 'We've met before,' he said. 'You were small.' He kissed Maureen on both cheeks and then held her by the shoulders. He said, 'Look at you.' She stepped back out of his grasp so that we could look at her. 'You have a beautiful mother,' he told me.

This was June of 1980. I was eleven years old and he was leaving for the summer. I have often wondered if he and my mother were sleeping together. He was twenty years older than she was, heavy-set, with a thick moustache. On the train into Paris, Maureen had assured me that Marcel was, in some ways, a great man. But I cannot help remembering his hands on her body, on her clothes where he could feel what she wore underneath.

He showed us to our rooms. He put Maureen in the large bedroom where he slept, where the bed was still unmade, and showed me into the guest room that had once belonged to his daughter, Claudia. There was a single bed, a hand-painted child's desk and dark carpet. He showed Maureen the priceless artifacts on the shelves that could not be replaced if broken and the wine in the cupboard that had survived both wars and was too precious to be drunk.

Maureen and I sat opposite Marcel at lunch. He gripped the bottle of white wine by the neck, and plunged it back into the ice bucket when the glasses were full. Without turning his head, he gestured out towards the street behind him and said the best shopping in Paris was just a few streets away.

'I have no interest in shopping,' she told him. 'And besides, I can't afford it, as you well know.' He laughed as if she had said exactly what he had expected her to say.

After lunch we waited at the table for him to finish packing. We could hear him banging closets and drawers until he reappeared wearing a hat. We followed him into the hallway and waited for the elevator. He stood amongst his luggage; my mother and I amongst ours. 'Be careful of the Arab children in the park,' he told me. He turned to Maureen. '*Petits voleurs,*' he explained. She smiled although she did not understand. She would look it up as soon as he had gone. He picked up his cases and stepped into the elevator. She blew him a kiss. '*Bon voyage!*' she called.

When he was gone, the reflection of Maureen and me looked back from the mirrored elevator doors. I wore a white canvas hat and a pair of favourite copper corduroys. Maureen had yet to remove her pink silk jacket.

'Don't listen to him,' she said. 'He's trying to impress you.

Only men need to impress children. You don't need to be any more careful with one person than another.'

She began her inspection of the apartment the way she entered a gallery: as if she had money to spend. She passed from room to room with increasing excitement. When she found one more impressive than another, she called out for me to come and have a look. There was a pink study with a fireplace and a pair of French doors looking out onto the street; a small toilet off the hallway containing a gold-painted sink; and the kitchen with three Thai-wicker umbrellas bound to form a single lampshade. She could not stand still and almost as soon as I entered a room, she left it. She was like a child receiving a gift long obsessed over – slightly panicked by a world in which dreams are realized.

Marcel had inherited his money. The apartment was large for a bachelor living alone, with both a guest room and maid's quarters. It was substantially larger than our place in New York, and had a view of the park across the street and, in the evenings, of the patches of setting sun reflected from the windows onto the tops of the trees. Marcel directed documentary films, usually about the Amazon. Several years later, Maureen took me to see one when it was playing in New York. I found it slow except for one gripping sequence when Marcel sits on a log with a spectacular view of a dam behind him. As he discusses the terrible outbreak of disease amongst an Indian tribe who worked on the dam with migrant labourers from San Paulo, he carefully inches the peel from an orange. He takes great care to keep it all in one piece. When he succeeds, he looks at the peel and nods with satisfaction before tossing it into the bushes.

He had agreed to let Maureen and me live in his home while

he was away making his next film. His daughter lived in an apartment on the ground floor. Claudia was twenty-seven years old, five years younger than Maureen. He said she would keep an eye on us.

When Maureen went out to dinner or to the theatre in the evenings, she paid Claudia to come upstairs and look after me. Claudia was tall and exceptionally long-limbed, her torso nothing more than a hesitation between arms and legs. When she rose from sitting contorted on the couch, she unfolded to a startling height. Her mother was Venezuelan, but something besides foreignness was foreign between us. Aside from the desk, all that remained as evidence that she had spent her childhood in the apartment was the piece of coloured glass hung from the window frame in the room where I slept, and a small brass travel frame, the size of a matchbox, that sat on Marcel's desk. The frame opened like a locket and contained two photographs: on one side, a young unsmiling Claudia wearing a pair of swimsuit bottoms at the edge of the ocean; on the other, a lean, happy-looking Marcel against an identical background. The pictures were taken on the same afternoon, roughly in the same spot, as if this had been the only afternoon they had ever spent together.

Whenever Claudia looked after me, she fried eggs with small cubes of smoked ham for my dinner. She sat next to me on her father's sofa, smoking cigarettes and arranging her rings and earrings into piles on the table. She taught me my first French words. She did not seem to mind that my mother and I were living in her father's apartment, or that I was sleeping in her bed. Later, as I lay in that bed, I would listen to her move around the apartment. She played the piano and, when she tired of that, she talked on the phone, laughing loudly. When she hung up, I felt a terrible silence as if she had gone out and I was left all alone. Perhaps she felt the same, for after a moment, she would make another call and when she had run out of phone calls she walked around, her footsteps indecipherable from the rattle of the windows, or the lives going on in neighbouring apartments.

At the end of August, it began to rain. Maureen sat each day at her desk in the small study near the kitchen. I spent most of the week sitting at the living-room window looking out. The building opposite echoed ours: red brick with a white balustrade, a black-speared fence guarding the edge of the pavement. I thought I could see figures in the windows, but it was usually just the reflections of the sky cramping in darkness overhead.

On the fourth successive day of rain, the skies calmed for about an hour. For a brief period the street became brighter, but very soon the clouds were shifting, threatening again. In the building opposite, lights came on in the windows and, with each, a square of reflected sky disappeared. I had the sensation I was not alone. I turned to find Claudia standing in the doorway. Her hair was damp. She looked at me, at first, as if she did not know me and then she smiled. '*Bonjour,*' I said.

A moment later, Maureen appeared in the hallway behind her. She held a pen in one hand, a cigarette in the other. 'Claudia,' she said. 'I didn't hear you come in.' Claudia turned and faced Maureen. 'You're still in your pyjamas,' Maureen laughed. 'It's the middle of the afternoon!'

Claudia looked down at herself thoughtfully.

'Are you just getting up?' asked Maureen. 'I don't blame you with this never-ending rain . . . Have you heard from your father? I have some mail. The envelopes look important. You can take them.' She turned away. 'I was going to make tea,' she said, and disappeared into the kitchen.

Claudia stepped out of her shoes, leaned over and arranged them neatly against the wall. We did not say anything to one another, which was not unusual. I believed that we had an understanding.

One night, when I was almost asleep, I had heard her on the phone, weeping instead of laughing. Street light came through the piece of coloured glass she had hung at the window of her old bedroom. Claudia came into the room without turning on the lights. After a moment's hesitation, she lay down on top of the covers beside me. I felt her legs and her breathing, the weight of her grown body. I watched her face soften into sleep. I reached out my hand and laid it over hers. I thought that one of us should stay awake in case my mother returned and discovered us there together, but soon I fell asleep as well. To my great relief when I awoke the next morning she had gone.

Maureen came back with a small pitcher of milk in one hand and a plate of inexpensive petits fours in the other. She put them down on the table and switched on a lamp. The light made the sky seem darker still. 'Perhaps you can tell me if we should send any mail on to him directly . . . How do you feel? You look pale.' She put her hand to Claudia's cheek. 'Petal,' she said. Claudia leaned forward and gave Maureen a kiss.

'Oh,' said Maureen, obviously surprised. 'Thank you.' Maureen looked old beside Claudia for the first time. Petal was my mother's name for me and Claudia was, in my eyes, a grown woman.

Maureen returned to the kitchen for the tea tray. Claudia crossed the room and stood beside me, looking out. She opened the French doors and went out onto the patio as if she wanted a closer look. She stepped over the potted plants and from the railing she stepped into the sky. She had come to us for the height.

For a moment, a breeze tapped the plants against the railing and then there was a version of silence, a flexing of the space that had swallowed her before Maureen returned. She was in the middle of saying something, but when she saw me she fell quiet. She looked around as if Claudia might have concealed herself in the shadows. She stepped out onto the patio and, without getting too close, peered over the edge.

Maureen held me on her lap while we waited for the siren. Small breaths of steam escaped from the teapot. She served the tea to the police once she assured them we were in no way related to Claudia. She wandered around filling cups, the policemen thanking her politely. She forgot to put out ashtrays and after some hesitation, the men went ahead and ashed in their saucers.

Marcel came home early from the jungle. Claudia's mother sat at the table in the living room where my mother had left the petits fours and the mail. Our bags were already in the hall. Maureen told her how sorry we were. The woman silently sipped her tea while Marcel stood at the window smoking cigarettes. They did not speak in our presence. Four bars had to be sawed away from the fence on the pavement when they cut Claudia's body free. Paris was finished. So was my mother's friendship with Marcel. And then there was the airport, the plane full of people and the sky.

Two

I am an American. I live in London. I spent my childhood circling the continent of Europe. My mother was writing a book about the most beautiful things in the world.

I think that I now possess the only complete manuscript of *Turned Back at the Border: An Art Guide to the Great Cities of Europe*. Maureen was too disorganized and in some ways had too much faith to have made a duplicate. The dedication is to me – *For Gordon, my faithful assistant (of course)*. To the front page she paperclipped two photographs of herself – potential dust jacket pictures, I imagine. The first was taken quite recently here in Cape Cod in cold black and white. In the picture she sits alert on her porch in a wooden deckchair. A corner of the wood-shingle house is visible behind her, a window stands open; it is warmer than it looks. Her face is thin; her hair has grown long again. She wears a coat over her shoulders. The smoke from her cigarette is washed away in the breeze, or perhaps it is unlit. Her expression is intently serious, as if a photograph of her was something rare – as if she were someone who had renounced the world for a life of contemplation. She looks directly into the camera, at whoever was taking the picture. I cannot help wondering who that would have been? I had not imagined anyone new in her life – she never mentioned anyone – but of course there would have been someone.

The second photograph, this one in faded colour, was taken many years before. A hat the shape of a wilted Japanese mushroom rests sideways on her head. On someone else it would look ridiculous, but Maureen had great style even if she made no effort to stay up to date. The frame is cropped tightly around her. The unrecognizable outline of a statue hovers over her right shoulder. Here, she plays the privileged, slightly clumsy American beauty overseas. Her bright painted lips are parted as if she had been in mid-conversation at the moment the picture was taken; but I imagine she wasn't. I imagine she held her lips that way when she knew she was being photographed. Her blouse is unbuttoned to just beneath the frame, revealing a string of pearls and the brown downward curve of each breast. Although I do not remember the picture being taken, it is quite possible that I was the photographer. Maureen taught me how to use a camera when I was very young – perhaps only in order to document our life together, and I now have a thorough record of it all. In both pictures Maureen is posing as someone she is not. It reminds me of one of the only things I learned in art school (Maureen insisted I attend): one cannot pose for a picture without first knowing what a picture looks like.

She had a passion for art and I was her companion as we went from city to city across Europe. She had a precise idea of the sort of life she wanted. Like some of her favourite painters who travelled the world in pursuit of good light, she envisioned her life in the casual, sunlit spaces of the Old World: beneath trees, at riverbanks, reading outdoors in the shade of a canopy. We covered the same ground multiple times. She would decide there was something in a painting she needed to see again, something she had missed. When we returned to the hotels where we had stayed months or sometimes years before, my mother would greet the staff, inquiring after everyone's health since our last visit. They usually had no idea who we were. No idea about this attractive woman leaning across the reception desk kindly inquiring how the concierge's family was getting along. She treated them like our personal staff awaiting our return and did not address them by name only because these were not the sort of hotels where name tags were worn. The concierges wore musty sweaters over their neckties; the bellboys wore denim and sneakers. In better times, the hotels had been private homes. Bells in the rooms called servants who never arrived.

I was not the sort of companion she wanted. I could not sit down to dinner and discuss the paintings we had seen together. I remember meals that consisted of long silences as she held a guidebook throughout the preliminary courses when she managed with just a fork in her right hand. Only when the entrées arrived, when both hands were required, would she rest the book face down for dessert; only then did we begin conversation. She respectfully believed that, despite being a child, I did not need constant entertainment; she presumed me capable, just as she was, of amusing myself. She busied herself thinking about art and about where we might go next. In her mind these were not frivolous times, not holidays.

I have been reading her book. I had not believed she would ever finish it. I have seen scraps in the notebooks she kept and from which she occasionally read aloud to me, but these seemed like notes, jottings, nothing more. I do not think I was unfair to doubt Maureen's ability to complete such a project.

Her discipline never matched her enthusiasm. She would discuss her book as if it were a living thing with anyone who would listen without having done any serious writing for several months. And she was never happier than when entertaining some tourist or businessman she found in a hotel bar. She was very pretty and easily held their attention. They sat on couches politely listening as she explained that she was writing a guidebook that would not only direct people to the great paintings, but would educate them as to what they would find when they got there. If she had her way, Maureen said, she would put an end to ignorant tourism. Perhaps a few lines from her introduction would put it best:

Who was it who who wrote that an examination should be posted at Dover and anyone who fails to pass, turned back at customs? Travel has become easier; the world has grown smaller, and the museums of Europe are filled with those who cannot tell a Van Gogh from a da Vinci much less a Vouet from a Vlaminck, and for someone passionate about art, as I am, this is deeply upsetting. I certainly do not intend that this work should take the place of night classes or correspondence courses. I am not an academic and aside from a series of well-received lectures at the Metropolitan Museum of Art in New York City, I am not a lecturer: I am a scholar as they existed a century ago. I am fascinated by the study of art and at that altar have dedicated my humble life. My interest has grown purely out of love. As my great tutor, Mrs Beryl W. Black, used to say, 'enjoyment is of the single greatest importance'. I would add, if you love art, no matter how crudely, then you have learned the first lesson of art. If you do not, you probably never will, so please, spend your holidays in the parks of

London, walk the Seine, eat pastries in Vienna, prowl the second-hand markets in Amsterdam, dance in the nightclubs along the Via Venito, or simply nap in your hotel room, but do not feel obliged to slog through the museums you cannot wait to be finished with. It is a sad affair for someone like me to see such a person slumped miserably in a coveted chair, checking his wristwatch to ascertain when he can respectably leave the gallery. Enjoy or, please, don't bother!

I remember Mrs Black. I can only recall meeting her once. I recognized her from the picture on her book that travelled with us everywhere. We were at a party in New York, I think, hosted by Mrs Black. She wore a large pair of coloured spectacles not unlike a pair Maureen wore for a short time. She sat down on a chair and held her hands out to me. I was an obedient child and came when I was called. She picked me up and put me on her lap. She was not at the time a part of our life, but there had been a year when I was a baby when she took Maureen and me under her wing. Maureen had enrolled in her class at the Metropolitan Museum of Art and proved to be an outstanding student, despite the baby who accompanied her everywhere, including the silent lecture halls. Apparently, I was an incredibly cooperative infant, almost without needs. Maureen could breastfeed and take notes at the same time. There were dinners with Mrs Black, cocktail parties. Maureen shook hands with Willem de Kooning. She sipped a gin and tonic beneath a famous Picasso and because no one else commented on it, she didn't either. She danced with older men in damp shirts and bow ties who usually invited her to come and visit their galleries. The lectures my mother gave were as a substitute for Mrs Black when she made a sudden trip to Europe. It was a way for

Mrs Black to advance Maureen's career. But there was a falling out. I am unsure if it was something Maureen did while in the charge of Mrs Black's lecture hall, or if there was some other indiscretion. Of course, I immediately think of Mr Black. Or perhaps Mrs Black had tried to define Maureen in a way she did not want to be defined. There are so many potential disagreements between teacher and pupil. I have no way of knowing. Mrs Black vanished from our lives and was referred to only in the most distant and reverent of tones. I believe, at a young age, I thought she was dead, not living in her spacious apartment on Fifth Avenue, where I spent many afternoons in my first year or two of life. And when we finally met at that party and Mrs Black told me, as she held me on her lap, how well she had known me before I was old enough to remember, it was with considerable confusion on my part.

The introduction to Maureen's book includes an 'extremely abbreviated' list of the books she found most useful:

> William Morris Davis's *A Handbook of Northern France*, from the Harvard University Press, 1918. Ford Madox Ford's *The Soul of London*, a pleasure. Lucas's *A Wanderer in London*, first published in 1906 and still the best guide available. Of course, Mrs Beryl W. Black's *The Promised Land*, Katharine de Forest's *Paris As It Is* and Moses Hadas's *A History of Rome*, *Guides Bleus Illustres Les Chateaux De La Loire* from the Librairie Hachette. The single best guide to Italy is Henry James's *Italian Hours*: he gets the essence of it . . .

The list continues for another half page, and then she goes on:

> I have included a guide to the most important works each city has to offer. There is also a general guide to the

important museums as well as an essay on my personal impressions of each city. I cannot explain my system for choosing the cities I chose and neglecting those I left out. It is not a science. It is certainly not meant as any slight to the residents of the fine cities I have ignored. I had no choice but to go on instinct. Hopefully, I have chosen cities whose artistic merits go far beyond the doors of their museums. Cities, where art is a way of life and where, quite frankly, I have felt at home. In this, I must disagree with Mrs Black when she writes, 'There is no shame in being a tourist.' In today's world, where the tourist track is so well trodden, there exist two versions of Paris, London, or Venice: one for the tourists and one where the rhythms of the city remain intact. It is not a question of shame. A guidebook is often essential, and one need not go as far as concealing it inside a newspaper or exchanging the cover with some contemporary novel written in a language one does not understand. But I urge you to hold still at times, keep conversation to a minimum, your guidebook tucked away in your bag and you may see something the tourist before you did not . . .

Most remarkable about Maureen's book is her success in recreating her voice. The lilting flirtatiousness, the mock casualness, the wholly unjustified tone of expertise: it is almost exactly as she spoke. It is a little like having her here with me again. The last time I saw Maureen was in Venice, now more then a year ago, standing in front of our hotel. It was a far grander hotel than we were used to. I had no idea that it was the last time I would see her and probably would have behaved differently had I known. We might have embraced or waved more vigorously, but then again perhaps we would have done nothing differently.

The house where I have spent the past week was Maureen's and it is a long way from Venice. She was not a guest here and could not rely on someone on the other end of the phone to change fuses or to tell her what to do with rubbish that was not picked up. Here, she did not depend on hired, uncomplicated people – who were, I think, her favourite sort of people. This was where she lived and it is a mess. I have been here just a week. I have slept in her bed and tidied up the kitchen. I found the manuscript in a box addressed to me beside what I think is a rented typewriter. I have walked along the narrow beach in the heavy winter sand and cannot imagine her living here. Maureen never had a home; she had an impressively practical yet glamorous set of luggage with faded unidentified monograms and frayed leather edges. For Maureen, a home like this would have more closely resembled a cell. And although she claimed not to have been banished to the grey Cape, that is precisely what happened. She said she had retired to finish *Turned Back*. But I know that my father's offer of the house and some economic support was conditional upon her agreement to stay on the Cape and to leave the hotels and rented apartments of Europe for good.

That my father was able, just like that, to buy a place near the water in a desirable, if seasonal, location, gives only some indication of the lifestyle my mother and I shared. I grew up with the trappings of money (if often without money itself) and while Maureen was quite capable of spending several hundred pounds on art books or on several attempts at the right hair colour when we were already short of next month's rent, there was always a sense of security to our lives. We had a means to money because we had my father, Theo Garraty of Palm Beach, Florida.

Maureen did not like to ask Theo for money. She put it off and when she finally sat down to write one of those painful letters, she became suddenly exhausted, a woman struggling to make ends meet, as if she had to get into character to write effectively. Although she had no reason to fear that he would ever say no, she laboured over each letter, performing furious calculations as she frugally smoked each cigarette down to its end. After the ceremonial depositing of the letter in the postbox, she told people that she was unable to accept invitations anywhere, even to lunch, until her fate was decided in America.

The off-white envelope would appear ten days or at most two weeks later. I remember the distinctive, elegantly handwritten address. Maureen refused to show me the letters that accompanied the cheques but, once or twice, I managed to sneak a look. He sent his love to both of us. He told Maureen he often thought of her or recounted news of an old friend of theirs, or about a place where they had been together. She read his letters without expression. 'He disapproves of us,' she used to tell me.

How to describe Theo? How to show all sides of something perpetually in motion? He exercises regularly, but remains slightly heavier than he'd like. His skin is always tan. He was considered slightly strange and was not well liked in school (this according to Maureen), but success has settled him. He is kind, and generous. All his stepchildren like him very much. They come to him for advice and money long after he is no longer married to their mother. He strikes up conversations in elevators, in airplanes, with the neighbouring tables in restaurants. He has certain stories he tells, almost indiscriminately.

Theo and I have dinner once or twice a year in the same old English dining room in the Berkeley Hotel where he likes to stay and where there are cages on the windows to prevent terrorists from throwing bombs in at the remnants of the ruling class. These dinners usually complement major life changes. My graduation occasioned such a meeting, as did his engagements and divorces. When he got married (the first and second time after Maureen) he invited me to dinner. He sat across from me, a man with his back up against the wall. He ordered noticeably more drinks than usual.

Theo appeared in very similar shape when we met at the end of one of his marriages, but he was noticeably happier in surrender. 'Some men, I think my wife would agree, should not be married. Maybe you too, Gordy. Maybe you'd agree?'

Reading Maureen's book I have come across a number of inaccuracies. For example, in the section on London there is a description of James Jacques Tissot's portrait of Frederick Gustavus Burnaby that hangs in the National Portrait Gallery:

> Tissot's very popular portrait of Burnaby shows the soldier reclining in his private chambers, his moustache freshly waxed, a cigarette raised in the air as if he were a nightclub singer. Behind him hangs a map depicting the progress of some of his most successful campaigns. The portrait helped establish Burnaby as one of the most popular public figures of his time. His escapades were legendary, not least because of his own notoriously fictional accounts which he published in paperback editions. He was nothing short of a super-hero for the boys and girls of the 1870s and 1880s;

just as the children of our day have their comic books. He continued to capture the imagination of the public and press alike until he finally died from a spear wound somewhere in Africa. I myself can confirm Mr Burnaby's effect on a child. When he was twelve years old, I took my son, who is relatively uncorrupted by television and the like, to view the painting. I told him some of the stories behind the figure and he spent the rest of the afternoon sitting crosslegged on the floor transfixed by the sinewy almost womanly figure in sash and uniform, stretched out on his divan amongst his books. I was hard pressed to get him away from it when the gallery closed, and for days after, it was all he spoke or asked about and when I put him to bed, it was stories about Mr Burnaby that he wanted to hear.

Judging from the badly photocopied image, I do not recall ever having seen the portrait. I certainly do not remember it or any other painting having had the effect she described. I only mention it to indicate my mother's willingness to distort the truth. You have to have known Maureen to understand the complicated insult that is in effect. She would have disapproved of the hero worship she describes. She had no patience for it. To suggest that I had an exaggerated fondness for Burnaby is, coming from her, a poke in the eye. Aside from the inevitable physical appreciation a child has for a hero, I can't imagine there was anything strange in my interest in this man – if I ever even saw the painting. And furthermore, from my experience, there is nothing womanly about this figure. He looks like one of those exaggerated upper-class Englishmen who, despite their ridiculous physical appearance, remain capable athletes and minor successes with women. I met one or two of these hypernostalgic and ineffective men at dinner parties when I was still

Maureen's escort and disliked all of them. They inevitably don't like Americans and have no shyness for stating the most absurd and outdated opinions. I have sat across from these sorts of men as they blurt out things like, 'Well, we all know the English write the best books,' or 'Doesn't it bother you that the blacks were savages a hundred years ago?' Maureen and I used to make fun of these men. She misrepresented me and I cannot help but think she did it on purpose.

I don't like the idea that Maureen continues to hold such influence over me, but the fact that she has already set down some record of our life together is certainly part of my motivation to record my own version of events. This will not take the form (as is often the case) of an inaccurately grim picture of my childhood. I understand enough of the world to realize that I was fortunate to be born into the life that I was. Maureen reminded me of this with regularity. She had to earn the life we shared and for me it was a gift.

I want to be true and accurate in my recount and I do not want to be accused of feeling sorry for myself. Something has happened, however. I find my life suddenly full of endings. I have wondered if this is a simple side effect of taking myself too seriously, but even with this check – stepping back and asking, 'Are you not simply taking yourself too seriously?' – I cannot avoid the simple fact that at the relatively young age of twenty-one, my life has already reached certain conclusions. So I have tried to make a short list of the places I have been, the windows I have looked out of, the cars in which I have travelled, but it feels as if I have only ever been in one room: this one, from where I am looking back.

Three

Dear Annie. I feel I owe her a letter of apology, at least of explanation. But I am not a letter writer. Is it better to know one's limitations, or to ignore them? I always thought it was better not to try at something at which failure was inevitable. What I have learned since is that you may surprise yourself; you may look up and find yourself behaving in a way totally unlike the sort of person you thought you were. For example, I married Annie when I was only nineteen and she was twenty-six. I had one serious conversation with Theo on the subject when he warned me that she would want to have children and settle down before I was ready; I would be burdened with responsibility and quite possibly crushed beneath the load. I dismissed his warning and am pleased to note that the trouble between Annie and me had nothing to do with our difference in age.

In September Annie went back to live with her father where she had lived when we first met. It was to be a temporary separation: a hiatus of a few months for us to get back on track. I put her two bags into the back of the car and put our dog Clara in the back seat. Strange, but I remember an excitement to the day as we drove up the hill, as if we were all going to the airport. I asked if she had remembered various items – her reading glasses, sneakers, her hairbrush – just as I would have had she been going on a trip. Outside her father's, I set her bags on the curb and we said goodbye. I refused her invitation to come in and say hello. Tom drives a taxi. He is a joyous man with broad features and strong stubby hands. Something about him has always made me uneasy: his fresh scent and tight trousers. Father and daughter have always seemed slightly conspiratorial together. They speak in a manner Annie has never used with me: with a real-world understanding that perhaps they feel I wouldn't be able to follow. Whenever we had him over for dinner he inevitably turned to me, usually when Annie was in the kitchen preparing the dessert, and asked, 'Still snapping away, then?' He would then lift a make-believe camera to his face and with a wink pretend to take my picture.

I realize I have not mentioned what I do for a living. I am what is called a 'back of book' photographer. Take a look in any discount catalogue from the last two years and at the back, amidst the acres of postage-stamp-sized pictures of household objects, there will be a few of mine. Little wine glass sets, miniature silverware displays – that sort of thing. My more artistic efforts line the walls of our London flat. A few sunlit portraits of Annie in the bedroom; her tan shoulders; her dark hair in the grass; a few sunsets, a few rolling rain clouds above the Heath in the living room. But I'm afraid that I am not very good. I can't tell my pictures from somebody else's. I have left the job. I no longer have any real need for money and I had not always intended to take the sort of pictures I do. When Maureen enrolled me in art college, it was with the intention of my becoming an artist. No one pointed out how far off I was.

Annie's father lived in a little block of flats on a small dead-end road jutting out into Hampstead Heath – a residential frontier surrounded on all sides by the nocturnal misdeeds of a public park. I wonder if he knew what went on at night just outside his window: what his daughter and I got up to not far away. It is the same flat where Annie grew up. He would never be able to afford it now. It has become a very popular place to live.

'You know where to find me if you need me,' she said. She turned and struggled towards the building with the two bags and the dog's leash looped around her wrist. I stood beside the car and watched her climb the steps. I think I may have waved. She put her key into the lock and turned and looked at me. She sighed and gave me a wonderful, reassuring smile. 'Off you go,' she said. And off I went.

The flat where we lived together for those two years was a place of tranquillity in a fast-moving life. A wedding gift from my father, Theo, it is in the part of London Annie and I have always liked. We had both been living nearby when we met. Annie lived with her father, and I lived in a small place in Swiss Cottage close to my art college. Annie made the place a home. She found a place for her collection of hand-blown glass on the window sill above the toilet. On her hands and knees, she redid the kitchen floor with Italian tiles she bought at a Sunday market. She lined the walls with books, and generously hung some of my very ordinary photographs.

The place became gloomy after Annie's departure. Like Maureen, I have never been much good at practical domestic tasks and fell behind in simple chores like replacing light bulbs. It is a garden flat and, in the winter months, gets only a pale light from the French doors leading to the patio and onto the steps of the garden. Neither of us are gardeners and we let the shrubbery do as it pleased. A public walkway runs along the back of the garden and from the living room it is possible to watch the bottom half of our neighbours hurrying past. The neighbourhood children often appear hunched at the rear of the garden gate sneaking cigarettes or depositing some incriminating evidence into our overgrown bushes. I have found cans of lager, even the odd pornographic magazine. I have never minded their enterprising visits. I am flattered by their trust in my discretion. I usually wander out to have a look at what small offering they've left me. In the summer, Annie and I used to cut a path out to the metal bench, and spent the occasional evening with a bottle of wine. The sunlight comes pouring through the French doors during the summers. It bathes the couch and the small dining-room table in one long slate of warm light, making the couch a very comfortable place to sleep away an afternoon. Annie and I were very happy there; it is an undeniable fact.

Our proximity to the Heath provides us with a wide collection of wildlife. We regularly have foxes nipping from the bushes to the torment of our dog. As Annie and I lay in bed one night, a large bird, what we presumed to be an owl, shattered our bedroom window. Even more remarkable, one morning about a month after Annie had moved away, I looked outside and found a peacock standing on the wall looking indignantly down into our garden. Its tail was demurely tucked away, but it remained an impressive sight. It stood there immodestly on our wall, its head undulating from side to side as if it were in a state of shock, as surprised to find itself there as I was to see it. Perhaps, looking down into our little garden, it had become suddenly aware that it wasn't in India or wherever peacocks come from. I watched the bird for several minutes and when I looked up again, it was gone. There was no sign of it. I remember wanting to tell someone about it and having no one to tell. Later that week there were signs posted along the street with a small cloudy photograph of two peacocks, one of them, presumably, the one I had seen, with an urgent request for information concerning its whereabouts. I called the number and although I assured the man who answered I had no further information but what I had told him, he insisted on coming over.

He was an elderly man with coarse, wavy hair covering only a triangular third of his head. He sat in our living room with a cup of tea. He made no comment about the room's relative darkness and as the afternoon wore on and I did not get up and turn on the remaining working lights, we slowly faded from each other's sight. This did not prevent him from talking, however, and his voice came at me from the darkness all afternoon. He had been an engineer before he retired. I sat there trying to imagine him in a hard hat. His wife was ill. I think he wanted my company in his unhappiness. He asked me several times where my wife was and I told him each time she was at work (which was technically true) and that she would be home soon, but I don't think he believed me.

He gazed outside, occasionally shaking his head as he recounted stories about his peacocks and the mischief they got into. They had never before gone missing for more than a few hours. He referred to them by name. I don't remember what they were called, except that it was incongruously ordinary; the sort of names one might give canaries or small dogs, but not peacocks. He had been robbed a few years earlier, he explained. Apparently, peacocks make wonderful guard animals. When threatened or startled, they become nasty and make a terrible noise. 'And,' he added, 'your average burglar does not know what they eat, so they're difficult to charm. They eat meat, interestingly enough. Famous for their ability to eat poisonous snakes without being affected by the poison.'

We shook hands at the door and he thanked me for the tea. He told me he would be in the pub on the corner that evening and would I be interested in joining him for a drink, his treat, in return for my trouble? I told him I would and he seemed very pleased and shook my hand again. I did not go and join him that evening, however. I saw him in the street once or twice after that and he nodded coldly, but did not stop to say hello. I never learned whether or not he found his peacock. I found his desire for my company unnerving. There are forty years between our ages and I didn't like the idea that he recognized himself – a sufferer – in me.

Four

The last time I saw Annie was just over a week ago, before I left London. We agreed to meet on the Heath. I wore my best pair of shoes. I don't know what possessed me to wear the shoes. Rain was inevitable. It was our first meeting since she'd gone; it felt like a special occasion I suppose.

On the pavement, my feet pinched reassuringly. I have reason to remember the details of that day. The streets were full of hammering men. Everywhere you look these days things are being built. According to the London news, we are enjoying a real-estate boom of unprecedented proportion. On Radio 4 there has been angry talk that England is going the way of America with apartment buildings and convenience stores, office softball in the park.

I waited for Annie sitting on our bench. The inscription in the backrest reads, *For Letitia Becksworth Who Fed the Birds Here 1918–1984*. For no particular reason, it is the bench where we've always met. We met there before we were married and during our little marriage as well. I looked across the flat stretch of earth towards the trees, in the direction I knew she would come from, and imagined what I would look like, sitting in the same spot, on the same bench where she had seen me so many times before. I wanted to look impressive, dignified, if alone. I leaned back, spread both arms across the back of the bench and crossed one leg over the other, pointing my shoe in the direction of the ponds. Time passed. We were to meet at two o'clock and two o'clock came and went. I began to worry she had changed her mind and wouldn't be coming after all.

When I was twelve years old, Maureen and I drove seven hours from New York to Montreal of all places, a vast greyness, to catch a cheap flight to Europe. I imagine that with the cost of rental car and petrol the cost was probably the same as flying from New York. Anyway, we never flew from Montreal again. It was early spring. The city had just emerged from a great freeze and there was a scorched light in the air. To make things worse, it was raining. Maureen's red hair hung in delicate curls beneath her knitted orange hat. We were late and in a rush, but had arrived with enough time to spend a few minutes in the magazine store. We momentarily separated. I left her with the trolley and our luggage and went to look for something to read. A few minutes passed before I heard her let out a scream. 'Someone's taken my bag!' I came around the stack of magazines and found her pulling luggage off the trolley and telling the embarrassed shop attendant that of course she was sure, and that she had turned her back for only an instant. When she saw me, she said it again, 'My bag, Gordon!' A crowd was gathering. 'Well, go out and have a look!' she said. I left the store to see if I could see anyone suspicious, only to find myself followed by another shop attendant who thought I was trying to steal the magazine I still held in my hand. Our passports and tickets were in her purse, as was her wallet and all our money. Finally, an airport official arrived: a man in a good suit and a red tie. Maureen all but fell into his arms. She had begun to cry. He pushed our trolley for us as we walked the length of the terminal. As we went, people stopped and looked at us, wondering what was wrong. He only stopped reassuring Maureen to snap seriously into his walkie-talkie in French. We sat in a security office for almost an hour as Maureen sniffled and filled out a form and then we were escorted to the Air Canada first-class lounge. Our flight left without us. Someone made Maureen a cup of tea and gave me a 7up. We were joined by a series of airport officials who tried to come up with a solution; did we have friends we could stay with? Could they fly us back to New York? Maureen looked at them seriously and told them that we had no one, that all we had was each other and that what was in that bag represented most of our worldly possessions. Just when she had silenced the last and most senior of the officials, she finished her cup of tea. She held out her empty cup and, instinctually, the official took it from her. 'Could I have a little more, please?' she asked. As I watched her grow increasingly comfortable in the luxurious surroundings and slowly extract for us two free nights in an airport hotel (time enough to have new passports issued) and tickets for a later flight to London, I was suddenly over-whelmed by the thought that I understood why Theo had left her. The realization seemed so terrible I could not look at her as she sat beside me. I remember staring into the magazine I had been allowed to keep free of charge. I was afraid she would be able to guess what I was thinking from my expression. I had understood what made her unlovable – why Theo had cast us off – but, years later, as I sat across from Theo at some dinner somewhere, I suddenly realized that it was she who had left him.

I have been told the fact that I have no real brothers and sisters is part of my misfortune. Siblings are the means by which children reassure themselves that it is their parents and not they who are partially insane. Annie and I have no children. Until quite recently – sitting on that bench, for instance, when I imagined what she would look like coming across the Heath, her skirt moving in time with the branches, a breeze offering an unexpected glimpse of her legs – I still felt hopeful about those things. If we did have children, would they be able to decide clearly who left whom? I feel Annie left me, and it was she who packed and sat down on the edge of our bed where I was still partially asleep. 'Gordon,' she began. 'I have something to tell you . . .' The rest dwindled off into silence; I cannot remember what she said, only that she got up and moved around the room and then came back to sit down again and was talking all the time. She said it was me who had left her. I stopped working; I stopped doing anything at all, she said. When we were in the room together, I was nowhere nearby. But if we had children, a son perhaps, and he boarded a plane with Annie, would he be able to guess?

Our dog, Clara, a blur of chocolate-coloured hair, came first, bounding from beneath the branches. She stopped, her head erect, and although I was much too far away, I thought perhaps she had a happy sense that I was near. Instead of bounding towards me, however, she pushed her face into the silver grass. Field mice torment her. She can hear them calling from under the ground. She digs for them, occasionally gets one, accidentally kills it and then seems to feel terrible. She spends several minutes throwing it up in the air, trying to wake it up again, before giving up and mournfully carrying it around in her soft mouth.

After a moment, Annie appeared behind her. She looked up and waved and then trudged slowly towards me. It took Annie a long time to cross the grass and I had a long time to watch her come. She wore one of her father's coats, rolled at the sleeves, reddish brown, and surrounding her like a cape. She held her arms folded across her chest and did not reach up to comb away her hair when the wind blew it into her eyes. Clara kept her nose pressed firmly into the dirt until Annie turned and said some encouraging word. It was inaudible to me across the windy Heath.

I stood up to greet her. Annie is very short so when she arrived she seemed still to be coming, a little way off on the horizon. She smiled brightly. 'Hello, Gordon.' There was an awkward pause in which, if we were that sort of couple, we might have embraced. But we were not that sort of couple. For a terrible moment, I thought we might shake hands, but instead she touched my arm, went up on her tiptoes and kissed my cheek. The first impression one gets when meeting Annie is of her size (she is five foot two) and of how well she compensates for this fact by being so well proportioned. Or perhaps it is only me who notices her size and her proportions as I am almost six foot three and together we must have looked at times, dancing for instance, an odd pair. Her skin is pale white, her eyes small and blue. Her dark hair is thick and curly. She photographs well, as I once told her, and which she said was a backhanded insult, although I did not intend it to be.

With the initial greeting out of the way we seemed even more like strangers than before. From across the park we may have looked to be engaged in the first stuttering steps of a love affair. She sat down beside me. Her fingers trembled as she lit a cigarette. The smoke poured out of her, disappearing immediately into the breeze as if it had nothing to do with her. 'Quite cold, isn't it?'

'Yes,' I said. I reached over and took one of her hands and warmed it between mine.

'It's good to see you,' she said. She removed her hand and patted me reassuringly on my knee. She turned on the bench so that she was facing me. She softened her gaze slightly, doing her trick of emphasizing the space between us so that I was suddenly aware of the warmth of her breath and the strands of hair leaning out towards me on the breeze. It was very persuasive.

We sat together in silence for a moment and then she stood up. 'Should we walk?' she asked. I said we should. She wore jeans and a pair of practical Wellington boots, not the skirt I had imagined for her. She pointed down at my shoes. 'Are you all right in those?' she asked. 'Maybe we should stay on the path.'

'I'm all right,' I said.

'You'll ruin them,' she protested.

'No, I'm fine,' I said. 'Really.'

'Well, if you don't mind.'

We walked in a long loop, through thick wooded places at times. Annie put Clara on the lead when we were near the pond. We paused and looked over the red-brick bridge into the shallow water. We passed the parking lot where there is a fairground in the summertime in which a very somber man was burning wood, his face blackened. An enormous flame leapt in and out of a barrel in front of him. He kept his eyes perfectly focused on the flame and, at moments, it seemed to be jumping up and playfully tapping him on the nose. He had an incredible amount of wood to burn; he seemed to be burning an entire building. We walked up towards the swimming ponds, past Kenwood House. In a crevice between two banks a great tree had fallen. Clara wandered in and out of its branches and lay down in the puddle where it had pulled up its roots. Half of the twisted branches were broken. If the tree were righted they would have fallen to the ground as sticks.

We walked all the way to the other side of the Heath, where the buildings sadly reappeared. The Heath is, unfortunately, smaller than I once thought. We didn't talk very much. We don't have children to talk about. We don't, currently, have a marriage, and all the day-to-day things married people talk about. We talked about Clara, our dear, but fairly stupid chocolate Labrador. We talked about Annie's family. We did not talk about my work as my failure to do any of it lately infuriates her. We did not talk about her work for she has never believed her sort of work was worth talking about. So for long periods of time, we said nothing at all.

From the foot of the hill, the people at the top seemed to be barely attached to the earth. We walked up the steepest side, looking up at them, dark figures with dogs, kites and pushchairs.

'It was lovely to see you,' she said when we had reached the top.

'You're not going?' I asked.

She shook her watch down on her hand and checked the time. 'I think I should.'

'Let's sit down for a moment.' I suggested. 'Please.' I sat down and patted the cold wood beside me.

'You said on the phone there was something you wanted to talk to me about.' She stood there a moment, I think hoping I would get up again, and then she sat down as if she were exhausted. 'I thought maybe it was about Christmas. I've decided I'm going to spend it with my dad. He's going to Portugal.' I looked up at her. I must have looked unhappy because she went on. 'Look, we've never particularly liked Christmas, Gordon. I always want to go away, and you don't want to do anything.' She waited for me to say something and then shook her head. Her pale cheeks were red from our walk. She rubbed my arm vigorously as if she had just given me an injection and stood up. She took the lead out of her pocket and called out for Clara.

'Maureen died on Sunday,' I said. I don't know why I said it. 'In America.'

Her back was partially turned, her words swept away in the wind. 'Well, that's where she lived,' I think she said. I know she felt I had trapped her. When she turned back she said, 'Gordon, I'm so sorry. You must be so upset.'

'I'm not.'

'Of course you are, Gordy.' She sighed heavily. 'What are you going to do now?' she asked.

'I'm supposed to make the trip.'

She sat down and rubbed my arm again, this time more gently. 'I can stay a bit longer,' she said. 'But let's keep walking, otherwise I'm going to freeze.'

Five

Jean Baptiste Greuze, French, b. 1725, d. 1805. One of the great moralists. His painting, *Broken Eggs*, is the most amusing of the moralist genre. He spent a great deal of time practising women's expressions at moments of great suffering and moral angst. These studies, seen in a series, however, appear to be a chronicle of the ecstatic moment. The painting, a clunky allegory for lost virginity, shows an older woman wearing one of these ecstatic, agonizing expressions Greuze was so practiced at depicting, as she has just been informed of her daughter's deflowering. The daughter, slumped on the floor, having just broken her basket of eggs, stares blankly into her lap. Beside her, her younger brother, presumably an idiot, tries futilely to put a broken egg back together. Of course, there are things that cannot be undone, Greuze tells us, but this is incomprehensible to the innocence of a child. Interesting, as if less were known about the moralizing and arch-Catholic Greuze, the image would be far more ambiguous. One could not be blamed for thinking the figures depicted here are, in fact, laughing at the child's stupidity, and revelling in the bawdy scene which, judging from the maiden's dishevelled clothing, had taken place moments before.

Losing love, Maureen used to say, is like falling from a window and breaking every bone in your body. You heal, but you never walk the same.

I have a photograph of Maureen and Theo taken when they were in university together: the two of them standing with another man, the wet green of summer trees, a hollow blue sky. In the picture, Theo is a nervous young man, about my age. He stands slightly back, his head turned gently to the left, away from Maureen, in the direction of a short man with well-combed, indisputably good hair. Theo's hands hover at the edges of his short-pockets. As if he had been told repeatedly to smile, just the corners of his lips curl reluctantly upwards. He seems suspicious.

Maureen's orange-brown hair moves loosely around her face and comes together somewhere behind her. The soft, glowing strands float in a warm light as the sun, sinking in the sky behind them, glistens in her hair in a saintly orange crown. She wears a sleeveless, bright red top with white horizontal stripes; her pale arms form larger stripes across her middle. She seems to be threatening to pull her shirt up over her head, but she might also have been pretending to protect her stomach from the camera. My guess is that it is June. She would have already been pregnant with me, although I don't think she would have known it. Large oval sunglasses cover her eyes and in her dark, open mouth she seems to be sighing, just before she might start laughing.

The plump, full lips are Maureen's as well as the skin: tight where the jaw joins the top of her neck and smooth across her clean narrow hands. The playfulness, the obvious joy she takes from being the woman alone with these two men, I can't place. She claimed to have no patience for men and their competitiveness, yet in the picture she takes her time, stretching in the warmth of their attention. And Theo, nervous, leaning back on his heels as if he were involved elsewhere, is unsettled by her.

In the photograph, Theo is thin. There is no indication of the size he will achieve. His arms hang weakly from the sleeves of a sweaty white T-shirt. His eyes are covered with dark lenses like Maureen's, but the distraction beneath is apparent. The man to Theo's left resembles an Italian film star: his vibrant black hair, his tan-creased brow and gold-rimmed glasses. He wears a bright blue collared shirt open down to the middle of his chest. He looks older than the other two. Perhaps Theo wishes he too had worn a shirt. Looking down at his dirty, sweat-stained T-shirt, he wishes he had dressed, like this man, more seriously.

Under his arm, the Italian holds a neatly rolled grey towel. The side of his shirt is darker where it has dampened the fabric. The three of them have spent the afternoon swimming in the lake which sits at the top of the long black water pipe leading, like a spine on twenty-foot stilts, down from the tree-line above. A month before, the lake was still frozen. The layer of orange afternoon sun across the water made it seem warmer than it was. Maureen wore her bathing suit beneath her clothes; a closer look reveals the outline of her shoulder straps under her shirt. After the three of them hiked to the top, she removed her clothes and hopped on her toes, from the little rocks out to the larger ones. A breeze came across the top of the lake. She crouched down to her knees. She held her arms tightly around her and listened to herself shiver.

Theo and the Italian rushed to undress before she changed her mind. Theo's body hardened itself against the cold; his skin grew reptilian. He was disappointed in himself; he did not want to go swimming. He had wanted to see her in her swimsuit all day, but now that the time had come, he felt no excitement for the summer's first swim. He looked at her: her skin taut on her thighs and on the arrows of flesh sliced from the fabric of the swimsuit above her hips. From beneath her white skin appeared a delicate design of blue veins like cobwebs beneath a frost. It struck my father as he looked at her, her soft behind sloping beneath her hips like a pod, a season's fur unzipped and folded down at her sides, that she was winter in summer's clothing.

The Italian charged into the water, waving his arms wildly. Maureen gasped and turned her head from the ray of icy droplets dangling in the air. You see, I can freeze the motion there again and keep my young mother from the unpleasant sensation. I can turn the water to ice, to flame in the afternoon sun.

The Italian continued until the water gripped him at the waist. Out past the rock where Maureen perched, that ray of water falling across her shrinking shoulders, until he spun around. 'Oop-La,' he called with a grin and let himself fall backwards, his chubby arms erect above his head, sending in the direction of my father one final bobble of his bouncing cock and balls.

Theo hesitated for a moment – this man was naked – and when he decided and determinedly yanked his shorts down to his ankles he was too late. She had already been struck by the foreigner's exuberance. She stepped out of her bathing suit, leaving it like warm, red flesh on the rock, leaned forward and unfolded noiselessly beneath the water.

For a prolonged moment they had both disappeared. Theo was alone. Silver skin flickered beneath the water until they reappeared, a pair of darkened heads on the sun-flecked surface. My naked father picked his way along the pebbly shore as they looked back at him and called him in. They appeared to be a great distance away.

Neither of my parents had a great fondness for people, but at that time, I suspect, things might have been different. On more than one occasion, Maureen described to me the first time she saw a Marcello Mastroianni film. Sitting in the darkened local cinema in north Boston, in an entire row of giggling teenage girls, Marcello flashed onto the screen and Maureen was changed. After her early teens spent watching American actors, seeing Marcello stumble and swagger across the screen was like realizing someone had been watering down her drinks all along. So *this* is what it tastes like . . .

The thought of Marcello troubled her as she lay in bed at night. When she thought of his lips hovering near her face, she tried to imagine the smell of his breath. It relieved her. She did not want anything so real and caressed by the thought that he was only make-believe, all twenty feet of him, she could safely unclasp her knees.

As a child, I had my own troubling thought. It inhabited my nightmares and visits me even now, late at night, in an insufficiently lit room when I have had too much to drink. It comes, I think, from a painting I saw, from something I passed in the long, sleepy hallway of a museum. More likely, Maureen had lodged me in front of it, her thin hands on my shoulders, the smell of cigarettes drifting from her fingertips. '*Look* at this one,' she might have urged. I cannot think conclusively what the painting could have been. I have looked for the image in paintings I see now. I have even, half-heartedly, been on the lookout for the image in Maureen's book. I have my theories. Perhaps the painting can be attributed to Francis Bacon, to the blurred disfiguring motion of some of his heads. I have never found the painting. Perhaps it no longer exists the way I saw it; the specific image, whatever it might have been, has been lost in the constant activity of remembering.

The image first came back to me while I was preparing for bed, perhaps the evening I had seen the painting. I was in a hotel room sitting upright in the middle of a vast double bed beside Maureen's, listening to the far-off sounds of her in the bathroom, or if she had gone out that night, to the sounds of the foreign streets that lay just beyond coarse yellowing white curtains. As tall figures move around in a grey watery background, their faces become unattached. The hard flat surface of the face moves a few inches in front of the rest of the figure floating hopelessly behind. Looking directly into the face makes the gap unapparent. The faces are expressive. They smile as if the nerves were still attached to the head, but between the face and the head there is only cold, dark shadow: a space in which, if one were bold, one could insert one's hand.

I think of the same space unravelling between Theo and Maureen as he stood naked and she floated in the arms of the Italian. How could he follow her into the water without becoming a fool? Theo watched them, quite unable to believe what was happening. The trees cast long shadows across the water. The sun slipped between the branches and the lake became a thick, gurgling gold. He could not tell how close the Italian had moved to her. He could not see his legs slip against hers in the cold. Their faces were not more than a few inches apart, silhouetted in the late day sun. But he could hear the sound of her laughter.

Never marry young, Theo once told me. It was, he said, the greatest mistake of his life. I was old enough to hear this sort of advice, but I was holding his hand when he told me so I wonder exactly how old I was. He was angry. We walked from Maureen's apartment to his rented car. My hands are more delicate than his. His are short, working hands, a mysterious package, presented to him from an ancestor who had laboured for a living. He does not know quite what to do with them; he seems to clutch a telephone too tightly, a pen appears to bend as if it will snap. As we walked, with my hand in his, I remember being afraid: afraid of making mistakes. I had not understood that errors of judgment last so long, that errors produce children.

Theo stepped into the cold and felt a pain in the roof of his mouth. His breath shortened and he felt the possibility of becoming dizzy. 'You must get in fast,' the Italian told him. The Italian had his arms around Maureen. Theo continued to move slowly. He looked old. He stepped carefully over the submerged rocks, concerned only with not injuring his feet. Maureen was overwhelmed with sympathy for him. She had, after all, agreed to come to the lake with Theo. They were tied together in ways they did not yet know. She rose from the water (she could stand) and walked towards him. He did not see her coming; he did not see all of her go hard in the slight, wet breeze. As she took him in her arms, acclimatizing him to the cold of her body, he let out a shiver. She held him tightly to her and fell, slowly, into the lake water.

Six

Henry Nelson O'Neil's *The Landing of Her Royal Highness Princess Alexandra at Graveshead, 7th of March, 1863* for her marriage to Edward, Prince of Wales. What is most curious about the painting is the positively discomforting horde of people he manages to fit into the frame (over fifty in all). The beautiful, demure Alexandra is dressed in sacrificial purple. Her parents, the future King and Queen of Denmark, stand just behind her, accompanied by an enormous entourage of men and ladies in waiting. It is as if a military escort has made a small gap in the crowd of spectators just sufficient for the viewer of the painting to get a look at the royal personage. The English crowd who has come to witness the historic arrival is delirious with pleasure. Several attractive young women, all dressed in matching white robes, coo at the Princess's feet; small boys clamber over one another for a look; the boats in the gaily coloured harbour in the background let up bursts of steam in happy unison. If you could get a clear look at the Princess's eyes they would surely be filled with panic.

Maureen married Theo in August of 1968 after her second year of college. The world was in upheaval, she said, and she was marrying the 1950s. I have been to the brightly lit church in Cambridge, Massachusetts where they said their vows.

Maureen and I stood on the steps as she acted it out for me: 'I stood here . . . your father here . . . your grandfather here . . . And here,' she tossed her hands in the air, 'I threw the bouquet.' Theo wore a morning coat. She wore a cream silk gown with embroidery at the neck. I have their wedding album. He looks shockingly, naively young and she is lovely. The photographs are crowded with people I cannot imagine ever having had a place in her life. The bride and groom smile politely. They look nervous, expectant, as if they were watching something that was supposed to be amusing but was not.

She left school and they moved to New York where I was born that February. Maureen's parents were pleased with the marriage. They seemed not to notice that she had left university without a degree. Theo came from a wealthy family, of the Garraty Trust, and possessed a certain shine and level-headedness that made it difficult to imagine that he would not do exceptionally well.

The marriage lasted just over two years. They told people that the split was mutual, but it was Maureen who had decided. Her father was devastated. It seemed to be worse for him than for either Maureen or Theo. He said that his daughter's inability to be happy with good fortune would always be a mystery to him.

Maureen and I set off for our first trip to Europe in 1972. I still have the passport; in the picture I am sitting on Maureen's knee and she is smiling enough for the both of us. I remember nothing about this first trip. Apparently, I fell down the plane's spiral staircase, which means, I suppose, that for the first and last time we were travelling first class. This extravagance is testament to Maureen's trepidation on that first trip. She had never before been out of the country. I like to imagine heartbreakingly beautiful stewardesses, white linen and silver pots of tea, and all the passengers dressed in evening clothes standing around the piano singing along, but I remember nothing.

We flew first to London and stayed approximately a year. I have no idea where we lived. Perhaps, as we travelled first-class, we also stayed in first-class accommodation. Maureen wore short skirts and pushed me around in a pram. There are pictures of the two of us. The earliest entries in her book include recommendations for which museum restaurants are most friendly to small children. After that year, we made our first trip across the Channel. It didn't last very long. We made just a few brief stops – a week in Paris, a few days in Amsterdam – and then returned, triumphantly, to New York. Maureen wanted to show her father and Theo that she and her young child had survived without them.

Our home, technically, remained New York City. Whenever we needed to, Theo allowed us to stay in the apartment we once shared on Riverside Drive. He was there only sporadically throughout the year and aside from those weeks the apartment was available to us. The cleaner, Dolores, has come once a week since before I was born. According to Maureen, Dolores, a mother of three and a native of Seville, was the envy of our neighbours who employed Filipino or Salvadorian cleaners. Maureen used to press her cheek against Dolores's face and wrap her arms around her shoulders whenever she got the chance. I don't know much about Dolores except that she had a few uninteresting stories about my behaviour as a child that she recounted whenever I saw her. She also wept whenever we left, which was often more than once a year.

Theo never made us move out. A box of my toys is still

stored in the basement. I am sure there is a pile of unimportant mail with Maureen's name on it sitting in the hallway even now. Maureen was never very happy there. Theo came through with his wives, and his wives left their impression – a new set of towels, a set of glasses – but they did not trouble Maureen. The apartment has not been comprehensively redecorated since Maureen and Theo moved in. Maureen chose the curtains, most of the furniture and a good deal of what hangs on the walls. She made an attempt there; I think that's what she didn't like about it.

For portions of each year, we would return to Europe and rent rooms in inexpensive hotels or, on longer trips, rent small apartments. My schooling was a travelling performance. I treated each new classroom, each new group of peers, as mere passing entertainment, barely worthy of my attention. At each school, Maureen masqueraded as long as possible as one of the other mothers. She pretended to be concerned about the curriculum and attended meetings, usually arriving flamboyantly late, clutching her briefcase. She pretended that we at least intended to stay at the school for a full term. I knew, however; I knew during a fitting for a new school uniform that after a few months, we would be off again. We would deposit the uniform in a plastic bag on the back of the bathroom door in the rented apartment. 'Someone might appreciate it,' Maureen used to say. And then we would creep downstairs in what I remember as darkness as if we were leaving bad debts. Perhaps we were.

Maureen found London agreeable. She practised hints of a false accent and picked up words and phrases that did not belong to her. When we were in England she called me *daarling* or Gordon. Gordy was my New York name. I think she wanted a European child. She claimed never to have liked America, never to have felt at home there. In restaurants, she insisted I pronounce each item on the menu correctly. 'Listen,' she whispered as we sat at our table. 'The only conversations you ever overhear are those of Americans. They don't have a sense of privacy.' Her great regret was that she had missed by fifty years the time when Europe was still open to Americans – when only the smart and the sensitive came across – and when, by merely opening your mouth, you did not immediately put people off.

During one particularly long stay in London, Maureen enrolled me in a school housed in a white Georgian town house off the Fulham Road. The uniform was a reserved crimson and grey. I entered in the third form into the class of a very kind older woman. She had a minty odour, like a clean floor. Her face was obvious and reassuring to a child, but was in fact quite ugly. She caricatured herself with too much make-up. Her wide mouth was painted too red, her almost nonexistent eyelids too blue. Her pink skin flaked where it was most active. She used to take us to one of the parks where we quite illegally picked flowers. 'She's an alcoholic,' Maureen explained.

I found a friend at that school; my first. Timothy approached me on my first day, with his rumpled clothes and dirty fingernails. He was carrying a large London *A–Z* under his arm and offered to look up my address. I had not memorized it yet, but knew a good thing when it walked up to me, and made something up. I must have remembered the name of some street I had passed because he very confidently pointed out the street and rough location of the house where I was supposed to live. He helped me negotiate the lunchroom and the playground and made people be kind to me. After school, he gave me one of his enormous candies that rendered us both speechless, frothing and red.

Timothy was dedicated and worshipful; it was my first taste of what Maureen had in me. It made no sense that he was following me and not the other way around. He was athletic and ruddy, with a large head and thin, wispy blonde hair. I was, much as I am now, too thin, with a grey complexion offset by hair a thundercloud black, even blue. Maureen has said I am handsome and I have, I think, grown into gravely hollow cheeks and an overhanging brow, but they meant nothing when I was a child. Timothy indulged my childhood addiction to rules and my refusal to do anything overtly wrong. He had had the air of a good-natured if sometimes badly behaved boy when I met him, but he gave that up for me and even tried, in vain, to tidy his appearance. Even when I solemnly rose from my desk and reported him for some indiscretion behind the teacher's back, he forgave me, and then, even better, allowed me to forgive him.

Timothy loved cars. He always kept a Matchbox car in the pocket of his trousers and spent much of his time rubbing the tiny plastic wheels up and down his thigh through the thin lining. Timothy had a particular fondness for American cars. He knew all the models and some of their technical facts: the pistons and horsepowers. I did my best to conceal how few years I had actually spent in New York and spoke about it as home. Later, when I got to know the city as an adult, I realized I had described the obvious places – the places one visits on a first trip. I wonder if Timothy would have caught on, perhaps not. He so wanted to hear my stories; he so wanted to believe in something better than his very glad and happy world.

'I think he's dense,' Maureen said.

I believe the smile put her off – that and the size of his head. We sat with cups of tea in the living room of the flat we had rented in Baker Street. We sat in front of the orange electric heater encased in the metal fireplace. On top of the heater, glass charcoals slowly glowed to life; Maureen's skin was flushed with the diamond colours. 'A nice boy, and you like him, but he's dense. A little, no?' She smiled warmly. I told her he was, but he made a good playmate. 'Well, that doesn't surprise me,' she said.

When Maureen and I would go out and do things – lunch in Chinatown, a trip to Greenwich – I'd ask if we could bring Timothy along. When she agreed, depending on her mood, she would either sulk, or behave wonderfully and make every moment of our time entertaining. She allowed us to eat and drink what we wanted and to ride on a separate tube car and wave at her through the window. Timothy thought she was marvellous. Other times, Maureen would refuse and ask, 'Don't you think the two of us would have more fun on our own?'

Timothy and I spent most of our time at his house. He lived on a square in South Kensington. The downstairs windows were lined with black metal bars. The front hall had a chess-board marble floor across which a boy could safely pick his way to the bottom step once it had been agreed that black was quicksand and white was safe, solid ground. Every room contained books and enormous windows filled with grey light. Timothy never questioned the fact that we never visited my home. He accepted the distrusting behaviour of a New Yorker. It added mystery, a pleasure to our friendship.

Timothy's mother was rarely at home. She appeared beneath a heap of shopping bags at the end of the day, or was there just briefly when I arrived in the mornings before she went out. She was always well dressed in skirts with matching jackets and earrings. She did not take much notice of me, but was always polite, always in a graceful rush. At times she made me feel as if Timothy had lots of friends around to play and that she could not quite keep their names straight in her mind. In the basement there was a self-contained flat. 'Perhaps you and your mother can live there,' Timothy once kindly insulted me. Timothy's au pair lived in the flat. She spent most of her time sitting in front of her television smoking cigarettes. She wore loose-fitting pyjamas through which one could occasionally catch a glimpse of her dark skin. She was very attractive and probably depressed. Whenever Timothy or I needed something she rose patiently from her flat to see what we wanted to eat, or where we wanted to be escorted, but otherwise, she left us to ourselves.

I would not play cars with Timothy. There was a pond in the middle of the patio behind his house where we threw pebbles at the carp. The garden seemed large, although it was not. The walls stood about six feet high, slightly taller than the garden shed. We climbed up onto the roof of the shed and looked into the neighbouring gardens. We stayed there for some time, keeping watch, until I gave the order for us to leap, rolling into a ball in the flower beds.

When it rained, we explored the interior of his enormous house. Timothy and I climbed the stairs on our bellies. We explored each room, carefully rounding corners, as if we fully expected to discover an imaginary enemy. At times we split up, each reconnoitering a separate room. Once, when I was alone, I found myself in the master bedroom where an armchair stood in front of the tall grey window looking out over the garden, and into the gardens of the neighbours on either side. Chimneys spread out in the distance over the rooftops all the way to the river. The cleaner had not yet come and the room was in luxurious disorder. Three dresses, as if she had had difficulty deciding what to wear, lay strewn across the chair, their backs unzipped, the interiors exposed. On the floor rested two pairs of shoes, each with a small circular stain in the middle of the insole. The bed had not been made. The sheets were folded open; I could see the impression of where she had lain and beside it, on the nightstand, a cold, half-full cup of tea. And there was an unmistakable smell of another person's mother. But, as I looked around the room again – into the adjoining bathroom, at the make-up, the stained cotton wool on the edge of the sink, the smudged mirror, the still-moist toothbrush and the overflowing laundry bin beside which lay a heaped robe – I saw not merely a mother, but a woman, as much a woman as Maureen. It sounds silly, but I hadn't thought of it. I don't know why. I had believed in two distinct groups, mothers and women, and that Maureen by some mistake existed as both.

Seven

Whenever Maureen grew tired of being a mother she would make the extravagant threat that she would throw herself under a red, double-decker bus. It was far-fetched; not only was she not English, but she resented having to use public transportation. Submitting herself to the wheels of a public bus filled with members of the public would have been a violation of her way of life. She made the threat throughout my childhood; whenever she felt hopeless or neglected, overwhelmed with the responsibilities or mundane tasks of her life. I never, except for one particular afternoon, believed she was capable of such a thing. It was a weekday, the sky a glinting silver, an underwater light falling across the city. People moved busily across Trafalgar Square. Tourists aimed their lenses into the sky at Lord Nelson atop his column. Buses revolved around the square. Timothy and I were dressed in our uniforms, Maureen in a brown corduroy skirt-suit with a yellow French-cuffed shirt underneath. From the elevated steps in front of the National Gallery, Timothy and I spotted the enormous black lions surrounding Nelson's Column, the fountains and the famous pigeons. Vendors sold small paper cups of seed and children stood with their arms outstretched, seed in the palms of their hands and sprinkled in their hair. When they felt the first set of clawed feet on their arms and on the tops of their heads, their eyes bulged and they let out small squeals of pleasure. I told Maureen we wanted to visit the square – to climb up between the lion's enormous paws like the other children, to throw pennies into the shallow fountains and to feed the pigeons. Timothy politely kept quiet while Maureen contemplated her watch and then her guidebook flagged with bookmarks. 'We'll have to see how we get along,' she said.

A particularly long day passed in the gallery: a show of Goya's prints and pencil drawings. His paintings are usually enormous – I remember specifically the image of Saturn chewing his son like a drumstick – but everything in this show was very small and hung a little too high for Timothy and me. We had to stand back to see. For a child, a gallery is a labyrinth. Just as we saw what we believed to be the exhibit's end, we turned the next corner to find another long hallway leading in the opposite direction. I was used to it, but Timothy was not. He tired quickly and rested on each available bench when we came to it. He propped his elbows on his knees and wore an expression of complete and painful exhaustion. Had he not been so polite, he might have complained, or made trouble.

If Maureen noticed Timothy's suffering, she did not let on. She wore glasses and held her notebook across her folded arm as she scribbled her notes. She got so close to some of the exposed prints, the resident guard would step forward a few paces, ready to pounce if she proceeded to kiss the surface of the print as it looked like she might. Maureen ignored them. She considered them a nuisance, an impediment to her work, as all artists need to feel there are powers working against them. But many of the guards in England are capable of arguing their interpretation of a specific work with great authority. Despite her better instincts, I have watched Maureen become embroiled in major disagreements and be matched reference for reference by one of those men or women whom she had wanted to consider beneath her.

There was a crowd in front of one of the drawings that particularly interested Maureen. It was a study for *A Dog*, one of Goya's most famous murals (described in Maureen's book as *forlorn and hungry in a lonely world . . . it seems to have misplaced its soul, if dogs possess them*.) Maureen stood in the crowd with her chin in her hand contemplating the pencil drawing behind non-reflective glass. Timothy and I sat down on a bench where we could watch her. She had a good figure, long legs and broad shoulders. I do not think we were the only ones watching. One group of people moved on and was replaced by another, but Maureen remained, standing almost totally still. It was Timothy who noticed that she was weeping. I had seen her do it before. Timothy touched my hand and pointed. He giggled nervously. Perhaps his mother never cried. We were far enough away that he could whisper to me without being overheard. 'She's crying,' he said breathlessly. I said, yes, she was, but not to worry, it happened sometimes and she would be all right in a few minutes. He did not seem convinced. What might happen to him, he seemed to wonder, in the charge of a grown woman who wept in public? I knew enough not to interrupt Maureen at a moment like that, and Timothy seemed to know the same by instinct. We watched as other gallery-goers noticed her tears and then quickly pretended not to, busying themselves with something on the other side of the room. I now understand the degree of affectation that was at work. But at the time – when I watched tears roll silently down Maureen's cheeks while she stood before Vermeer's *Girl in a Red Hat* or Hopper's *Sun in an Empty Room* – I presumed there was something in those paintings that I could not see, but one day might.

When we finally emerged from the building, I was surprised by the same grey sky. No evolution had occurred from morning to afternoon. Maureen held Timothy's hand in one hand and mine in the other as we crossed the road and descended the stairs into the square. As we walked, I contemplated the four black lions, each covered with a clambering group of tourists, the vendors handing out paper cups full of wet seed and the children wearing pigeons on their heads.

Maureen gave Timothy and me fifty pence each and walked us over to one of the vendors. We each bought one of the small containers of seed and then found an empty piece of the square and sprinkled seed on the pavement. Our generosity was rewarded and a small crowd of pigeons began pecking frantically at our feet. I poured some of the seed into my open palm and immediately felt the fleshy tug of a bird's claws on my wrist. I looked over to show Timothy only to discover that he already had a bird on his head. He grinned at me until another bird landed beside the first. He swayed under the weight as if he might fall down and then steadied himself and began, tentatively, to smile once again.

I turned to look for Maureen. She was standing away from the fray, laughing at us. I began carefully to walk towards her, balancing the bird on my wrist. 'Keep that thing away from me,' she said. I had almost reached her when the bird suddenly had its fill and with a furious snap of its wings, rose up between us and flew away.

What happened next needs to be explained in the context of the time. It was a nervous city. All the rubbish bins had been removed from public spaces. There had been several bombs, some of which came with warnings, and some of which did not. There was a sound, what might have been an explosion, but that might also have come from one of the construction sites near the river. The people in the square lifted their heads. It came from the direction of Downing Street and the government buildings. And then the sound was heard again, but this time it was closer and someone in the square decided to run.

Three hundred people ran from one side of the square to the other. From the sky, it would have seemed that the wind had suddenly changed direction, the way pigeons in flight move like a single plastic bag in the wind. They came running towards us. I remember the slow adjustment in Maureen's face as she began to understand the situation. She snatched my hand where the pigeon had rested and we began to run. At the stairs, people crowded against the walls, and took the steps two at a time. A policeman tried to come down the stairs, but he could not move against the crowd. He had lost his helmet; his thin brown hair was askew as if he had just been roused from bed. He fought the tide for a moment and then changed his mind and let himself be carried away up the stairs. I remember Maureen's knees as they came out of her skirt beside me. I felt the stone wall against my side. I could not see the sky from the crowd of bodies; it seemed to have gone black.

When we got to the street, the crowd opened up and the sky returned. The people ran across the street like a river overflowing. The drivers in the cars did not know what came at them. Some of them tried to accelerate and men angrily beat their hands against the bonnets of the cars.

We crossed safely to the steps of the gallery where we stood in a huddled crowd. Minutes had passed without another explosion and the crowd had grown quieter. Men slowly wandered down the steps of the museum and looked around for anyone they might help. Embarrassment at the earlier panic slowly surfaced. People looked at one another. Had anyone acted bravely? As we stood, awaiting the police, Maureen looked down at me and smiled. I smiled back. And then her face clouded over and she said, with horror, 'Timothy.'

We rushed back into the street and through the traffic. Drivers had begun to get out of their cars and stood looking around wondering what had caused the charging crowd. People continued to stumble up the stairs from the square. Two men supported a woman as she bled into a handkerchief. 'You've just fainted,' they were telling her.

The policeman would not let us go back down the stairs. 'But we've lost someone,' protested Maureen. He took on a grave expression and took us to the side where we could look over the wall down onto the square. I expected to see bodies. The only casualties dotting the square were hats, bags of shopping, a walking cane on one of the steps. The pigeons were frenzied over all the spilt seed, and there amongst them, still clutching his little empty cup, was Timothy, crying, and talking to a policeman who had thoughtfully removed his hat and dropped down to his knees to talk to the boy at eye level.

On the way home, Maureen tried to calm Timothy. We ate pizza, and bought him an ice cream for dessert and although Timothy had stopped crying, he would not allow Maureen to wipe his eyes. I respected him for this. He was still breathing unnaturally. He could not forgive Maureen. He had never met anyone like her. He felt, I imagine, that he had been wronged in a way that no one had ever been wronged before.

I stood out on the pavement while Maureen explained to

Timothy's au pair what had happened. I think we narrowly missed the arrival of Timothy's mother. At first, the au pair smiled politely and then she suddenly pulled Timothy closer to her, as if she imagined Maureen capable of doing him harm. The au pair dropped to her knees just like the policeman had. She looked at Timothy, who I saw give a great, dramatic sigh, and then she gave him a heartfelt kiss. She did not look again at Maureen for several moments, although Maureen spoke continually, and then, apparently, she said something curt, for the door soon closed. Maureen looked at her reflection in the gleaming black door and then gave a sigh of her own. She came back to me and took my hand. She looked defeated. I thought she might start to cry, but instead she asked, 'What have the Irish got against us?' I told her I didn't know. We walked up to Queen's Gate where we flagged a cab, a rare extravagance. She held me closely to her all the way home.

Nothing changed between Timothy and me. The next day at school, we were, as usual, inseparable. It did not last. Maureen soon announced, quite abruptly, that we would be moving back to New York. She barely mentioned that day again. I can remember only once a few years later when she recounted the story to friends. We were at a restaurant, the guests of someone she had met at a class in New York. I was the only child there. I can measure out a great stretch of my childhood sitting in restaurants surrounded by adults. 'I was terrified,' she said. 'I think Gordon was as well. And coming to the edge and looking down at that little boy . . . I have never felt so empty before. I wonder if I would have felt better had I looked down and not seen him there or, God forbid, if something terrible *had* happened. Of course, later, I would have felt much worse. But at the time, I just can't tell you what I felt.' Everyone nodded in agreement.

When we returned home that evening, Maureen mentioned him again. She walked around getting undressed for bed, hanging her clothing. I could not understand why he was on her mind. Somehow, she had gotten the news about Timothy. He had been on holiday with his grandparents, she explained. They had pulled over on the side of the road so he and his grandfather could relieve themselves in the trees. Timothy had become confused and went around the wrong side of the car. It was a narrow hedgerow, and another car came whipping around the bend. Maureen stopped her movement, her back and forth to the bathroom. She shook her head. It was one of her gestures, as if she were trying to dislodge something that teetered precariously on one of the shelves in her mind. 'I'm sorry, Gordon. I didn't know how to tell you.'

Eight

Death of the Virgin, artist unknown, approximately 1350–1360. Anyone who knows anything can tell you that this woman is no virgin. Judging from her dishevelled state, the artist and the model might have been wrapped in an embrace just moments before.

From *Turned Back*

I have been thinking of all the deaths I have known. I have imagined Maureen's. I have imagined her last few hours in the hospital. She disliked hospitals intensely.

When I was fourteen, Maureen's father, Roger, walking down his street clutching a paper bag full of groceries, felt a sharp pain behind his ribcage. It was a cold and sunny day. He was a thin man with a full head of white hair. He wore a canvas fishing hat and blue scarf. A plane passed overhead as children yelped and cried in the playground across the street. He leaned against a lamp post for a moment. According to the teacher who saw him from the playground, he said something she could not hear, what looked like a single word, and fell to his knees still holding tightly on to his groceries. His heart stopped and if that was not enough, with the supply of blood and oxygen to his brain suspended, he suffered a simultaneous stroke, forehead pressed against the pavement.

I did not know him well. I met him only a handful of times in his home just outside Boston. I was twelve the last time I saw him. We sat in the living room. Maureen sat on the little wooden bench that curled around the empty fireplace. She glanced nervously around the room. She pointed at the flaking yellow paint. It hadn't been changed, she explained, since she was a child. 'Neither have the curtains,' she nodded, sitting on her hands and rocking her hips back and forth. 'Nor the lampshades.'

Maureen hated going to see him. When she was young, he worked long hours, appearing late at night, a depleted figure on the edge of her bed. Maureen said he had no extraneous interests. The phone never rang for him. He could not stand to be idle and holidays and weekends were torture. He was terrified of poverty. At every moment, he felt failure approaching. He worried. As a direct effect, his looks had gone by the time he was halfway through his thirties. They went inwardly, as if a drain had been unplugged inside him. He still had his thick dark hair, his broad shoulders, his elegant hands, but he had decayed. His arms were weak, as if they had been broken many times over; his gums receded; his skin gathered in pools in the hollows of his face.

From when Maureen was young Roger warned her to weigh very carefully the prospects of the man she chose to marry. He told her she was attractive, and would be popular. She could not afford to be a fool. After finishing high school early (where she was considered exceptionally bright and in possession of certain creative talents that would set her apart) Roger bought her several new outfits and they drove the three hours north to her university together. She watched the abandoned farmhouses go by, the dead trees, the tufts of animal fur on barbed-wire fences. She found the landscape was dramatic; she could be happy there. As they walked around the campus passing the young men in tweed blazers and white trousers, Roger warned her about deciding rashly. 'This is a very good school and it costs a lot of money.' He kissed her forehead and she waved goodbye from the steps of her dormitory. She was free.

When Roger returned from the kitchen with a vodka tonic for Maureen and himself, and a glass of punch for me, he sat in his armchair. With his fingers, he had dug out two small pits in the armrests where the stuffing was apparent. On the mantel there were framed photographs of my dead grandmother which, disturbingly, had been taken in the same room when it was warmer and better lit. Another picture was of a crying baby. 'As a baby, your mother either cried or laughed,' Roger explained when he saw me looking at the picture. 'It was like that from the moment she was born.' I felt sorry for Maureen when I imagined her childhood in that dreary house. In front of the fireplace an antique porcelain doll – jet-black hair, red lips, and black eyes – sat in a miniature rocking chair. Perhaps he had arranged the chair next to him when Maureen was small, the doll in her lap, as he told her his troubles.

On these visits, Maureen always wore something expensive to torment him. She balanced her glass on her knee as she told him of our recent travels. 'We've just been to the Fitzwilliam Museum. We took the train out of London to Cambridge,' she said. 'A very impressive collection. Lots of Blake. Mother always liked Blake.' Roger slurped his drink loudly. 'We've also just taken a trip to the Muzeum Narodowe in Warsaw. The place is full of Olga Boznanska. You probably don't know her. She's really an Impressionist but she didn't like to admit it.' She dismissed him with a wave of her hand. 'Boy, Warsaw is grim.'

'I hope you're as rich as you think you are,' said Roger. 'I'm sure Theo likes to hear about you two flitting around the place spending his money.' He turned to me. 'You must remember me to your father, Gordon, the next time you see him.' He could not stand her. Maureen's pleasure, her defiant radiance was enough to make him hate her.

Roger lived the rest of his days alone, and in near-poverty. When he died he had over a hundred thousand dollars in the bank. He left a small portion to Maureen and distributed the rest amongst relatives he had not seen in years. They probably remember him fondly. I found him frightening. As we sat together in his living room, the morning sun slung in triangular shapes from the dirty windows like white sheets partitioning the room, he seemed to be willfully and angrily dying in front of us. So it came as no surprise when I came home from school one afternoon two years later and found Maureen packing more violently than usual.

I had never before been in a hospital. The ambulances, the people smoking nervously on the pavement out front, the bustling lobby and over-sized elevators seemed to me, above all, realistic.

Maureen and I sat together in the waiting room. The families of four or five other patients sat staring at the television or looking silently out of the windows at the industrial part of the city. The room was impossibly quiet. Every hushed conversation, cough or adjustment in the squeaking, fake-leather armchairs reverberated around the little room. On the three or four blonde wooden coffee tables lay a standard array of out-of-date magazines. The people in the room could not have looked less comfortable. Most sat stiffly in their chairs shyly avoiding eye contact as if a nurse might enter at any time and ask us all to disrobe. I remember one woman in particular. She was very young. Her new husband had been in a terrible car crash that morning. His car had skidded on ice and leapt right into an intersection. She wore a sweatsuit with little pictures of cartoon characters on the breast and one side of the hip and sensible white sneakers. Her hair was done in wet curls and she wore glasses. She wasn't crying. Her hands shook violently. I didn't notice them at first, as she kept them firmly under each arm. Occasionally, she brought one forward to comb some of the curls from her face. The women of her family hovered around her ready for her to break down. Between her feet she kept a brightly coloured duffel bag full of clothes. Just prior to our arrival she had announced that she would not leave before her husband awoke from his coma. Her family was trying to get her to come home, but she was resolute and, I remember thinking, wrong. He would not wake up and then how would she ever go home?

Maureen sat on the edge of her chair. She did not watch the television or the others in the room. I offered her a magazine and she shook her head. She stared into space or at a spot on the wall opposite and swivelled her jaw thoughtfully back and forth. I felt completely powerless to appease her anxiety and wanted to desperately.

A red phone, a dramatic spot of colour, hung on the wall below the television. Every quarter hour or so, it would ring. The jolly nurse on the other end would ask if the family of one patient or another was in the room, and then she'd tell them to come through to the ward. When it began to ring, a profound feeling of hesitancy arose in the room. We all looked around at one another until someone finally presumed no one else would answer and got to their feet. It usually meant two people found themselves standing and the phone continued to ring while these two came to a silent, polite agreement as to who would answer.

Finally, it was our turn. Maureen picked her way across the room, careful not to touch anyone. She smiled graciously and took the phone from the elderly woman who had answered. For just a moment, she looked at the receiver as if she were considering wiping it clean. After listening silently to what was said on the other line, she hung up. She gestured for me to follow and the two of us walked out of the room and down the hall. We went through a pair of doors marked ICU and continued until she paused at another smaller door and looked through the window.

'Okay, Gordy,' she said. 'You might feel sick.'

'I won't feel sick,' I said.

'You might.' She fiddled with her dress absent-mindedly, smoothing the fabric along her thighs and then across her flat stomach. She looked up into the window again, as if she hoped to check her reflection. 'Lots of people feel sick.'

I nodded, and she pushed open the door to reveal a wide circular space connecting a series of smaller doorless rooms extending off the main body of the ward like tentacles. In the middle of the large room, an enormous round desk stood covered with computers and paperwork. Sequestered behind the computer screens sat nurses and doctors. Their skin had turned rosy pink from the electric lights above their heads. Some of the nurses looked up as we entered, and smiled. I thought we probably looked clumsy in our civilian clothes. The nurses seemed like more efficient, happier human beings, and only when they were close enough that I could see their jewellery and other poorly chosen particularities did they resemble real people.

It seemed to take us a long time to cross the room. I looked into the little rooms as we passed. In each, a bed sat framed in the window beneath a television set. Each contained a strange, wounded body. In one lay an elderly woman with cobweb-white hair surrounding what appeared to be a weightless skull resting on the pillow. Her eyes were closed. The television above her head flickered across the crumpled sheets. Her husband, wearing a green baseball hat, sat beside her watching the television. His hand lay absently on the bed beside his wife's. In the next room a man lay breathing through a respirator. The curtains were drawn across the windows and the light beside his bed was switched off. A row of flowers sat shadowed on the table in front of the window. A bouquet for each member of the family who could not make it, or for those who had been there and about whose visits he knew nothing. In another bed, long curly blonde hair spilled across a pillow. I could not tell if her eyes were open, but she was turned towards the window.

The room was quiet except for our footsteps, the conversation between doctors and nurses, and the beep and groan of mysterious machines. Until then, Maureen had moved without urgency. As we crossed the large room, however, I realized that now I could barely keep up with her. Only then, when we were just a few feet away, did she feel the need to see him. I was in such a hurry to keep up I did not realize that I had begun to feel light-headed until we got to the side of his bed. The antiseptic smell in the room was suddenly very powerful and I felt dizzy. I put my hand on her arm to steady myself, and felt her start.

Perhaps she thought it had been her father who had touched her.

I had not yet looked at my grandfather's face. From beneath the pale blue sheet on the bed, came a long angular foot, lumped with painful-looking purple veins and yellow nails curling over the tops of his toes.

'Go to the bathroom,' Maureen said sensibly.

I turned and walked back the way I had come. The same nurse smiled pleasantly as I hurried from the room as if to say she saw this all the time. I pushed through the door, crossed the hall into the bathroom and sat down on the toilet seat with my head lowered between my knees. The smell, the sterilized rot of the human body, had settled at the back of my throat, and as much as I spat into the toilet bowl I failed to shift it.

When I no longer felt dizzy, I splashed water over my face and into my mouth and stood still in the middle of the green-tiled room to see if my stomach had settled.

Before I entered the unit again, I looked through the glass in the door. Roger's bed sat directly opposite, all the way across the room. Maureen was leaning over him. She seemed to be listening intently.

I pushed open the door and the same nurse looked up and smiled once more. I decided not to look at any of the other patients as I crossed the room. As I passed, I heard the man in the baseball hat laugh gently at something on the television.

Maureen was not moving. She did not seem to be speaking. I paused, and thought perhaps that I should not intrude, but she had never expressed a desire to be alone with him.

When I stood beside her again, she reached for my hand. Roger's face was covered with coarse grey stubble around a blue oxygen mask. The skin of his lips fell inwards as he mumbled incomprehensibly beneath the steamed plastic covering. He had his teeth out. I had never known they were not his, and was amazed he had allowed himself the expense. Above the mask, his nose dripped. His thin hair was uncombed and his eyes, staring past his daughter, emerged from his grey skin a startling, terrified blue. Maureen held my hand in one hand, and with the other pushed his hand firmly against the bed. He kept reaching to remove the oxygen mask.

'No, Dad,' she was whispering. 'You should keep that on.'

The skin that draped over the fragile bones of his left hand appeared yellow and dry. It lay quiet, already dead. From the deep crevasse between the tendons of his fingers sprouted lumps of dried black blood around the IV tube. A sickly orange urine bag was hung off to the side, in an attempt to conceal it behind the IV bag.

'Granddad, you should keep that on,' I found myself echoing Maureen.

'You all right here?' asked a jolly voice from behind us. We both turned to see a nurse smiling at us reassuringly. She looked tired. 'You all right, Roger,' she asked rhetorically. 'What are you up to?' She walked around to the other side of the bed, wheeling the IV and urine bag out of her way with startling force. She leaned over and removed the mask from his mouth. 'He can keep this off for a while. If he gets short of breath we put it back on. Just let me know if you don't think you can do it yourselves. My name's Helen,' she smiled. 'All right, Roger?' she spoke louder when she addressed him, and stroked his hair reassuringly.

Roger licked his lips and blinked his eyes.

'His skin gets so dry,' said Helen. She took a jar of Vaseline from the cupboard next to his bed. 'Here,' she handed the open jar to Maureen who took it thoughtlessly, blinded by the authority of someone in charge. 'Put some on his lips.'

Maureen looked horrified and moved the jar ever so slightly back towards the nurse. Helen had, over her years, clearly come to understand the importance of involving relatives in the processes of both healing and dying. She did not know Maureen. Helen extended her own pinkie finger, the nail painted pink, and swirled a few times around an imaginary jar of Vaseline. Maureen followed her example, and lowered her own finger into the jar. 'That's right,' urged Helen.

Maureen removed her finger, its end covered in the silver slime. She lowered her finger and smoothed the substance over Roger's lips. He continued to lick his lips, his angry tongue touching Maureen's finger.

'There you are,' said Helen. She patted me on the shoulder. 'Give me a shout,' she almost whispered, and wandered off.

When Maureen turned her face to me again, two black-stained tears hovered in her eyes before they leapt, one after the other, in narrow grey lines down her face: perhaps only at the unpleasantness of it all.

Roger began to speak. He was clearly unaware of us. Most of what he said was incomprehensible, until he said, clear as could be, 'The headlines of life.' He began to mumble a seemingly senseless stream of words, saliva dripping onto his chin.

'I don't understand you, Dad,' said Maureen. 'Gordy,' she turned. 'I don't understand.'

I listened, trying to understand what he meant by headlines. I thought I had misheard him until he said it again. 'The headlines!' As I watched him getting angry, at one point lifting his only live hand and hitting the bed beside him, I imagined him watching a nine o'clock news of his life: BOY BORN . . . BOY

DREAMS AT SCHOOL ... BOY MARRIES ... BOY FAILS TO BECOME WHAT BOY WANTS TO BE.

Maureen rose from her chair. 'I don't understand a damn thing he says,' she said, indicating her father who was now swinging his one good fist above his head.

Helen reappeared and rubbed Maureen's shoulder. 'Why don't you two go on back to the waiting room a moment.' Without another look at him, Maureen obediently turned and walked across the room towards the double doors. Once again, I had to hurry to catch up.

We walked right past the waiting room. She paused only long enough for me to go in and retrieve our coats from the plastic hangers. She did not speak until we were outside walking down the asphalt ramp of the parking lot towards the car. 'I can't believe he's going to die so angry,' she said. 'Stupid, stupid man,' she said in a suddenly more English accent. She removed a handkerchief from her bag and dabbed at her eyes. He didn't look like he was going to die to me, I thought of telling her. But she was right. Having completed his speech, he sputtered himself from life that evening.

Helen telephoned as I lay in the large bed in the airport hotel where Maureen and I shared a room. Maureen had stayed in the bar after we had had a dinner of enormous steaks and mashed potatoes. When she came in later on I think she knew as soon as she saw my expression, my hands folded gravely over the top of the sheets. I waited until she came and sat on the edge of her bed to remove her shoes. I told her that Roger had died. Helen had assured me he had been comfortable. She had sat beside him and reminded him of the people who had loved him. Maureen began to weep. 'Oh, Gordy,' she said. 'That poor man.' She got up and walked across the room in the darkness. 'I'm not going to end up like him,' she said and closed the bathroom door behind her. I fell back to sleep as I listened to her weep and smelled the smoke from her cigarette drift slowly from beneath the door.

I have no reason to believe that Maureen's time in the hospital was in any way similar to Roger's. Her operation was judged a great success. They decided to keep her under observation all the same. 'Your mother is not the most exuberant character,' said Doctor Auddi over the phone. He sounded about my age, but I'm sure he must have been much older. Perhaps the years of study had halted the ageing process.

'But strong,' I interjected.

'We want to watch her,' he said.

The cancer did not spread. It did not come back. They waited six months before they declared her out of danger, long enough for Annie to leave me. As if to belittle the experts, the cancer waited until backs were turned and then came back at speed. By the time she complained again of headaches, by the time she sat in a booth in a coffee shop in town, refusing to get up, refusing to answer any questions, it was too late. They looked through the scanner and found her brain riddled with the disease, like wet, black bandages covering her skull. Her brain had been eroded from within. I could not speak with her on the phone. It was nearly as swift as if she had been decapitated. Her body made machines tick and respirators go up and down with nothing but a bloody stump at the top of her neck. When they contacted me to tell me that they could not explain it – they had never seen a cancer come back so quickly – there was nothing, no one left for me to come and see.

Nine

Jan Vermeer's *View of Delft*, c.1660/1661. Despite what they have done to the city of Delft since Vermeer's death, I remember it the way he portrayed it ... The painting is a triumph of technical ability ... The city occupies only the lower third of the canvas; the blue sky and hulking cumulus tower above, dominating the majority of the painting. On the near bank two worried women discuss, no doubt, the goings-on amongst their neighbours or, perhaps, what is happening to their city. And from appearances, they have reason to worry. The bright sky has a strangely ominous effect. The mud-coloured buildings are darkened with shadow and reflect in ghoulish forms in the surface of the river. The contrast between earth and sky is as stark as heaven and hell. It is the bright blue sky that throws the world into darkness as if to suggest that the world would not be hell without a better world above us.

Annie was engaged when we met, to a hairdresser. I was nineteen and she was twenty-six. One of the men who worked in the greengrocer a few doors down from the American-style delicatessen where she worked told me both her age (she was older than I thought) and that she was, as he put it, 'off limits'. I saw her fiancé only once, from the back, when he dropped her off at work on the back of his motorbike. He wore light denim jeans and a matching denim jacket. He removed his helmet to kiss her goodbye. He shook his head like a lion. He had a great deal of textured, airy hair like a pop star. I was not deterred.

I used to come in and see Annie almost every day. I ordered sandwiches from her, pounds of cheese and slices of ham or roast beef. Months passed before I made conversation with her. I had enrolled in a second-rate art college and lived in a flat Maureen had rented for me with Theo's money. It had a narrow bed, a kitchenette, a wooden desk and a dresser, all of which came with the apartment. It was situated on the top floor of a three-story house not far from the college. Maureen found it for me in a single afternoon of looking and signed the lease immediately.

Maureen took me shopping for towels and bedding, to the bank to open a student savings account and to the chemist for shampoo, soap and condoms, which I had not yet had a use for. Maureen installed what she bought on the small, square wooden shelves above the tub. She contemplated the sunset-orange beach scene on the condom packet and then put it carefully away as if the contents were fragile or as if the couple depicted lounging in the sand could be disturbed. She appeared in the bathroom doorway and looked at me. 'Look, Gordon,' she said gravely. 'I want you to know I am willing to discuss any questions you might have.'

I told her I had none.

'Well, don't hesitate to ask if anything comes to you,' she said.

'I won't,' I said.

'What else?' she asked, looking around the apartment. I sat back on my sponge cake of a bed. She had bought an orange bed cover, which made the bed resemble even more a dessert one might buy in a hospital or a bus station. As I sat, I seemed to slowly sink almost to the ground, the ends of the bed curling gradually around me like rising bread. 'Let's see,' continued Maureen. She had removed her gloves and handed them from one hand to the other. 'Are you going to be all right with this? Are you going to be all right alone?' she asked. I felt her looking at me, but I didn't answer. I felt she did not expect a response; she had made her decision to go. She turned out of the doorway, back into the little bathroom. From where I sat, with the bathroom door open, I could see her from the corner of my eye. The toilet faced the bed. She placed her gloves on the sink. She raised her skirt, tugged it around in front of her, and cradled the fabric under her arm as she shimmied out of her tights. She sat down and looked around at the yellow walls and brand-new blue shower curtain still creased from the packaging.

I got up from the bed and walked across the room where I wouldn't be able to see her. I looked out of the window beside the protruding eave above the bed. Across the street the buildings looked similar to mine with storefronts on the ground floor. Beneath my window there was a bus stop and my window was just high enough to see the dirty tops of the double-decker buses as they passed. I heard her hum for a moment and then she stopped. 'You need a frying pan, Gordy,' she interrupted herself. 'We didn't get you any pots and pans!'

She appeared in the doorway leaning against the door frame once again. 'Are you listening to me, Gordy?'

'Sure,' I said. I did not look away from the window.

'You don't have anything to cook on,' she said with greater urgency.

'Don't worry, Maureen . . . I'll get that stuff.'

She came across the room and stopped beside me. I had no

choice but to turn and look at her. She smiled and dragged the back of her hand across my cheek. 'You feel abandoned, is that it? I can't stop in London just now,' she said. 'I'll try to arrange it so that I have enough work here to spend some time soon. I wish you were coming with me, but it's time you had your degree. Don't you think? I envy you. I'd like to stop and study for a few years. But I can't. I have work to do. You understand, don't you?'

Maureen left for a more extended tour of the continent. She called and she wrote letters. I have them all. They are carefully dated along with a notation of where she was when she wrote them, probably to make it easier on whoever would one day write her biography. She said that she would come through London regularly. She said she would stay with me on a pull-out cot when she did in order to save money. *Theo won't support me forever now that you're on your own*, she wrote.

I was lonely at first. I had never been alone, never without Maureen, and at first I did not know what to do with myself. I was not good at making friends at college. Some of the students were very political and went regularly to rallies of one sort or another. Occasionally one of them would thrust a badge onto my lapel that I would dutifully wear for the rest of the afternoon. Others sat in the bar carving small designs onto the backs of their hands with knives. Another group wanted to paint pictures of nature and move to the country and live self-sufficiently. The teachers weren't much better. The lectures lacked inspiration, and although I am unsure how much of Maureen's 'research' she bothered to substantiate, her presentation as I have read it in her book is often more gripping than the dry and sometimes embittered instruction I received.

I did my best. I went to a few dances where I danced stiffly with some pretty girls. I performed the assignments quietly and unremarkably and, when possible, with little contact with my classmates. I spent a good deal of the time at home sinking into my bed, or looking out of my window. I occasionally went to the museums, not to see anything in particular, but to wander amidst the subdued lighting and whispered conversation where I felt strangely at home and was reminded of Maureen. I am not sure I could really claim to have missed her in the longing way people describe. I had simply lost the only real motivation that had compelled my life in the direction it had been going. It is a feeling, I imagine, experienced by virtually everyone of that age: I felt adrift.

That Maureen overlooked the purchasing of pots and pans is not surprising. She was never a great cook. We ate out more than the average. She had a few recipes that she prepared with regularity: spaghetti with capers and canned tuna fish, a shepherd's pie, a spring vegetable risotto for entertaining. These meals were some of the great consistencies of my childhood.

I bought myself a single pan, hammered a single nail above the electric stove, and hung the pan in a ready position. From its place on the kitchen wall, it stared at me, urging me to use it, urging me to make my new house a home. Despite the pressure it applied, over the months that I lived there I don't think I did more than fry a pair of eggs, and even that unsuccessfully. I survived on food I bought from the delicatessen where Annie worked.

Annie claims never to have noticed me. 'Do you know how many students we'd get?' she answered when I asked, long after we had become a couple, if she had looked forward to my daily visits. I had hoped that we had been engaged in a silent flirtation, but she claims to have no memory of me, which goes to show how much I know of flirtation. She had not noticed me, until I entered one day with my camera. While she guided the lump of meat back and forth over the spinning blade, I asked if I could take her picture.

She looked around and gave me what I thought was an irritated expression, the sort of discouraging expression, I imagined, practised by barmaids. I thought I had ruined my chances already and resolved to take my meat and flee, never to come back again.

She finished carefully slicing the meat and then returned the lump of ham to its place on the shelf. She stood up very straight, adjusted her fringe with just her small finger so as to avoid dirtying her hair and posed with a hand on her hip. 'All right, then,' she said. 'I won't smile.'

I fumbled to get the camera to my eye. I had taken to carrying a larger format camera. Maureen had found a Rolleiflex in a market in Berlin. It's one of the best-made German cameras. I still have it. She bought it for almost nothing and it is worth, I'm told, a significant amount of money. I was just getting used to it at the time. It's held at about chest level, and there's a magnifying glass to help with the focusing. The top is open and the mirror, usually inverted in modern cameras, is fully exposed, so through it everything is backwards.

She exhaled and rolled her eyes. I thought she was growing impatient, but when I knew her better, I recognized it as self-consciousness. I snapped once unsuccessfully and then wound on and took the picture with an almost imperceptible 'click.' 'That's it?' she asked.

'Yes. Got it, I think.'

'It doesn't make much noise.' She wrapped up my slices of

ham, closed the wax paper with a piece of tape and wrote the price on the outside.

'Thank you,' I said. 'And thank you for the picture.'

'You're welcome.' She didn't even ask why I wanted it. Perhaps it made sense to her that strangers wanted her photograph. I turned to walk away, but she called after me. 'You can't just disappear with my picture like that,' she said. 'You'll bring me a copy, won't you?'

When I stood in the darkroom at college and watched her face slowly appear in the reddened liquid, I was overjoyed by what I had created. Despite her promise not to, an involuntary smile had flickered to life at the instant I closed the shutter. She seemed to be smiling directly at me. I had botched the picture with my trembling hands, or perhaps it had been her nervous, unsteady little head on the end of her narrow white neck. Her face was there, clearly recognizable as the woman I had watched, to whom I had paid unnoticed visits for months; but she was slightly out of focus, blurred beneath her eyes, as if she had been gently rubbed out with the end of a pencil.

When I returned to the delicatessen the following day, I requested half a pound of Cheddar cheese sliced into medium-thin pieces, and when her back was turned, slicing the cheese, I put a brown envelope containing the photograph on the counter. As she turned back to hand me the cheese, she caught sight of the envelope. She took it gingerly between the palms of her hands, careful not to dirty it. She pressed it against her belly as she unclasped the metal binding with only the very ends of her fingers and peered inside at the photograph.

'I'm glad you didn't forget,' she said.

'No,' I said. 'I wouldn't.'

'I'll look at it later. I don't want to get anything on it.' She smiled. 'Thank you.' It had not before occurred to me that she was vain.

'I'd like to know what you think,' I said. 'Could you let me know? I'm studying photography at the college. I like the early photographers, myself . . . Julia Cameron, Brassai.' I smiled idiotically and felt myself begin to redden. 'Different centuries,' I continued, trying to reclaim what I was afraid might have been pretentious conversation. I only made myself feel worse, but kept talking in the hope that if I did not allow her to speak I might get things under control again. 'I'd like to know, if you'd tell me . . . Perhaps you'd like to have a drink,' I finally got out.

She looked at me carefully, perhaps considering my intentions. 'If you like,' she said.

I waited across the road from the delicatessen in the newspaper shop reading the headlines of the evening papers and flipping through fashion magazines. I didn't want to get to the pub before her and wait, and become nervous. I knew I would end up drinking too much and having to leave for fear of embarrassing myself.

When Annie came out of the shop, she wore a pink wool car coat buttoned up tight beneath her neck. She carried a black bag slung over her shoulder and the brown envelope under her arm. From where I stood across the road, my face partially concealed behind a luxurious-smelling magazine, I could see that she was smiling. I hoped the photograph was responsible.

I followed her down the road from across the street. She wore childish black leather shoes with covered toes and buckles. She kept them close together as she walked and pressed them tightly shut when she paused at a curb to let a car pass. Her manner of walking would become familiar, but at the time, I was struck by it. It was as if she was carrying something between her knees. She had let her hair down. I had never seen it that way before. It curled beside her neck, at the collar of her coat. Her face shone in the cold.

At the corner, she stopped and stepped into the chemist. It was the chemist where she now works. I did not know what to do, whether to walk ahead to the pub and wait for her there, or to follow her in and meet her coincidentally. I decided that a trip to the chemist together was a sophisticated intimacy, one that I wasn't ready for, so I stepped into a phone booth and picked up the phone. I felt like a detective. Married men hire detectives to watch cheating wives, or vice versa, but I was following another man's fiancée. I watched the entrance and pretended to be listening to someone on the other end of the phone, even nodding and smiling at something they might have said. The shop windows glowed out onto the darkened evening street, but I could not see Annie.

When she emerged, she looked up and down the street as if she were deciding which way to go. She pulled the shoulder bag further up towards her neck, and arranged the collar of her coat beneath her chin. She frowned as if she were personally offended by the cold and walked down the high street, past the toy shop and then the video store and turned left towards the pub. Once she had gone a safe distance, I hung up the phone and followed.

I gave her, by my watch, five minutes before entering the pub. When I had my hand on the door, it suddenly occurred to me that she could have been sitting inside by the fire watching me wait outside. Before I had time to worry sufficiently, two men came roughly through the doors almost knocking me to the ground. When I entered, Annie looked up as if she had been looking up every time the door opened. She smiled politely and indicated the chair opposite her. Her formal smile meant that this was an appointment rather than an engagement. I immediately felt it was a mistake to have come. In front of her sat a half-full glass of Baileys and a half-smoked cigarette, the filter lined with freshly applied pink lipstick. Beside the ashtray rested the brown envelope containing her photograph.

'Hello,' she said. The way she spoke was somehow different in the pub and in that one word she conveyed more sophistication than had existed in any of our previous exchanges. I can remember the sound of her voice. Although blue smoke drifted from between her lips, it made her throat seem narrow and clean. 'I think it's a lovely photograph . . . Really lovely. Sort of sad.'

'I didn't mean to make you look sad,' I said. 'I'll get us a drink.' I pointed down at her glass, still more than half full.

'Baileys, please,' she said and drank the rest of the liquid. She handed me the glass and looked up at me. Her eyes watered slightly.

It took me a long time to get the barman's attention. I ordered, and took a large sip of my pint before returning to the table. I focused all of my attention on not spilling any of either drink, but as I approached the table I could see she had the photograph out of the envelope.

When I put the drinks down, she did not look up. She guided her cigarette to her lips and said, with a gust of smoke, 'You've also made me look quite pretty.'

I craned my neck over to take a look at the picture from her angle. I was standing above her looking down at her looking at a picture of herself. The image was black and white. The large window to her left was a washed-out grey. The lights above her head were bright white, but without form, like snowflakes falling across the lens. Her hair was tied tightly behind her, and her eyes looked larger than they were. She looked young, younger than she looked, even then.

'What's the matter? You don't think I could look pretty?'

I looked up, and saw that she was smiling at me, with more familiarity this time. I walked around to the opposite side of the table and sat down. She took a drink of her new Baileys and continued staring at the photograph.

'I knew you'd look pretty,' I said. 'You are pretty.'

'Thank you,' she said. 'You're very sweet.'

'I'm not saying it to be sweet. I mean it.'

A group of men were playing pool in the back room. Throughout the evening they grew steadily more drunk and steadily louder. They let up cheers when one of them won or lost or just made an especially good shot. As we spoke, when they let up a particularly loud cheer, Annie would look over my shoulder to see what the commotion was about, and I would be forced to look as well, to keep up the momentum of our conversation. We had three or four more drinks each. I suppose we got to know each other over the few hours we sat there. She asked why I was living in England, and where I had lived in America. 'You get to travel a lot, then?' she said. 'I'd love to travel. I've been to Spain once.' She thought for a moment and then glanced up at me. 'And I've been to Paris.' I wanted to ask about her engagement, but I didn't. Once when I said something she found amusing she put her hand on the back of mine, and left it there a moment or two before moving it away. I almost asked her then, but decided against it.

Several times she put the photograph in and took it out of

the envelope. She held it slightly off the table to be sure it wouldn't get wet, down at her side where I couldn't see it, as if she was looking at a kitten in a box. 'Funny, isn't it?' she said. 'I'm not sure it looks like me.'

'You never know how someone's going to photograph. You can compensate once you know. You can get parts of someone. You can get at it, but not all of it.'

'Oh, I know that,' she interrupted. 'You just get a bit of what's floating on top.' She finished her drink and stood wobbling slightly on her heels. 'I'll get another.'

'I'll get it,' I protested, but she silenced me with the open palm of her hand.

'I want to get it.'

I let my vision dissolve over the orange and red flames in the fireplace, and felt that I was drunk. The windows above the empty seat where Annie had sat were steamed against the cold outdoors. I turned in my chair to look at her, weaving slightly, at the bar. She had left her coat heaped on her empty seat. She wore a conservative black skirt, and a cropped grey wool V-neck sweater. She turned and glanced back at me. When she saw that I was staring at her, she looked away.

'What is it about pictures?' she asked as she put my drink down in front of me. 'I've never seen a painting look as sad.'

'No,' I agreed. 'My mother disagrees. She says a photograph can't do half of what a painting can. Tristan Tzara, this man who used to write about photographs in the twenties when people didn't understand them as well as they do now, said a photograph presents an image to space which is more space than space.' She looked puzzled. 'It's specific, but not. Perfectly clear and static yet ephemeral and inconstant. Intangible in another way altogether, almost *because* it's so specific.' I trailed off because she no longer listened as much as just watched. I had been reading about it in school and was interested in the theory of it all. I can't believe now that I ever was. 'I don't know,' I said.

'Oh, Gordon,' she smiled. 'The way you talk.' She was smiling again. I think she found me slightly ridiculous. She was just looking at me. She looked so lovely at that moment. She leaned forward. I thought she wanted to whisper something to me, but when I leaned in to hear what she had to say, she kissed me. When she stopped, the billiard players let up another cry and she looked up again over my shoulder. 'They're rooting for us,' she said. I turned in my chair to see several drunken men raising drinks in our direction.

'Well done, son!' one of them called.

The air outside had grown colder since we had gone into the pub. As we walked along the pavement, ribbons of grey steam curled from our mouths around our faces. I looked down at her hand out of its pocket, swinging limply beside her. I reached for it before thinking, or rather, the thought of what I had done came back to me like an echo or a memory in that drunken way that thought follows action. She did not flinch. She held my hand softly. We walked that way together, my hand in hers. Occasionally I'd look over at her to see what look she had on her face, but she just looked ahead, smiling happily. I remember thinking how absurd it seemed that I should be already holding her hand. But I was enjoying it, just as I was the way I allowed her to lead us wherever we were going.

She led us to a corner of the blackened Heath. The wet asphalt path reflected the orange street lights in pools of colour between long black stretches. We walked deep into the park,

past several empty benches and a line of tall oaks planted a
determined distance apart. Behind the trees, a field opened up,
and the moon made the sky brighter between a pair of rickety
goalposts. I don't remember where – and I have since wandered
around that part of the Heath trying to remember – she pulled
me off the path into the dark, wet grass. She began to kiss me,
slowly at first, and then (it may have been the drunkenness)
with what seemed to be increasing speed, her face darting at me
from behind her pink coat, as we turned dizzily around until
we tumbled over. I felt the leftover rain seep through my
trousers. She carefully undid my belt, unbuttoned my trousers
and pulled them down just slightly so that the zipper wouldn't
rub uncomfortably against my skin. And then she raised her
skirt and stepped out of her tights. I remember looking at them
there on the ground beside us, cold and curled, the life of her
seeping out, as she pulled a packet of condoms from the pocket
of her coat. She threw the white paper bag from the chemist's
into the darkness. She opened one of the little blue packets and
helped me put it on. She smiled, and then slowly, without a
word, lowered herself onto me. Her feet were flat on the
ground beside me. I put my hands on her thighs, but she didn't
look at me. She kept her eyes closed, her lips parted as if
she were feeling around for something in a sack. I began to
concentrate on the sensation. She felt warm and kind, like an
underwater hug. As I watched her raise and lower herself,
her bent knees propelling her rhythmically up and down, the
thought came to me that she had embraced many others. For a
moment I had the feeling I needn't be there at all. Then, all at
once, and all too soon, the sensation swept over me. I lifted my
head slightly and she met my brow with her hand and stroked
my hair. She smiled down at me with sympathy and reassur-

ance, as if she were a doctor who knew just how I felt – my shyness, the sudden remembered coldness of the air – but she'd seen it all before. And I found that profoundly comforting. 'Thank you,' I said.

We lay there together. A little breath of wind passed over us: a cold piece of silk lain down upon us and then lifted off again. She kissed my neck and I looked into the dark sky at the trees' bare branches above us. We lay there together in silence for a time, her knees pressed into the cold ground beside my arms. We reassembled ourselves silently beside one another. She tied a knot in the condom, and threw it into the bushes. It made me momentarily sad the way she tossed it away. I strained to see where it had gone, but couldn't find it in the moonlight. I redid my trousers in time to watch her put herself together. As she stepped into her tights I caught a glimpse of her white skin and black hair and realized, with a pang of remorse, that I had not yet seen her naked.

We began to walk back the way we had come. She leaned on me. I felt tired as well, and suddenly nakedly sober. Above all, I felt proud to support her head against my shoulder. I put both arms around her and gave her a little squeeze and Annie stopped. We had not gone twenty yards from where we had lain together. She turned and faced me. I thought the hug had upset her and regretted my excitement. 'Gordon,' she said. 'Can I ask you something?'

'Certainly,' I said.

'I don't mean to offend you.' She was reluctant. 'Was that your first time?'

I felt I had no choice but to tell the truth. 'Yes,' I said with as much dignity as I could gather.

Annie's face instantly clouded over. 'Oh, Gordon,' she said. 'Why didn't you say something?'

'Why?'

'Well, it shouldn't have been in the park like that.'

'Why not? It's as good a place as any.'

'I suppose.' Annie did not look at me.

I took her by the shoulders and looked confidently into her eyes. 'Annie,' I said. 'That was quite unlike anything I've experienced.'

She smiled. 'Well, of course it was.'

'No. I mean unlike anything at all. A totally different thing altogether. Not just more of something else, but something completely unique.'

Her expression softened and I felt with both surprise and excitement that my look had landed in the right place.

'Annie,' I continued. 'I've been thinking about you for months. The only reason I come into the deli at all is to see you.'

'Really?'

'I think I might love you.'

'Poor Gordon,' she smiled.

An instinct I did not know I possessed compelled me to lean towards her. I had seen it in numerous paintings, and in numerous films, and this is how I account for the fact that I knew what to do. As I moved slowly towards her, I was conscious that this was something I should remember: our first kiss.

After I had released her, I noticed that Annie's eyes were no longer closed. She was looking across the field behind me. There was a man standing there. He stood quite still wearing a hooded jacket. He held a stick in his hand. It seemed, from the way he stood, that he had been watching us for some time. 'Do you think he saw us?' I asked.

'I don't know,' she said. She laughed. 'Heathcliff out wandering the moors.'

I laughed as well, although I didn't know why. I didn't know who Heathcliff was at the time. I thought she meant her hairdresser fiancé, which frightened me. When I realized he wasn't going to charge towards us and challenge me to a fight, I felt sad for him. He had begun to swing his stick back and forth, swatting at the moist grass at his feet. I wondered how she could say such a thing. I didn't know then how much Annie loved to read.

I waited two full days before I stopped in to see Annie at the delicatessen. I stood across the street and watched her clouded form through the blue frosted glass. I had the feeling that I should not go in. If I made the effort to see her again, I felt, I would be ignoring some unspoken adult agreement. When she had bid me farewell that evening on the high street, she made the separation easy; she did not mention any further arrangements. She was, after all, engaged.

After pacing the pavement opposite for several minutes I resolved that I would handle the matter casually. She could not expect me to stop shopping there, I reasoned.

It took me fifteen minutes to work up the courage to approach her. I meandered through the aisles, staying close to the shelves, reading labels, and collecting unwanted items in my wire basket. When I changed aisles, I took a peek at Annie working behind the glass at the meat counter. When I saw one of her co-workers, I was convinced that they looked at me strangely, as if she had told them the funny story about what had happened in the park and what I had said. By the time I approached the meat counter I had accumulated far more than what I usually allowed for my weekly grocery allowance.

'There you are,' she said before I had raised my eyes to her lovely face. 'I thought you'd forgotten me.' I wanted to tell her that I had not forgotten her, that as I lay in my narrow orange bed at night, I pictured the slowly inflating outline we had left in the wet grass. 'You had me worried,' she said firmly. She finished wrapping wax paper filled with cold meat for the little old woman standing in front of me at the counter. Annie avoided my gaze and took a long time putting the cap back on the marker and the marker back in the breast pocket of her coat. A bouquet of stray flicks of ink spread out around the pocket on her chest.

'Have you come to ask me out?' she asked. One of the older men working further down the counter glanced at me over his glasses and then looked disapprovingly at Annie. I looked at my shoes.

'Have you become shy since I've seen you last? You weren't shy the other night.'

'Did you get home all right?' I asked.

'No trouble,' she smiled confidently.

'I should have found you a cab.'

'No,' she picked up a large slab of the smoked ham that I like so much and dropped it on the stainless steel slicer. She wore plastic gloves and held one hand on the meat as it slid back and forth over the spinning blade and in the other she caught the ribbons of meat and piled them neatly on a piece of wax paper. 'So where are you taking me?' she asked.

'I don't know,' I said.

'Where do you take your girlfriends?'

'How about the Ritz for tea?' I asked. It had leapt into my mind. I had been there only once with Maureen and we hadn't enjoyed it. They made me buy an expensive red necktie in one of the hotel shops and I spent the time miserable, scratching at my neck as Maureen looked around the room critiquing the unpleasant decor. 'You'd think they could at least get some inoffensive flowers,' I remember her saying. But it had come to mind, and I could think of nothing else.

Annie wrapped up an enormous lump of ham and wrote a price on the paper with her thick black pen. When she tried to put the pen back in her pocket, she still had the cap between her lips and added another stripe to the bouquet.

'Here you are,' she said when she had recapped the pen. She had charged me only fifty pence for an amount of food that should have been far more expensive. 'That would be nice,' she said. She smiled unconfidently for the first time. She looked down the counter towards the older men slicing cheese and filling paper cups with black or purple olives. She removed her plastic glove, wiped her fingers against her white coat and placed her hand open on the counter. I put my hand in hers and she stroked my skin with her nails. 'This evening?' she ventured.

Ten

Maureen tried to be supportive of my study of photography. She was responsible for my initial interest in the subject. She gave me my first camera when I was ten. She gave me my first set of charcoal pencils and a sketchpad a few years before, but I never took to sketching. It was my responsibility to document our travels together and between us we have a fairly detailed photographic record of most of the places we went to and of our own respective physical changes as the years went by. I have, in fact, used some of those pictures in an attempt to accurately describe these events as I have put them down. She brought me that camera that I used on Annie when she came back through London from Berlin. She gave me a lesson in its mechanism sitting on my little bed. She showed me, just as the market vendor had shown her, how the film was loaded, using the empty roll of the last film to wind on the newly exposed film. She wore a hat with a slight veil covering her eyes. It was one of her favourites. I had seen her wear it many times before, but I remember noticing for the first time, as I sat beside her, how absurdly out of style it was. Through the veil, she looked down at the camera in her lap, trying to remember the market vendor's instructions. She let her fingers move over the camera, hoping that they would remember (when she could not) the manoeuvre she had so easily performed standing at his stall in

Berlin. 'You'll have to figure it out yourself,' she said, handing me the camera in two pieces. She had lost patience with re-attaching the back. 'You'll need a tripod, he said. When you can't use one, you hang it around your neck.'

She got up from the bed and with great ceremony lifted the strap over my head. I had not yet managed to get the back closed. 'You have to hold very still. This isn't like one of those modern ones. You have to be more careful but, ultimately, you'll get better pictures.' She was trying to convince me just as the vendor had convinced her. She could always be convinced that something older, something that had survived was, as evidenced merely by its survival, better. 'Try it on me,' she smiled. She crossed the room and leaned on the window sill where she struck a contemplative pose, turning partially towards the traffic outside.

'You can't stand there,' I said as I continued to fiddle with the camera. 'I don't have a light meter, you'll come out silhouetted.'

'Where then?' she asked

I guided her across the room and had her sit at my table. 'Sit there,' I said. 'Pull the chair out, and cross your legs.' She followed my instructions. She wore a short pink skirt. 'Put the light on,' I said and walked into the kitchen. I took a saucer from the cupboard and put it down in front of her. 'Have a cigarette.'

She retrieved her handbag from the bed. She took out a packet of cigarettes and a lipstick before returning to her chair. 'Are you gonna make me look like an old film star?' she asked. She sucked in her cheeks. 'They used to have their teeth pulled for those cheekbones, those valleys.'

'Take off the hat,' I said.

'Do you think?' she asked

'I do.'

She unpinned her hat and lay it down on the table beside her. She opened her shirt one button further and adjusted her necklace so it was visible.

'Don't move,' I commanded.

'No,' she agreed. She turned her head, showing only slightly more than her profile to the camera, and opened her eyes very wide as if she were a little innocent thing lost in the world.

We took the whole roll, twelve pictures in all. She was very serious about each pose, trying a different expression for each one. When we were finished she was in a very good mood, and afterwards she offered to take me to lunch.

As we stepped out onto the street she adjusted her hat and unfolded the veil down over her eyes. 'Why do you wear that hat?' I asked. 'It's a little silly.'

'You don't want me to be recognized, do you?' she asked.

She was not as supportive about Annie. I told Maureen over the phone that I had met someone. 'Oh good,' she said. She let out a tremendous sigh, as if it was a great relief for her. 'Oh, Gordy, wonderful news. Just wonderful.'

When Maureen next came through London, just before Easter, the three of us had a casual lunch together in a pizzeria facing Hyde Park. Maureen had spent the morning in the Serpentine Gallery. A show on contemporary British sculptors, Maureen explained to Annie, had brought her back through London. 'I'm doing a book, and this fits quite neatly into the sequence.' Annie listened attentively. 'Some of your country's finest sculptors are there at the moment.'

Annie nodded. 'I think you're very fortunate to be able to travel like you do.' She smiled confidently.

'Have you been to see the exhibit?' Maureen wanted to know.

'No,' said Annie.

'I think that's a shame.' Maureen turned to me.

'I don't know much about art,' said Annie. 'I appreciate it, but it's not one of my interests, I'm afraid. I don't have the time.'

'Annie loves to read,' I interjected.

'I work,' said Annie matter-of-factly.

Maureen stared at Annie for a moment. 'You have an interesting face,' said Maureen.

'Do I?' asked Annie.

'In America people tend to judge a face by what it isn't. If someone's nose is not too big, eyes not too small, lips not too flat, they qualify as good looking, when there's really nothing to them at all. Blink your eyes and you've forgotten them.' Maureen closed her eyes to show how this could happen. She kept them closed longer than I expected. 'You have an interesting face,' she said and finally opened her eyes again.

'Well, thank you,' said Annie.

'It's meant to be a compliment.'

'I think you have a beautiful face,' said Annie.

Maureen waved away the compliment as if Annie had offered to refill her wine glass.

'I can see you in Gordon,' added Annie

On the way home Annie was quiet and then, as if she had considered it for a long time, she announced that she liked Maureen. Maureen responded by letter: *I don't object to the fact that she's not good-looking. It's her ambition, Gordy. It's palpable beneath her English-rose skin. She's too damned eager to please and will drive you mad. Trust me . . . Love your old gal, Maureen.*

Maureen's letter did not surprise me. During lunch I had watched Maureen stare at Annie. She watched as Annie pushed her hair back and slipped, with nimble fingers, a few loose stands beneath her hair clip. I saw Maureen's eyes slide dangerously across Annie's soft face, and down her neck, and I wanted desperately to brush them off. To stamp on those ugly thoughts like insects. I watched Maureen look at Annie's hand, which she had the rather annoying habit of sometimes resting on the table, lifeless, beside her plate as she ate. As I watched, I knew that Maureen was busy making ugly calculations.

'Ambition,' I said into the telephone, 'is not the same as wanting to please.'

'Same church, different pew,' said Maureen.

'Maureen,' I said. 'Be nice to her.' There was a long pause. 'Maureen,' I said again. And then she promised she would treat her kindly.

Eleven

I remember a summer day walking in New York long before I had ever laid eyes on Annie. It was unusual for Maureen and me to be in New York in the summertime. Maureen did not like the heat. She spent her days sitting silently in one of the old chairs in the darkened apartment, as if the temperature made it impossible to read. In the late afternoons she walked across town into the park towards one of the museums. She considered this a great effort. When she returned in the evenings she collapsed on top of her bed for a nap and called out for something cold to drink.

We met for dinner in the apartment every night at eight thirty. We ate something she had picked up on her way home or else she asked the cleaner, Dolores, to make a tortilla and leave it in the refrigerator. She claimed that Dolores made better tortillas than Maureen had ever tasted in Spain.

In that hot summer I was free to move around the city by myself during the days. I had spent the afternoon in question browsing the bookstores along Fourth Avenue. There used to be a great number of them, many with fairly good selections of antique photographs. I once collected them and don't know why I stopped. I still have them. One of my favourites is a complete book of Eadweard Muybridge's stopped-motion pictures. They have a vaguely erotic quality about them: pairs of flesh-white wrestlers with faces frozen in exertion and horses floating above the earth with rippling chests.

I worked my way from Fourteenth Street down to Ninth Street going in and out of stores. I was sixteen and had a very specific sort of picture in mind. I ended up buying a collection of German semi-nudes from the 1920s. The pictures are attributed to 'Anonymous'. I remember the book because its racy red cover and black print were what initially caught my attention. It was entitled *Frau Allein* or, 'Woman Alone', and looked like a political manifesto. The pictures themselves interested me because of their alluringly amateur quality. It seemed to me that the subjects (housewife-types of different shapes and sizes) knew the photographer intimately. The pictures seemed to have been taken in the women's homes, as if he had come around and rung the bell and had, over tea, persuaded these women to take off their clothes or merely open their blouses or lift their skirts.

I had the book under my arm. I was between Fourth Avenue and Broadway walking along in the desolation of the late-afternoon city heat. The sky, gleaming and expansive at the western end of the island, was a blinding slab of blue, like the reflection off a boat's hull above the Hudson. From behind me I heard a series of muffled collisions, as if the largest pedestrians had begun forcefully walking into one another. I turned to find the street behind me almost empty, the last remaining people darting out of sight into doorways. I think for just an instant I imagined it had something to do with the book I had bought. Until I noticed the sky. It had become a mossy-grey behind me. I had never seen such a sky. An instant later, the raindrops, whose muffled collisions I had heard against the metal rooftops, made it to the street. My clothes stuck to my skin, the red binding of my book bled in my hand and my feet slipped in their shoes.

I ran across the street and took shelter with another man in a doorway and together we watched the downpour, the street flowing like a river, sweeping the city of its refuse.

It was like that: I realized my feeling for Annie in an instant – like a change in the weather.

When I had known Annie for just a few months, we took our first of several trips to Dorset for a visit to Sasha, her older sister. She lived in a small village, a twenty-minute walk from one of the most pleasant and tranquil rivers in the world. Their mother had come from there.

We set off from the station on a warm Friday afternoon. Along the way we picked up school children at almost every stop. The corridors were lined with them gazing out of the windows at the green fizz of passing landscape and blowing cigarette smoke through the small opening at the top of the glass. Games of flirtation were played along each corridor: school bags stolen, sweet wrappers flicked back and forth, bursts of cruel laughter. While I was only a few years older than some of these dishevelled boys with their shirts hanging out or the girls with their pleated skirts and perforated knee socks, I felt a generation apart. After all, I was with Annie.

At the station, I held both bags in one hand and Annie's hand in the other as we waited on the platform. She stood up on her tiptoes and searched amongst the crowd. The station was quite full, mostly with commuters and noisy school children. They passed around us: the commuters, silent and determined, on their way to the car park; the students, still buzzing from the pleasures of the train journey, on the way to the bus stop. No one seemed to be waiting for anyone like us.

'Do you see her?' asked Annie. She scanned the station anxiously and then looked up at me. 'Well, do you?'

I told Annie that I had never seen her sister so I didn't know what I was looking out for, but when I saw Sasha, I recognized her instantly. She looked like Annie, only older, a little taller and not as pretty. She emerged from the crowd smiling with a self-deprecating curve of the mouth. Annie released my hand and rushed across the platform. Sasha opened her cardigan to receive her and they embraced passionately.

We drove to Sasha's small house in her powder-blue Volkswagen Polo. The car made pained sounds of determination from a place directly beneath my seat. I sat in the back smothered with luggage and several bags of shopping as Annie talked continually, interrupted only by bursts of not entirely natural laughter. Sasha watched the road and occasionally smiled. Once or twice I caught her glancing at me in the rearview mirror. I smiled and she looked away.

After I had put our bags on the guest bed I returned to the kitchen. Annie had gone to wash up and Sasha and I were left alone. She rested her hands in the pockets of her over-sized cardigan where she fiddled with a collection of moist tissues. She had the habit of dabbing at the corners of her eyes and then blotting her forehead, as if she were an old woman suffering from cataracts and hot flashes when really she was just thirty-two. She seemed depleted and unhappy. Wilted with resignation, it seemed to me, but Annie said that in fact it was stubbornness, a lack of compromise that had hurt her sister.

We stood there watching the slow kettle. A row of souvenir mugs stood along the window sill behind the sink. In each she had arranged a few dried flowers. Through the windows, I could see her well-tended garden. She was obviously very proud of it so I told her it was lovely.

'Oh, I need a garden,' she said. 'I don't know how you two live in that filthy city.'

'I've always lived in a city,' I told her. 'Perhaps I should give country living a try one day.'

'You should,' she said and offered me a biscuit.

'I imagine it takes some getting used to.'

'Yes. I suppose so. But then you begin to notice things in a way you didn't notice them before and you can really feel time passing.'

'I'm not sure I'd want that,' I said.

'No. Most people don't,' she said.

Annie returned and we all sat down at the table for tea. Sasha warmed her hands around her mug despite the double-glazed windows that made the room almost uncomfortably warm. 'Annie says that you're a photographer?'

'I'm hoping to be,' I said.

'He's very good,' said Annie. 'He'll take some pictures of you.' She turned towards me. 'Won't you?'

I'd never known Annie to be the excited one, the organizer. 'If you won't mind,' I said.

Sasha nodded, looking down into her tea. It was an indulgent, motherly gesture, as if she were not quite listening.

'Get your camera,' said Annie.

I don't think I've ever mentioned Annie's mother. She disappeared when Annie was six and Sasha was twelve and left them in the charge of their father. She wrote birthday cards that first year, postmarked from Denmark, and was not heard from again until she died seven years later in Leeds, of all places.

'Now?' I asked.

'There's no need to take pictures of me,' protested Sasha.

'I want some,' said Annie. 'I hardly have any pictures of you and they're all from about ten years ago.'

'Well, not now,' said Sasha touching her sister's hand. 'I look awful. Not now.' Having quieted Annie, Sasha turned again to me. 'You're at art college?' she asked, her hand still resting on Annie's.

'Almost finished.'

She nodded again. 'But you're an American?'

'That's right.'

'The accent's difficult to detect.'

'Actually, I've spent a good part of my life here, or in Europe.'

'How's that?' she asked.

I glanced at Annie. I thought she would have supplied Sasha with all those details, but apparently she had told her very little about me.

'His mother travels all over Europe,' said Annie. 'She's working on a book.'

'Oh?'

'A guidebook and she travels for research,' said Annie.

'She never stops travelling,' I said.

'Annie would like that. When she was little, Annie said she was going to join the navy. She wanted to see the world.'

'Did she?' I asked.

'Yes she did.'

After tea, the three of us walked out of her drive and then along a narrow road. We had to walk in a single line, Sasha in front and me at the back, pressed up against the hedges to avoid the cars whizzing past. I thought of Timothy. After a few moments we turned into a break in the hedge, about the width of a single car, where we could all walk together. Annie and Sasha linked arms and I carried the picnic supper they had prepared. We followed the two troughs of flattened grass on either side of a flowering median until the pass opened into a large field. At the end of the field flowed the gentle river on which canal boats floated slowly past and brought with them the smell of cooking meat and sometimes music.

As we sat, the air seemed to be floating horizontally with its collection of petals, insects and pollen. I remember picking tiny leaves from my sandwich. The evening was so still I could hear Annie and her sister chewing. They chatted away on many different subjects, about people I didn't know, or things that had happened long ago. They recommended books to one another with varying degrees of imperative. Sasha would name a title, the author and then put both hands on her chest. 'This book,' she would say and shake her head as if she could no longer risk speaking for fear of bursting into tears. I thought they both sounded overblown and a little silly. I may have let this show. At one point, Sasha turned to me and said, 'You're not a reader, then? Some people just aren't, I suppose.'

'No. I guess not. Not like you two.' I watched Annie's head where it lay in Sasha's lap and felt slightly jealous. We sat in silence until Annie or Sasha sighed and commented how lovely everything looked. Even the cold bottle of white wine that Sasha had provided failed to inspire a sustained three-way conversation. Finally, I resorted to the most tired of commonplaces and asked Sasha about her work. Sasha worked for the council as a home-care nurse. I imagine she spent her time making reassuring cups of tea, puffing up pillows, and stealing pensioner's cigarettes. On that first visit, after we had all complimented the scenery numerous times, the conversation turned to politics. Sasha was very down on Margaret Thatcher and her attempts to privatize everything. I didn't know much about it. I had no strong opinions on the subject one way or the other. Sasha was talking about the hideous repercussions for the country and, perhaps, for nursing in particular. I am not confrontational. I can't have been listening very closely for, had I realized how strongly she felt about it, I would have kept my mouth shut. 'I don't know why everyone gets so upset about Thatcher,' I said off-handedly. 'All round, she seems to be making England a nicer place to live.' I have very little interest in politics and get most of my information from the headlines or conversations I have with those who are more informed. I may have been quoting Theo, but he would have said something like, 'a damned nicer place to live', but I can't carry off that sort of talk.

Annie and Sasha glared at me. Annie looked disapproving while Sasha was obviously very angry. She twice raised her hands in front of her face before clapping them together ceremoniously. She shook her head as if to clear her vision. 'I don't think you have the slightest idea what you're talking about, Gordon.'

I had no idea what to say. 'You really don't,' added Annie, nodding sadly.

'She may have made it a nicer place to live for you and your mother who, as far as I can make out, don't work, but for the rest of us, she happens to be making it very difficult indeed.'

There was a long, cool silence as the river trickled past. Sasha's anger seemed slowly to subside as poor Annie made polite chat. I resented Sasha's self-righteousness, especially over something I cared so little about. I could hardly have explained that to her, however; it would only have made things much worse.

We stayed out by the river until almost dark. That was always my favourite part of the picnics. As the sun went down, the tame English landscape was transformed. The ball of fire in the black trees, the tan grass and wispy sky – Dorset suddenly looked like Kenya.

As we rested in the guest bedroom before dinner, Annie reprimanded me further. 'Don't talk about things you don't understand, Gordon,' she said. 'Especially with people who do.' This is sound advice that I am happy to pass along. I might add, do not say anything at all if you feel, as I have felt for the majority of my life, an inability to feel passionately about public things. But that was how I was raised. Maureen had no politics except to judge things on aesthetic terms.

After dinner the three of us sat around the table smoking and finishing a bottle of wine. I was trying to repair the damage I had done with Sasha at the riverbank. I made repeated efforts at conversation, mostly unsuccessful. I even made an apology, which she accepted graciously. The whole experience was exhausting and it was getting late. I decided to leave the two of them together to catch up without my interference. I rose from the table, thanked Sasha for her bland cooking and kissed Annie goodnight.

Annie and Sasha sat up late chatting at the little kitchen table. I could hear them whispering from where I lay in the guest bed. I tried to sleep, but just when I began to drift off one of them laughed and the other made a shushing sound. As it got later I began to wonder what they could possibly be talking about for so long. I very gently peeled back the sheets and stepped onto the cold floor. I moved gingerly towards the door and after another moment's pause, pushed it partially open. A small band of light from the candles fell across my shoulder and I could hear their voices more clearly.

'He's an *idiot*,' said Annie.

When I heard her say that, I felt sick. I had been lying there worrying that they had been talking about me and now I was sure: I, obviously, was the idiot.

Sasha laughed. 'You've always loved each other. Since you were kids.'

'He had his chance,' continued Annie.

'He loves you,' said Sasha. 'He calls and tells me. He's pathetic, actually.'

'He tells me as well and I don't care . . . Besides . . . Now I've got Gordon. He loves me and I would like to be happy and I—' She stopped in mid sentence. 'What is it?' Silence. And then it suddenly occurred to me: I've been seen.

'Gordon?' called Sasha.

I said nothing. Irrationally, I froze (I may even have closed my eyes like the child I remember myself being) and hoped I was invisible.

'Gordon?' Sasha called out again. For what could have been a full thirty seconds, there was only overwhelming, deadly silence.

'He's asleep,' said Annie finally.

The relief I felt at that moment has never been matched in my life. She had not seen me. It was not me she had called an idiot. Someone else, but it didn't matter because she had me. I could not have been happier. I thought nothing of what Sasha had said about them loving each other since they were children. Everyone has their moments of conviction; that's how I think of it, not as stupidity or denial, as it may seem, but as conviction: an overwhelming desire to believe in something.

I pushed open the door and yawned wildly. A delicious feeling of exhilaration pushed at the back of my eyes. I must have never seemed so awake. 'What?' I asked groggily. 'Were you calling?'

'I thought you were in the room,' said Sasha.

'In the guest room,' I said, thumbing over my shoulder.

'No, in here,' she said coldly. Her hair was now down around her shoulders and she looked even older than she had that afternoon.

'No,' I said. 'I heard you calling and got out of bed. Did you need something?'

'No, darling,' said Annie. 'Go back to sleep. I'm coming now.'

I turned and walked back to the guest room. I was wide awake when Annie came in. She disrobed quietly thinking I had gone back to sleep. When she lay down beside me, I rolled over to her and began to kiss her.

Sasha and I exchanged an icy handshake at the station. She glared at me as Annie hung around her neck. Her distrust of me had been confirmed by what she thought she had seen the night before. That look she gave me at the station was the moment she wanted to make it clear that she didn't care for me, and it wasn't lost on me. I knew it each time we came to visit and Annie knew it as well.

Annie and I sat in the train compartment watching the landscape turn slowly grey the closer we got to London. 'What did you two talk about so late?' I asked.

Annie shrugged. 'Just catching up.'

I don't know why Sasha is so bitter. Annie told me a story about her sister's early devotion to some depressive boy with whom she had gotten herself pregnant. The baby was terminated. Annie claimed that Sasha wanted to keep it, but this may have been wishful thinking on Annie's part; she disapproves of abortion. The boy is probably at least fifteen years older than I am, so I should probably not refer to him as a boy, but this has always been the way I've thought of him: that is, sympathetically. He felt that he wasn't making enough money to begin a family. Apparently, it hadn't been Sasha's first termination.

With the baby, unbeknownst to Sasha and her lover, went their fondness for one another. They hung around for a while, kicking at the emptiness between them. The real difficulty, according to Annie, was that they still vaguely recognized one another as the people they had loved. Like recognizing a childhood friend in a station somewhere and finding, upon shaking hands and inquiring into one another's lives that you don't like each other at all. Annie said that Sasha still thought about this young man.

'How can you stand her?' I asked.

'She's my sister. We didn't have a mother. We're very close.' She shook her head, turned and looked determinedly out of the window.

Annie was silent for a time. I stroked the back of her head but she kept moving away. 'Sasha doesn't approve of you either. When you stand in the room, she's not sure you're really there.' Annie laughed unconvincingly and a small drop of saliva appeared on the glass like a fleck of rain.

The moment when I realized my feeling for Annie came as we wound our way back into London. I had wandered down the train to find us something to eat. The snack car had run out of almost every item on the menu. The steward was totally uninterested in serving me. He dragged his hand over each sandwich as I pointed through the dirty glass and I had to point out the two cans of lemonade, one after the other, in the fridge. As it was Sunday, the train was free of students and quiet. I studied each of the sleeping or reading passengers as I passed the cabins on the way back to ours and decided that there was no woman on the train as attractive as Annie.

When I finally made it back to our compartment, I found Annie asleep. She had let her hair fall across one eye and the skin on her cheek creased slightly where she rested her face against the seat cushion. I glanced tentatively at the large man with swollen forearms and scrubbed skin sharing our compartment. He never looked away from the window or changed the angry expression with which he watched the passing landscape. I put our snacks on the small, white plastic table marked with grey initials. Someone had shakily scratched another Annie's name. I dragged my finger over the letters and the crushed heart the artist had added beside her name.

As soon as I sat down next to Annie, she switched positions and laid her head in my lap. I was content watching the houses standing in their little gardens. They seemed startled, as if the train had interrupted them in an act of privacy. I was happy thinking of the people inside having something to eat or watching television. As we passed one house, joined in an endless series to others exactly like it, I saw a young woman squeeze a full-sized double mattress through her window. It snapped open in the air and landed soundlessly on the patio. She leaned out and looked down at it and then we sped past out of sight. I once read that moments like these define modern human existence. The world passes at such a rate it is almost impossible to know anything for certain. For every action witnessed, any number of details or gestures go unseen that make it impossible to decide what an action really means. Was the house on fire? Was she a prisoner in need of a soft landing for her escape? Had she discovered a betrayal that had taken place on that disgusting mattress? Or did the mattress simply need getting rid of and why bother carrying it down the stairs? I was concerned by the possibilities. It is far more reassuring to imagine simple lives passing behind darkened windows. I was content with this thought until I looked down at Annie again. This was the moment I have alluded to. She had fallen into a deeper asleep; her skin had slackened, vibrating partially from the motion of the train. Her lips were parted, her eyes held effortlessly closed. She was truly sleep and I was horrified. The usual competence and energy in her face, the privacy, was nowhere to be found. I hardly recognized her. I could see into her open mouth, her crooked teeth, the velvet ribbon of tongue and the dark, cave entrance of her throat. I suddenly felt overwhelmed by the thought that everything would not be all right. Terrible things could happen to such a face, I decided. I put my hands around her chin and her forehead and tried to hold her still, but it didn't help. I had to wake her.

She blinked and looked up at me without recognition and then, only slowly, she began to look awake. 'What is it?' she asked, glancing up at the window.

The man sitting across was now watching us. When I returned his gaze he frowned and looked out again. 'What is it?' she repeated. 'What's the matter?' She looked up at me with alarm.

'You looked so . . .' I paused. I didn't know how to say it.

I felt really very emotional. 'I don't want anything terrible to happen to you.' The man looked at us again and let out a small, incredulous chuckle. Annie reached up and awkwardly cupped my chin in her palm.

'Don't worry,' she said. She was being kind, although she seemed irritated to have been woken. She moved her hand back and forth over the stubble on my jaw until her grip slowly slackened as she drifted back to sleep. I shook her once more and she emerged again with that same expression of under-water horror. 'What?' she asked.

'I'd like to marry you,' I stuttered and glanced up at the man sitting across from us. His hairless eyebrows rose above his pink face.

She looked at me for a long moment. Her face did not change from one second to the next and then she put her small hard hands on the back of my neck. She smiled, but suddenly tears bubbled up and overwhelmed her expression. They were tears of joy, she explained, but she looked miserable. She pulled my head towards her and kissed me. I cannot be sure if it was my breathing or perhaps Annie's, but I think the man might have let out a sigh before turning back to the window, to the landscape that had been replaced by the first dreary neighbourhoods of the city.

'Do not be a fatalist,' said Maureen when I told her this story. 'Your father is a fatalist, it's simple-minded.' Although she did not say so, it is also un-American.

I had called to tell her that Annie and I were engaged. Maureen wanted to know if I was in love with Annie and I said that I was. She asked me how I knew and I recounted the story, exactly as I just have. She said I had it all wrong: 'Love,' she told me, 'is not fear of what you might lose.'

'Have you never felt that you had something that it would just kill you to give up?' I asked.

'Oh, Gordon,' she said. 'You've never felt that strongly about anything. Not even as a child. You've always been quite self-sufficient. If I've done anything for you, I think that might be it.'

Twelve

Annie, you will remember, was engaged before we met, to the hairdresser, the Heathcliff on the side of the hill. His name is Graham. They grew up in the same block of flats and played together as children. I've never met him. I saw him just that once when he dropped Annie off at work and shook his great mane. We used to see his motorbike parked in front of Annie's father's place when he was there visiting his mother. When I asked about him, she said that he had been understanding when she broke off the engagement. On a few occasions, she thought he might have been following her. Once, we had to duck into a fast-food restaurant in Leicester Square from where she could watch until she was sure it wasn't him. He turned up at the deli once. Annie asked him firmly but kindly to leave. One of the middle-aged men who worked beside her behind the counter had escorted him out onto the street. And there were numerous hang-ups on the machine that I attributed to Heathcliff.

'Why?' I wanted to know. 'Why, or how could you become engaged to someone else? Did you love him?'

We sat together on the sofa watching the lower halves of people passing on the pavement outside.

'There is a religion, and don't ask me which one, because I don't remember, but there's a religion where they believe that everyone has a ray of light leading from us up to heaven.' Annie lifted an imaginary hat from her head and held it at arms' length above her. 'It's just a flimsy narrow ray of light, but when you marry someone, when you intertwine your lives . . . When you fall in love . . . Your two rays join and become a bigger one.' The hat grew in her hands to about the width of her shoulders. 'Your connection to heaven is bigger, you see?'

'And children?' I asked.

'The more children, the bigger the ray.' The hat spread to the width of a souvenir sombrero. She was hesitant to have children, however, and so was I. We spoke enthusiastically about the prospect with other people: in a few years, we said, when things are more settled. When we were alone, we avoided the subject. I don't remember ever having a conversation about it. The way we might have not wanted to talk about the possibility of stopping smoking.

'But did you love him as much as you love me?'

She tilted her head to one side, and smiled. 'Gordon . . . It wasn't a very official engagement. We were kids. I probably wouldn't have gone through with it even if we hadn't met.'

Less than a year after we wandered onto the rainy dark Heath after that first night in the pub, we were married. It was important to her that we get married. And I, believe it or not, still have faith in marriage. Somehow saying those simple words, even if it is a conscious lie, connects two people like fish snared on the same shiny fishhook. I have heard people say that repetition of the Lord's prayer can take you somewhere spiritual even if you have no intention of going. I think marriage works like that.

After our first rainy union, however, I wondered about her seriousness. As we walked out of the Heath, she leaned against me as if she was very drunk. I looked into the sleepy brown houses reflected in the pond and considered what had happened. In the darkness, a phrase played repeatedly in my mind – something Maureen had told me by way of helpful instruction on making love with a woman: *listen*. And I had tried to listen, to flatter – for listening is flattery, according to Maureen – but it had been tumultuous, over quickly, and in the murky shadow (yellow lamp post bobbing between black wooded claws) difficult to see. For certain, Annie was the more experienced of the two of us; in the matter of sex that would not change. When we shared a bed, for all my listening, I often had the feeling that Annie went unsatisfied. She told me I was wrong, but if this is to be a true and accurate record, I cannot avoid remembering what makes me unhappy.

I had the selfish habit of drifting off quickly after we made love and more than once I awoke, who knows how long after I'd fallen asleep, to a faint movement across the bed. I would open my eyes and greet Annie's, but she was there only a moment. Her eyes closed and when they reopened they were foreign, lazy, warm weather. She would move her legs forward and breathe a little fever against my skin and then I would feel that rumble, only slight at first, but growing, as if a train was quietly passing. Perhaps her foot would touch me accidentally, and then her body went rigid. 'Kiss me,' she would say and I would press my lips against hers and feel her shiver and kiss me hungrily as if I could have been any man in the world.

We never discussed these late-night encounters. I never brought them up, but this was what we had in store for us as we walked out of the Heath that first evening onto the silent high street. We had walked for about ten minutes when she suddenly stopped and stepped away from me. I thought she had realized she was missing something, a favourite earring lost in the muddy park (for which I would have happily gone back and searched until dawn if she had asked) but she mentioned no such item. Her expression was suddenly clear and sober. She checked her watch and looked up and down the street as if she thought we might be spotted amongst the deserted shopfronts. 'I have to go home,' she said.

I had the terrible feeling that the night might not have been as exceptional for her as it felt for me. She was, I feared, like one of those people you meet at parties who are capable of serious conversation with almost anyone.

'I live with my father and if I don't let him know I'm not coming home, he gets worried. He can't go back to sleep. He sets a little alarm clock and if I'm not there to switch it off in time, he goes a bit mental.' She smiled sweetly, acknowledging that she indulged him. 'Will you be all right?' she asked. She stood up on her tiptoes and kissed me on the cheek. 'Okay, then?' She kept her eyes on me a moment longer, waiting to see if I would object. She crossed her arms tightly over her chest, nodded once, turned and walked off down the high street. I watched her walk, looking down at her feet as she went, stepping patiently around the stray pieces of rubbish bubbling out from the neat piles of black plastic bags at the curb. When she was still close, I could see her shoulder blades jutting out in the back of her pink coat. As she got further away, the pink faded to grey when she was between street lights. Beyond her, I could see the series of dazed, blinking orange lights on the pedestrian crossings and the lighted, empty interior of the number 46 bus creeping up the hill. I watched her go, quite unable to believe she would not look around, but she did not, not even when she turned the corner in search, apparently, of a cab, or a night bus, or going some place else, because the first time she took me to her father's I realized that he lived in exactly the opposite direction from which she had walked that evening.

Thirteen

Those who argue that totalitarianism and tyranny are responsible for the most beautiful things in the world are quick to point to Paris as an example. The highly organized city is, to many, the most beautiful in the world. The organization of Paris came to full fruition in the nineteenth century under the Emperor Louis Napoleon. Like the kings before him, he took enormous pleasure in straightening roads and lining up monuments. The beauty of Paris is certainly not the result of *liberté, égalite, fraternité* and it is testament to the importance a Frenchman ascribes to the aesthetics of his world that he exchanged a king for an emperor when it looked like democracy might darken the city of light. Do not be fooled by the apparently bohemian climate of the more popular neighbourhoods; the French are one of the most nationalistic of peoples. But it is an aesthetic nationalism and, thus, forgivable. They view the rest of the world merely as a point of comparison: a way to be sure that the city of Paris is, indeed, more beautiful than any other.

Annie and I were married on the sixth of June on the forty-fourth anniversary of the Allied invasion of Normandy. There was a commemorative aerial display above London with both antique planes and new. They kept flying in complicated formations over our heads. They came in clusters of four or five, guns glistening in the early-afternoon sun. You could see them coming, once you knew to look for them, a long way off in the distance. They appeared not to be moving until they were very close, and then they passed no faster than a pack of sea-gulls floating hopefully behind a passenger ferry.

Annie wanted to be married in a church, but I refused. Maureen raised me as a strict agnostic. The point, for Maureen, was not simply that you would never know, but that you would do well not to ask. 'If you were supposed to know,' she used to say, 'you would.'

We agreed on the registrar's office on the King's Road next to the library, across the street from a discount department store that sold items at half their usual price due to minor production flaws. Annie chose it because it is the most regal of all such offices. A large clock juts out above a wide stone staircase. The wedding party was to congregate at a quarter to eleven and Annie would appear as the clock struck the hour. Tom, Annie's father, gave her away. There were four brides-maids wearing matching floral dresses of a fleshy variety of pinks and reds, and holding matching bouquets. Apparently, it is uncommon in England for bridesmaids to be grown women, but Maureen had told her that that's what was done in America, and Annie had liked the idea. Sasha, of course, was the maid of honour. Elise and Mary, both of whom worked in the deli, and Liza, a friend of Annie's from school, made up Annie's part of the group.

Theo was my best man. He came to London for the wedding accompanied by Louise, his third wife. I wore a grey wool, single-breasted suit that Theo took me to have made for the wedding. He said it was time that I owned a suit, something classic. Theo wore a dark blue double-breasted suit and gleaming black shoes. He simply wears a suit better than I do. He looked as nervous as he did at one of his own weddings. Or rather, he looked irritated, as Theo's nervousness usually comes out in irritation. Several times he stopped pacing and flicked a comb through his hair. And then he removed a handkerchief and flamboyantly blew his nose. The nose blowing always came after the hair combing, as if one triggered the other. When he saw me watching him, he said something encouraging like, 'Not long now.'

Louise wore a sensible blue dress, belted at the waist, with short puffy sleeves, and a smart blue hat that concealed half her face. She stood off to the side behind the bridesmaids looking neat but inconspicuous – the effect she usually went for. She did not want to be there, but had made an endearing stab at enthusiasm as we shared a taxi from their hotel.

'I was all nerves too,' she told me.

'You were not,' said Theo. 'And Gordy's not either, are you, boy-o?'

'Your father certainly was,' said Louise. She gave Theo a quick flirtatious glance that he pretended not to see.

We had hired a photographer: a young Turk about my age. He wore purple suede shoes and kept to himself. He was so successful at making himself inconspicuous, I periodically forgot about him only to be startled when he stepped forward and took my photograph.

And that constituted our group: Theo, Louise, the brides-maids, the photographer and me, a flower in my lapel, standing on the King's Road waiting. It was one of the most uncomfort-able twenty minutes I have ever endured. When one of the sets of planes passed overhead and we all looked up, it was a merciful reprieve from the growing tension.

The photographer took several pictures as we waited. The best of them appear in our wedding album. There are a few of Theo and me with the blue stone steps of the registrar's office and the fleshy bridesmaids' dresses behind. In some I am wearing a ridiculously optimistic grin. In others, Theo and I wear very similar nervous expressions. In almost every other aspect we do not resemble one another in the least. He is broad, formidable and tanned, his arm pressed against the small of my back. I am slight and look jumpy, my arms folded across my chest. But in our expressions we seem drawn in by the same thing. An anxious squinting creases the middles of our faces, as if they could be folded neatly down the middle and filed away somewhere in a file for nervous grooms.

Maureen was late. We had already assumed our rehearsed formation in front of the registrar's office: Theo, Louise and I off to the right of the staircase, the bridesmaids in a row on the left. The sky was a thick watery blue and made the sun seem small. It had not rained in days and the pavement felt hot, as did the passing cars. As the time for Annie's arrival came and went, I thought perhaps Maureen was not coming. When I told her over the phone that Theo would be at the wedding she had expressed irritation. And when I added that he would, of course, be bringing Louise, Maureen could not contain herself. 'Why should he bring a spectator?' she asked. 'It's not as if she'll object if he doesn't.' She had threatened not to come, but she put it differently. 'Wouldn't you prefer it if I didn't come? I have a great deal to do here. And you could be with your father. We could have our own private celebration later on.' She was calling from Vienna where she claimed to be busy with the

Austrian Impressionists. Theo and Maureen had not met face to face for five years, since I was fourteen. At that age, to everyone's relief – not least my own – it was decided that I was old enough to travel by myself. No longer did Maureen and Theo have to meet to hand me from one to the other. I found those meetings terrifying, shadowed with the fear that one would tell the other something I had let slip out, some betraying intimacy that the other should not know.

I spotted Maureen amidst the crowd of shoppers a little way off down the street. She seemed to be running or, more accurately, floating – it was a more delicate movement than a run – as if she were coasting on a small set of wheels concealed beneath her dress. Her hair flowed behind her. Her pale face was flushed as she paused at the corner to let a car pass. Her hair was still wet from bathing, and batted back and forth across her shoulders leaving two dark damp patches above each breast on her silk cream dress. It was the most formal dress she owned, cut for the evening, for dancing, from an almost impossibly thin silk, as thin as the skin of a grape. I had not seen it in years and not to take anything away from her entrance (she looked wonderful) it fit her differently than it once had. As she crossed the street, she looked up – she had slowed, now, to a walk – and fixed her eyes on me.

As she strode towards us she seemed to have nothing left of the anxiety she had expressed over the phone. She looked, in fact, more relaxed than I had seen her in many years and I thought, *She has put it all aside for me, for us today.* She drifted away from the passing crowd tripping over themselves as they gaped at the assembling wedding. Louise, who had not until then seen Maureen coming, recognized her instantly, and moved over to the side of the building as if she hoped to blend into the stone. Theo continued to grin bravely as he watched Maureen come. His cheek muscles twitched, and his eyes narrowed. I knew that her tardiness and flamboyant dress infuriated him. Louise personified the stoic opposite of such an entrance. *There is a subtitle to everything Maureen says or does*, Theo once told me, *it's 'look at me'*.

Maureen ignored the rest of the wedding party, as if it were a private meeting between us. As she came, I suddenly noticed she was not alone. A thin man in a green jacket and grey trousers trailed behind her. He was about Maureen's height, if not shorter, with golden hair combed to the side. His face had aged in the deflated manner that often befalls pretty, suntanned men. As if the bones themselves had receded, leaving the sandy skin hanging limp like a wet paper bag someone had tried to preserve by hanging it to dry in the sun. A pair of sparkling blue eyes glowed beneath this face with such life they seemed as foreign as an injury. He was at least ten years older than Maureen. At first, I thought that he was a stranger who had been so struck by her he had decided to follow wherever she was going. Just before she reached us, she turned and waited for him to catch up. She put her arm through his, and together they came towards us.

Before Maureen could introduce me to her new friend, Tom's gleaming black cab swung to a stop at the curb. It had been shined into an immaculate black mirror reflecting the distant clouds. White ribbon was tied to the front of the bonnet crossing over at the top and attached to the door handles so that when Tom opened his door, the ribbon buckled in places and was pulled taut in others. I could see Annie sitting in the back looking at her shoes. With the cab's arrival (momentarily blocking traffic) a small burst of tooting horns went up from the cars behind before the drivers saw the white ribbon, and realized someone was getting married.

'Here she is!' cried Sasha before she was silenced by one of the modern jets passing overhead. The sounds of the engine echoed down the street, shaking, for a moment, concentration from the event at hand. Maureen and her friend looked up, as did Tom before straightening his tie and gesturing at the drivers behind who had honked. He pulled his jacket firmly down and looked inside for Annie to give the ready signal. When he got it, he swung the door open in one dramatically rehearsed gesture. He reached in and helped Annie onto the pavement, and then turned and snapped the door closed.

Annie took a moment to collect herself, adjusting her clothing and taking several short breaths. She was so full of nervous energy she seemed slightly blurred, like a mirage. She wore a sleeveless pink crocheted dress, high on the neck, down to just above her knees, a matching handbag balanced in the crook of her arm, a pair of perfectly white gloves and a white pillbox hat, with a short bejewelled veil covering her eyes. When she had everything in place, she finally looked up at me. I do not feel capable of describing my feeling at that moment. The planes passing overhead. The traffic slowing down for a look. Her look of trust, as if I were the only one who could guide her from the cab to the safety of those stone steps. Perhaps it is enough to say that I felt the urge to put out my arms to catch her, as if she was about to take a running leap towards me.

The ceremony took place in the cramped office up the stairs where papers were signed and birth certificates exchanged for a marriage certificate. With our entire party, the room was at capacity and felt very hot. I could feel the heat from those pressed in behind me. A fan rotated, ruffling and re-ruffling papers on the desks. The branch of a tree brushed against the dirty windows, fracturing the sunlight into a handful of golden coins falling continually down the wall. As we listened to the young woman read our vows, I concentrated only on Annie standing beside me. She looked straight ahead, listening attentively to everything the woman said. I could not now repeat a single word of it. I could hear people coughing, shifting on their feet, and the creak of the fan. As the heat in the room steadily increased, I felt a droplet of sweat gather just above my hairline. It hung there, gathering volume until finally it slid across my forehead, lodging itself in the corner of my eye.

Before I knew it, it was time. I plucked the tiny gold ring from Theo's hot hand and slid it onto Annie's finger. She wrapped her arms around my neck and pressed her small lips against mine. As we kissed, those in the room let up a cheer of approval, followed by polite applause.

We came down the stairs out into the warm, early June sun, and perfect strangers passing on the street paused to welcome us into the married life. Little buckets of confetti had been arranged near the entrance so that anyone could join in. Annie squinted into the crowd and waved. She moved slowly down the stairs, savouring each cool step. Her loveliness seemed to have increased, reflected in so many eyes. At the bottom of the steps, I paused to kiss her again. I suppose I felt some expectation from the crowd that I should. They let up an even bigger cheer than we had received in the privacy of the office.

We climbed into the cab and Annie slid over next to me. Her father started the engine and, as we pulled away from the curb, we squeezed our heads through the same window and waved. At that moment I felt totally convinced that no two people were more deserving of marriage, no two people had such a clear idea of their lives. Even as I looked out of the window and saw Maureen standing quietly beside her mysterious friend and, a few paces away, Theo waving his arms above his head as if he were waving in a plane, I was convinced.

Tom sat in the front chuckling quietly to himself as if we had successfully held up a bank. Annie withdrew her feet from her shoes, and curled her legs under her dress. She laid her head on my shoulder and I rested my hand on her spine where she had perspired just slightly through her dress.

'What's so funny?' she asked.

'Nothing's funny,' said Tom. 'My daughter just got married . . . I can be pleased, can't I? Right, Gordon?'

'Right,' I said.

He checked us in the rear-view mirror. I could tell from his eyes that he was smiling. He lit a cigarette and tossed the packet over his shoulder through the open glass separating the passenger compartment from his. Annie retrieved the cigarettes from the floor, put one in her mouth and then one in mine. She leaned forward and took the gold lighter from her father's extended hand and lit our cigarettes. I opened the window wider and felt the passing breeze on my face.

'Are you happy?' asked Annie.

'Oh, yes,' I said. I had the sensation of starting a long trip, although we did not have far to go at all.

'I do love you,' she said. As we kissed, Tom tooted the horn, and some of the other drivers passing in the other direction tooted their horns in response and some waved out of their windows, and others waved from the street.

We drove towards the Albert Bridge where there was less traffic, and the wind picked up, ruffling Annie's veil where she had folded it above her face. I felt profoundly relaxed. Tom continued to smile to himself, and Annie smiled with her eyes closed, like a cat pretending to sleep in the sun. We passed the cast-iron statue of a boy swimming behind a dolphin, his narrow fingers wrapped around the fin, his legs extended into the air behind as he followed the creature into the imaginary deep. We pulled onto Cheyne Walk, and drove along the little street between the gardens and the red-brick town houses until we reached the pub.

I was surprised to find no one waiting for us out front. Tom opened the door and leaned in for Annie. She stepped out ahead of me and immediately began adjusting her hat and her hair. She was very serious again, as if that relaxed creature remained curled up on the seat in the cab. The garden across the street was in full bloom. Pink flowers mingled with the thick green bush running along the inside of the metal fence. Nothing of the park inside could be seen but, as I waited for Annie to be ready, I could hear the sounds of children playing.

'All right, darling?' asked Tom.

Her lips were parted with concentration as she struggled to get a few errant strands of hair beneath her hat. Tom and I stood on either side of her, our hands in our pockets. He grinned at me warmly, but as if he found me slightly funny. He turned his head quickly to one side, made a snapping noise with his mouth and said, 'I'm a happy man.' And then he leaned across Annie and took me in his arms.

'Oh, Dad,' moaned Annie. But she was slightly muffled by the sleeve of his suit-jacket against my ear. I put my arms around his soft waist, and thanked him – for his daughter, I suppose.

'Come on you two,' said Annie. She draped her arms over us, and shook her head. 'Break it up.'

Tom let go. He wiped at the corner of his eye and smiled again, but he still seemed to find me amusing. He always seemed to. Annie took his arm, but he untangled himself from her and put her arm through mine.

We stood for a moment in the entrance to the pub before Tom announced our arrival. 'Here we are!' he said. Everyone in the pub turned to look at us. Annie held tightly to my arm, and straightened her back. The three tables our party occupied at the rear of the bar let up a cheer, all arms raised with a glass. Annie and I smiled politely at our welcome, and started across the bar. The front of the pub, lined with tall, elaborately etched glass windows, was filled with lazy sun and cigarette smoke. The old wood of the bar had recently been replaced with blonde pine giving it the feeling of a bar in a ski resort. Music (something I can't remember, but that had been very popular that summer) played quietly beneath murmured conversation. On the television, cars silently raced around a track. As we moved through the room we had to pause as Annie turned and smiled her appreciation to each person who mumbled their congratulations, or raised their glass in our direction. It was a weekend afternoon crowd, friendly and mostly sober.

In the rear of the pub, not in a private room but on a slightly raised platform, sat our wedding party. They occupied three different tables. All four bridesmaids sat crowded around one table engaged in conversation with Theo. They leaned in closely, their mouths slightly open, poised to burst into laughter. I could tell from their faces that he had been making them laugh for some time. They were a polite and enthusiastic audience, showing, as they leaned over, varying lengths of shadowy cleavage. Even Sasha seemed to be enjoying herself. She probably didn't realize that Theo was related to me. At Theo's right sat Louise. She had removed her hat, which had left a faint circular dent in her hair. She held the shocked and worried expression of someone who had swallowed her drink stirrer, which I attributed to the fact that she sat opposite Maureen, who was leaning far over the table chatting enthusiastically. Next to Louise sat the mysterious man, my mother's new friend. With the same expressionless smile he displayed at the registrar's office he was watching Maureen and sipping a Coke.

Theo stood as we approached. He held his arms outstretched as if to gather us into his grasp from across the table. 'Here they are,' he said. Everyone smiled at us and we smiled back. For a moment, that was all we did; and then Theo struggled his way out from behind the table. 'Let me get you something to drink.' He put a great arm around Annie and she smiled graciously, not the smile of someone who looked in danger of disappearing into the inner pockets of his suit jacket. She seemed happy at the feel of his touch. Theo has the ability to make everything feel all right. Ever since I was a child, if he told someone where to sit it was inevitably the right place; if he advised what to order from the menu he never steered anyone wrong and if there was a question, whether or not he understood it, he would answer clearly one way or the other, and for a moment at least, sometimes for many years, you did not question that in following his advice, or in letting him confirm what you had already believed, you had done the best thing and had been right.

He gave Annie a little tentative squeeze and then guided her gently into a chair he simultaneously arranged at the centre of the three tables. Annie beamed as she took her place of honour. 'Tom, will you give us a hand and we'll get some champagne,' said Theo. Maureen turned sideways in her chair to face Annie. She held her hands flat on her thighs and grinned.

'Hello, Maureen,' said Annie with a mischievous smile.

'Come here and give me a kiss,' said Maureen, reaching for Annie's arm. They exchanged enthusiastic kisses on each cheek. Maureen did not immediately release Annie's hand. She held it over her knees. As I stood behind Maureen, I noticed that her dress had a very low back, a lower back than I remember it having, and that sitting up straight with her good posture, a long and very beautiful portion of her back was on display. I could feel Tom notice it beside me as he put a glass of champagne down in front of Maureen and then Louise. Theo was simultaneously delivering glasses of champagne to the bridesmaids. Before they could return to the bar for more glasses, a door opened, and a young man gingerly slipped through rattling half a dozen champagne flutes on a tray.

'Oh, fantastic!' exclaimed Theo. 'This will save us going back and forth.' He took his seat at the corner of the table amongst the bridesmaids.

We all watched as the young man closely studied the quivering glasses and the quickly darkening cork top of the tray. He placed each step with care, as if he were crossing an icy street. No one said anything as we watched his slow journey, and he seemed to be aware of being watched. His face flushed, not with embarrassment, but with irritation at having been asked to perform a task that was not usually his.

When the young man finally got to the table, Theo leaned back in his chair and held up his hands defensively, apparently anxious that the tray would end up in his lap. The muscles of the boy's narrow arm flexed strenuously until he finally got the tray safely on the table. 'Well done,' said Theo patting the young man on the back. At my father's touch, he seemed to relax slightly, and smiled as he quickly removed all the glasses from the tray and arranged them in a cluster in front of Theo. When he stood and exhaled, however, the annoyed look returned to his face. He slouched off, but just before he went back through the door, he shook the tray violently, spattering the floor with spilt champagne.

'A toast,' said Tom, rising to his feet. Everyone raised a glass. The young man paused by the door, holding the tray against his knees, dripping champagne onto his shoes. 'I'd like to toast my darling Annie,' Tom began. The pub suddenly grew quieter as the other patrons ceased their conversation and turned to watch. 'My youngest daughter,' he smiled. 'And one of the most lovely, sensible, kind-hearted women in the world. If your mother was here, she'd be very proud. You've made Sasha and I proud.' His voice cracked and he looked at Annie. Annie nodded to her father. 'And to Gordon,' he shifted his gaze to me. 'Just the man to look after her.' I also nodded, confirming, I hoped, that he had the right man. 'I wish them every happiness.' He raised his glass and we all did the same.

'Here, here,' said Theo.

'Bravo,' said Maureen.

There was a pause as we all looked at one another, wondering if there would be another toast. Annie gently squeezed my hand and I realized that it was I who should speak. I pushed my chair out from behind me, and stood, holding my glass raised. Annie looked up at me with great affection. 'I'd like to make a toast,' I said. 'There are several people I could thank.' I darted my eyes from Tom to Theo to Maureen. 'And I could describe how I feel about Annie, or how we met, or what I think is going to be ahead of us . . . but I won't.' A few around the table giggled dutifully. 'I'd like simply to raise my glass.' I turned to look at Annie. 'To my wife.' A couple of the bridesmaids oohhed. 'I married her because I love her. So to call her my wife makes the most sense possible.' We all raised our glasses together and I sat down.

'Well done,' said Tom quietly.

Annie rubbed my hand appreciatively. We were quiet again as everyone waited to see if there would be another toast. When it seemed that there wasn't, people began lighting cigarettes, and a cloud of smoky relief wafted up towards the ceiling.

'Annie,' said Maureen, after a moment. 'This is my friend, Gerhardt.'

He was instantly standing. He leaned down, took Annie's hand and brought it to his lips. 'My congratulations,' he said in a perfect English accent. The bridesmaids stubbed out their cigarettes again and Theo broke off his amusing story, presuming that Gerhardt was going to make a toast. When Gerhardt realized what was expected of him, he waved both hands in front of his face. 'No, no,' he said. 'But thank you all for allowing me to come.'

'Thank you,' said Annie as Gerhardt sat down again.

'And you know Louise?' Maureen asked.

'Of course,' said Louise. 'We met when she came over with Gordo.'

Maureen hated that name for me, but she didn't show it. She reached for Annie's hand and held it in her lap.

'Annie, come over here,' interrupted Theo. 'I want a picture of us.' He stood and walked towards the dormant fireplace. I only then noticed the portrait that hung above it. The picture depicted a grisly scene from the industrial revolution; a factory with a hellish glow coming from the green factory doors, the dark figures of labourers toiling inside, and in the foreground, the fierce, chinless factory owner glaring out like an angry god.

Theo gestured for Annie to join him. 'My new daughter and I,' he said.

Annie rose and joined Theo beneath that horrible painting. 'And then me,' Maureen called after her. She turned to me and said, slightly too loudly, '*My new daughter . . . imagine.*' I could feel Louise bristle.

'Congratulations, Gordon,' said Gerhardt. We shook hands across the table, but he did not stand. He had the most perfectly shaped hands. Like the little casts proud parents sometimes make of their infant's hands, they didn't look quite real. 'I have heard a great deal about you.'

'I wish I could say the same about you,' I said.

'Oh, yes,' said Maureen with apparent surprise. 'You two haven't met.'

'No,' I said. Sending my own inconsequential smile in the direction of Gerhardt's. 'I'm sorry we didn't get a chance to shake hands before the ceremony.'

'I'm so sorry to have been late,' she said. 'We had to get out of the cab and run, the traffic was so bad.' She glanced in the direction of Gerhardt who nodded confirmation.

'Gerhardt is a friend from Vienna.' She took my left hand and pulled me into the chair Annie had given up. 'Come sit closer,' she said. 'We share many interests, Gerhardt and I.'

'Oh good,' I nodded.

'Oh good,' Maureen mimicked and patted my hand. She gently pinched the skin on my hand and pulled it up.

'Well, interests are good,' I continued. 'You have to have things to do on rainy days.'

'Ah yes, rainy days . . . Marriage is full of rainy days,' she said, squeezing my hand again. And as an after-gesture she leaned forward and kissed the side of my face. 'My boy.' This was when Maureen began to worry me. I did not have her full attention. These were not private gestures, nor were they only for Gerhardt's appreciation.

I turned and watched Annie standing proudly between Theo and Tom. The two fathers took a moment to toast one another. They clinked champagne flutes over her head, as if she were a little vessel being sent off to sea. In all the photographs, the portrait of that angry man looms above. The effect is quite distracting.

Maureen finished her drink and stood. 'Now me,' she called. 'Time for a photograph of Annie and me.' She threw her head back and walked gallantly towards my wife. Theo and Tom instinctively slipped off to either side out of her way. Maureen moved with such determination, she swept up a little breeze, trailing her long hair behind her. Her dress clutched at her body, at her still youthful, muscular thighs, her breasts and her thick square hips. This was the way a woman who wanted to be intoxicating crossed the room. The power to intoxicate had never been far from her grasp, but she hadn't reached for it in a while. Intoxication would not have been necessary to gain the attention of Gerhardt. From the way he watched her, following her every move, her every expression, it seemed he would have fallen for her before she even knew he was looking. She was fumbling now to get a proper hold over what she had always imagined would be ready, whether she reached for it or not, and it was coming back with more difficulty than she expected. Perhaps she had chosen too wide a target to entrance; she wanted the entire group. As she swooped across the room towards Annie, and then turned, spinning Annie around and facing us again, a slight hesitation appeared in her gestures. She wondered if she might look ridiculous, if the dress she had worn was too young. Worst of all, she had begun to think that her self-doubt was apparent. To intoxicate, total assurance is necessary. And to try to intoxicate and fail is to fall from the greatest height.

She held Annie tightly to her. Annie is so small she looked like Maureen's child, pressed against her skirts. They smiled practiced, camera smiles as the flash splashed against them. Each wave of light revealed the grey ash in the dormant fireplace and seemed further to disturb the angry industrialist looking down at them. They began to laugh. At one point, Annie reached behind her to put a hand around Maureen's neck. It was an awkward, if well-intentioned gesture. The discrepancy in height meant that Annie's hand, arranged where it was, pressed more against Maureen's jaw than her neck. The gesture ruined two photographs, as Annie's little wrist managed to conceal part of Maureen's mouth. In fact, at a quick glance, it looks as if Maureen is playfully holding Annie's wrist in her teeth. Maureen finally removed Annie's hand and held it in her own. After a few more snaps, Maureen called to me to come and pose for a picture between them. It's a lovely photograph. Annie's face is pressed against my chest, and Maureen has her arms wrapped around us. She looks really very proud.

The afternoon wore on, and the pub grew darker, while the sun-struck street was still apparent out of the windows. We all had a number more drinks, and Annie, as she does, began to look sleepy. Theo's face had turned a deeper red, although not yet as deep as Tom's, and Louise had switched to Perrier. Maureen had been drinking vodkas and was becoming drunk. You knew she was drunk when she began to suggest that she might be capable of bad behaviour. She never *actually* said anything terrible, but liked to make it seem that she would. She looked at Louise, for instance, and asked loudly, 'So, where's your hat?' When Louise, steadying herself for a challenge, held up her hat and said, 'Why, it's right here, Maureen,' Maureen told her it was a lovely hat and asked where she had bought it so that she might buy one herself. Or when she commented, 'Who, please God tell me, chose the bridesmaids' dresses?' and I told her Annie had, she exclaimed how lovely they were. She was so convincing that she managed to eradicate any memory of the critical manner in which she had asked the question. At first, she could actually convince people that they had misunderstood her. It was how I knew that Gerhardt was a new friend. He seemed to be anxious about Maureen. As she leaned provocatively back in her chair in search of a new target, he showed visible signs of nerves, and I felt the day winding to a close.

'Where are you two going for your honeymoon or whatever?' Sasha asked.

'Oh!' exclaimed Maureen with sudden clarity. 'The honeymoon!' She brought her chair back to the floor with a crack.

'We're going to the Lake District,' I said, not wanting to acknowledge Maureen.

'I wanted to go abroad,' said Annie.

'I've rented a small cottage near a lake. We're going to go for long walks and take photographs and sit by the fire at night,' I said, sounding, it strikes me now, like a travel brochure.

'I forgot to tell you,' said Maureen. 'Our wedding gift!' And then Maureen surprised even me. She looked at Gerhardt. 'We're taking a trip to Venice at the end of the month, and we're inviting you . . . We've got the hotel rooms and everything . . . Yes?' she checked with Gerhardt again.

Gerhardt nodded. Apparently, he was exceedingly wealthy, or deeply in love and prepared to pay for the whole trip.

'I've got some work to do there,' she continued. Everyone around the table remained silent, and she continued to talk, sensing what she imagined to be their awe at such a generous gift. All except Theo who snorted audibly when she used the word 'work'. She registered this. She glanced down the table at him and he smiled and raised his glass. Ostentatious gifts were usually Theo's and she had outdone him. 'Will you come?' she asked Annie.

There was a long silence. It must have been hard for Annie to know what to do. Honeymooning with my mother and her new friend did not appeal to me. Annie, however, was twitching away beside me, until she finally burst out, 'Oh, Maureen . . . Venice! I'd absolutely love to!'

'Oh good,' said Maureen, and turned her smile on me.

'What about work?' I asked Annie quietly.

'I'll get time off for *Venice*.'

'We're staying at the Europa & Regina,' said Gerhardt. 'It's right on the Grand Canal.'

'A very good hotel,' nodded Theo, duly impressed. 'Very nice.'

'Oh, God, thank you so much, Maureen,' gushed Annie.

'Not at all,' smiled Maureen. 'We'll be lucky to have you.'

Annie squeezed my hand and said, 'We can go to the Lake District another time.'

'Of course,' I said.

Around the table people continued to discuss Maureen's gift until Theo tapped his glass and struggled out of his chair. He was not going to be outdone after all. This was when he announced that he would be supplying the down payment on our little flat. He had already said something discreetly to me, but he now felt the desire to share it with the table. I think, most of all, it was for the benefit of Maureen. Annie was totally overwhelmed by my family's generosity. She barely got out any words of thanks. She walked the length of the table and kissed Theo. 'Thanks, Theo,' she almost whispered, and as she came back down the table, Maureen stood and extended her arms and Annie thanked Maureen again.

We made our goodbyes on the street in front of the pub. Tom climbed, rather drunkenly, behind the wheel of the cab, and waited at the curb. I shook hands with Theo. I thanked the photographer, and kissed each of the bridesmaids. The day had seemed to turn sour for Sasha, who was red-eyed and morose. Annie kissed everyone goodbye. Her cheeks were pink from the alcohol, her eyes heavy. I kissed Maureen, and felt her shivering slightly beneath her thin silk dress in the cool evening. 'Goodbye, love,' she said as our faces were pressed together. I kissed Louise, who seemed to have had the worst afternoon of all of us. She looked completely exhausted, a condition that seemed to be exacerbated by the hat she held in her hand. Over her shoulder I watched Maureen say goodbye to Theo. They shook hands.

'Goodbye, Maureen,' he said softly. He looked like a young man, gazing at his feet.

'Have you put on weight, Theo?' asked Maureen.

He looked up and seemed himself again. 'In the last ten years? Probably,' he laughed.

'No, I mean around the eyes.'

He laughed.

'They'll close if you're not careful, and you'll be blind.'

'You look very well,' he said. We left them there talking though I wanted to stay and watch. We climbed back into the cab, and Tom drove, straight as an arrow, off down the street – Annie asleep before we reached the corner – back towards our flat.

Part Two

Fourteen

If Paris is, as a whole, man's most beautiful creation, Venice is his most unlikely. Like something dreamed or imagined, it is sinking before our eyes. I have often felt, when wandering the quieter alleys, that I can hear the air seeping from the bricks as they slowly disappear into the lagoon.

Our honeymoon kept having to be put off. The original plan for the end of June did not happen for reasons I am even now unsure of, but I do know the postponement came from Gerhardt and Maureen. Summer is no time to visit Venice. September and October are the city's busiest months and Maureen always felt that to see art through a crowd is not really to see it at all. We thought of November, but Annie and I had already agreed to visit Theo for Thanksgiving. December is of course a slippery month and January and February were very cold. Maureen and Gerhardt went to New York in April. And then it was May, almost a year since Annie and I had been married.

What did we do for that year? This is what frightens me most. I remember moments, but piled up, they account for less than a week. I remember London, the buses and the road-works. I remember travelling from one place to another, looking out of the window at the streets filled with people. I remember waiting for trains and going to films. I remember walking on the Heath. Annie had lunch four times a week in the pub on the high street. One particular afternoon, I surprised her there. I bought drinks for her friends. They teased me good-naturedly and Annie leaned against me and held my hand in her lap. When it was hot that first summer I walked around the corner one morning to get the paper. When I returned, I found her stretched out in the garden weeping. She held a book against her chest; she couldn't stand the way it ended, she told me. That night, we walked up the hill for an Indian meal. It was still light after ten and as we walked home after dinner, aside from the men standing around outside the pub, it felt like the middle of the afternoon. Annie didn't feel well. She hadn't eaten much. When we turned off the busy road onto our street on the way home, she steadied herself against the letterbox and was sick in the gutter. Her shoes were splattered with yellow grains of rice. In September we drove out to the country. We'd risen early. Annie slept in the seat beside me. The yellow street lights and then the first blue light nested in her hair. At the farm she stood on a wooden fence, looking down at a mass of wriggling brown and black bodies and chose our little dog. On the way home it trembled in her hands on the back seat and wet her dress as we passed into London.

We saw Maureen only once over that year. She came to London and stayed in a hotel near Hyde Park. Gerhardt paid for her trip. His money came from the family business, the production of professional uniforms: nurses, waiters, blue-smocked French electricians. Maureen and I spoke regularly over the phone. She was living in Vienna and through letters provided me with regular updates on the progress of her book.

Gerhardt had said she possessed great talent. He talked about financing a small private publication if it failed to attract the attention of a major press, perhaps even if it did. I had long ago given up believing anything she said about the book. I told her all about my exciting photographic career. I began by doing portraits, crying babies in matching sweaters, weddings; but I wasn't much good at handling the subjects. They looked at me and their looks were asking if they looked all right, and somehow I never succeeded in convincing them that they did.

Gerhardt and Annie did the actual organizing for the trip. When Maureen and I spoke, we never discussed those details. Whenever one of us broached the subject she said, 'I'll pass you to Gerhardt.' And I said, 'I'll pass him on to Annie.' As if those details were beneath us.

I think it took me several months to realize that the fact that he was always on hand to be passed the phone meant that he and Maureen lived together. Maureen had not lived with a man since Theo. There had been men over the years with whom she had spent time; it was not uncommon for her to find her way into someone's apartment for a short period (Marcel's for instance), but the apartments were usually uninhabited. I had no idea what Gerhardt's home would be like. I hoped it was large. Gerhardt was ten years older than Maureen and although still quite young, he was retired and would be at home all day getting underfoot. When I asked about her living situation she was not forthcoming. I said, 'So, you're living together?' And she responded, 'We're very near the museums.'

We had a pleasant flight. The grey day we left in London was transformed the instant the plane nosed its way through the final layer of cloud. The metal wings baked in the sun, a warm light drifted through the portal windows and half the passengers dropped off to sleep around us.

After what seemed to be barely any time at all, the plane lowered over endless sunny fields and we walked in a group across the hot black tarmac towards passport control. We stood in line together, the young couple on honeymoon. I wore a lightweight sports jacket that I liked to think of as casual. Annie had had her hair cut shorter. She wore it held back from her face with a pair of sunglasses balanced at the crest of her brow. She had chosen a practical grey dress with large square pockets over each hip and a hemline that hovered at her knees. She wore dark stockings, a pair of black buckled shoes and a maroon cardigan. She had re-applied her lipstick as we taxied closer to the terminal. She looked lovely but subdued as she watched the family in front of us fall into disagreement. The father spun around and waved his finger very close to the faces of his children. The veins in his neck stood erect with rage. 'Enough!' he said through closed teeth and then he glared at us as if he expected us to intervene on his children's behalf.

'Do you see?' Annie whispered. 'When you get people away from home, they turn on one another. I was on a flight once, from Malaga. When we arrived in London, two policemen came on board and removed a man from the rear of the plane; he had struck his wife.'

When it was our turn, we stepped forward together. I handed our passports to the young, unshaven man sitting behind the glass partition and folded my hands on the counter. He glanced up at them and I took them down. I wanted him to ask if we were a family, but he did not.

We collected our bags and walked through customs towards the bar. We reported to the Hotel Informatzione desk, as

Gerhardt had instructed, where an attractive young woman ticked our names off from a list she had in front of her. 'The Hotel Europa & Regina?' she asked. I nodded. She said that Maureen and Gerhardt had not yet arrived. They were expected in just under two hours. I looked at my watch. The woman suggested we have a coffee. We went into the bar and had sandwiches and espressos. There were no stools, so we ate standing. The bar was full of water-taxi drivers, all wearing sunglasses. Everyone seemed to know each other, the barman included, as if it were not an airport bar at all, but an intimate local establishment.

After a cigarette, I pushed our trolley outside and found a place on the wooden pier in the sun. Annie sat on the luggage, her legs delicately folded. I sat beside her on the ground, keeping a firm grip on the trolley to avoid her rolling away. We held our faces up to the warm sun and listened to the water beneath us. 'That's nice,' she said. 'Gerhardt suggested we look towards Venice if we had to wait. He said you have to pass through Marco Polo airport, which is one of the ugliest parts of Italy, to get to Venice, the most beautiful.'

'You two have become very friendly,' I said.

'Yes, we have.'

I stood and revolved the trolley so that Annie could sit on her perch and look out across the water. It was what one might do for a toddler in a pushchair to keep them amused. Annie laughed lightly to herself and then, with disappointment, said, 'You can't see the city from here. I'll have to correct Gerhardt.'

'No,' I agreed. There was just the expanse of blue water nicked by grey and the lesser islands, Murano and Burano, in the distance. 'I hope he doesn't spend the entire time telling us what to look at.'

'Don't decide you don't like him before he arrives. I think he makes you jealous.'

'What do you mean?' I laughed.

'You had Maureen all to yourself as a child.'

I sat down with my back against the railing looking in the other direction, perhaps to spite Gerhardt.

'You'll finally have the opportunity to play out some of those Freudian scenarios,' she laughed. She leaned over and stroked the top of my head.

'Is that what you've been reading?'

'No,' she said. 'That's basics. Did you know that you two almost talk the same?'

'And what do you mean by that?' I asked.

'You're the most hopelessly old-fashioned people I've ever met.'

Behind the airport stood several blocks of government housing. Tall, white stone buildings with drying laundry draped from most of the windows. The lower windows were lined with black metal bars through which dangled the occasional arm attached to the shadowed figure of someone watching the tourists arrive for their holiday. They were ugly buildings, unlike anything found in the city of Venice. These were what Gerhardt suggested we did not look at. There used to be a poor section of Venice. The word ghetto was invented there. I don't think any such place exists today. The farmland we saw from the air supplies Venice with produce; the government block supplies the city with labour. One might think the city is a collection of only the attractive things in life, but people are leaving. The hotels, I've heard, are having a difficult time getting young Venetians to stay and work.

There was a breeze, but the white early afternoon sun kept

us warm. It hung strangely low in the sky, at about equal height with the top floors of that large white building. The lagoon chattered behind us. A constant stream of water taxis and *vaporettos* came and went. I opened and closed my eyes, listening to the assortment of languages drifting past from the tourists and felt that warm suspended sensation of skimming along the edge and into the shallows of daylight sleep. A man laughed endlessly. The breeze buffeted parts of his laughter higher, dropped others to a point near extinction, and it would seem he had stopped, as if he had not been laughing for a very long time, as if there had been no laughter at all, until another breeze lifted the sound again.

I woke in stages, in tides. The laughter, I began to realize, was the creak of the wooden pier in the current. The boats and the people walking past became sharp for an instant before they again drifted away. Only when a jet erupted into the sky did I lazily open my eyes and look at Annie, who seemed even more half-lidded than I, and then we drifted off again.

When I next opened my eyes, I did not at first recognize the two people walking towards us. They wore matching green Austrian hats with the rear rims folded up and long pheasant feathers jutting up from the side. Maureen had tucked her hair up beneath her hat, and wore the front rim low, almost covering her eyes. She wore a coat, an expanse of blue fabric, tightly tailored at the shoulders, but a sweeping wave around her lower half. In my semi-dream state, she seemed to be floating above a mass of leashed, blue dogs. Gerhardt wore a crumpled raincoat over a jacket and tie, and pushed a trolley with a pile of mismatched cases and an enormous umbrella thrust sideways between two bags. They stopped and stood over us, blocking the sun with their hats.

As Annie greeted Gerhardt nearby, Maureen dropped down in front of me. Her face was more made-up than usual and, if it had been her intention, she had succeeded in looking younger. 'Are you asleep?' she asked. She leaned forward and gave me a gentle kiss on my cheek.

'Come on,' said Gerhardt. 'We have a taxi going.' He reached down and helped me to my feet. He gave my hand a formal shake. He met my eyes with a sincerity that suggested he had rehearsed the moment. His eyes were even more aquatic and unreal than I had remembered them. His skin was not the same sandy complexion it had been when I'd met him a year earlier. I imagine Maureen had put a stop to the sunbeds. He was now more of a polished pink and, without the glowing tan, purplish and veiny at the end of his nose. His hair (and I have always wanted to describe someone this way) was flaxen; his teeth, although I doubt they were his own, were bright as bone. I had not been wrong in remembering the sense of depletion in his face, the way it dropped off from his prominent cheek-bones, and then surfaced again in his buoyant lips. He patted me gently on the shoulder, and then pointed in the direction he wanted us to proceed.

Maureen and I pushed one of the trolleys behind Annie and Gerhardt. The wooden boards of the pier rattled beneath the trolley's shaky wheels, turning this way and that, sometimes bringing us to a jolting halt. Maureen seemed very happy. Her clothes were expensive and as we walked she removed her hat and patted it against her knee revealing a new hairdo. It was short, with bangs cut just above her eyes and tints of an unnatural red. The style was uncharacteristically modern and, I thought, Germanic, but she made no explanation. 'I can't believe it's been so long, Gordy,' she said, and shook her head with sorrow. 'Terrible.'

We loaded our bags into the water taxi, handing them one after the other to the driver. He stood inside the boat sweating with irritation until a bellhop who had come out in the taxi from the hotel (the words Europa & Regina were embroidered on his jacket) came running along the pier and jumped on board. He soothingly patted the driver's back and pushed him away, resuming the loading of our bags himself. When the red-faced driver had wandered over to join the other drivers at the bar, the bellhop smiled, and said, 'He's angry.' Gerhardt answered him in Italian and the two of them shared a joke they did not explain to the rest of us.

In the boat Maureen and I sat down opposite Annie and Gerhardt on the long blue-cushioned benches running the length of the cabin. We were the first on board. The floor was carpeted and draped in sunlight from the salt-specked windows. We rocked slightly in the tide.

'I like your hair,' Annie told Maureen.

Maureen tossed her head back. 'Good, isn't it?' she said. They smiled at one another and fell awkwardly silent.

I stared at Gerhardt. He was still so unfamiliar. He looked down and swept his hand along each of his thighs as if he had just finished eating something that had left him covered in crumbs. 'You've never been to Venice, have you?' He turned and laid one of his long hands across Annie's knee. He kept it there.

'No,' she grinned. 'I'm really looking forward to it.'

'Well, you're going to love it,' he continued. 'It's the most enchanting place on earth.' He looked around to be sure the coast was clear before reaching into his pocket for a small airplane-sized bottle of cognac. 'I stole this so that we could have a toast,' he said. 'Our first in Venice.'

'Oh, you didn't,' said Maureen.

He broke the metal seal and took two long sips.

'This is not a school trip,' protested Maureen.

He extended the bottle towards Annie, swallowed what he had held in his mouth and frowned. 'Ghastly stuff,' he said. Annie tentatively raised the bottle and said, 'To Venice, then,' and took a swig. We all drank. Even Maureen drank. She pointed the bottle at Gerhardt and said, 'To you, dear,' and took a small sip. She shuddered with the heat of the liquid as if she had felt a chill. Gerhardt opened another bottle and passed it around again. 'One more before we have to share our boat,' he said. This time Maureen refused. She took a book from her bag and put on her glasses.

Slowly, the boat filled with other hotel guests. They were all couples like us. The driver had great difficulty convincing several suspicious men that the hotel had paid for the boat and that there would be no excessive charge upon arrival.

After we had waited for some time, I heard the sound of someone running along the pier. I turned to see a colossal suitcase appear in the rear of the boat followed by another of equal size and then a woman's voice thanked the porter.

Gerhardt leaned forward, careful not to crush his hat resting on his lap, and called out, 'It's already paid for.' The woman came inside, paused in front of us and smiled politely. 'It's paid for,' Gerhardt repeated.

'Thank you,' she said. She stepped carefully along the rocking cabin and collapsed into the only remaining empty seat. She looked exhausted. 'Sorry to hold everyone up,' she said without looking up. She swallowed her words in a way that made it difficult to tell immediately that she was an American. She removed a book from her bag and leaned over to shine an imperceptible stain from the end of her shiny black boot. The boots had pointed toes and needle heels. They were for a younger woman. From her slightly fallen face, I guessed she was around fifty. They seemed to be a very new and well-considered purchase.

Soon after, the engine started and we slowly reversed away from the pier and then turned equally slowly until we pointed out into the open lagoon. We passed a row of other taxis, bobbing up and down, raising and lowering their drivers who stood like hood ornaments on the bows. When we were further out, the speed increased and the front of the boat lifted itself from the water.

We had unwisely chosen our seats directly next to the engine; conversation was virtually impossible, so we sat in silence. At the top of the varnished wooden steps I could see the driver. Behind him the airport grew smaller along with the tall white building until they disappeared from sight. Gerhardt sat erect beside Annie. He frowned and looked at something out of the window between Maureen and me. The first few times he did this, I turned, but failed to see what concerned him. He leaned forward and glanced up at the driver. He seemed agitated, as if he was concerned the driver was taking us the wrong way. Before long, he stood as best he could without cracking his head against the low ceiling, and darted out of the doorway and up the stairs. Some of the other passengers watched him go with interest. Maureen turned from her book and looked at his green hat, which remained where he had carefully placed it on the bench. It seemed to take her a few moments to register that he had actually gone and had not shrunk to a size so small he could be concealed beneath his hat. And then she went back to her book.

Outside, Gerhardt stood beside the driver, holding himself steady on a railing and squinting into the distance. The driver looked over at him and Gerhardt nodded approvingly. He steadied himself on his feet and reached into his inside pocket for a pair of dark glasses. He looped them over each ear and then stepped forward and lifted his head defiantly into the wind. Lagoon water slowly flecked his glasses, but he didn't seem to mind. His hair snapped and wavered. He clenched his jaw and surveyed all around him like a conquering general. He looked perfectly comfortable on the high seas. I would not have been surprised to learn he had a drawer full of naval decorations somewhere, except that he was Swiss and, of course, the Swiss don't have a navy. His tie leapt from his jacket and floated in the breeze. Occasionally, he reached behind him and tried to smooth it inside his jacket again where it would only stay for a moment or two before springing free again. I was the only one watching him. Everyone else in the boat was either engaged by their companion or by something they read. Even the latecomer, who sat in the least desirable seat with her back in the direction we were going and so had the best view of the driver and Gerhardt, was engaged by a paperback mystery. I alone watched as Gerhardt removed a third cognac bottle from his coat pocket, took a long drink and then tried to get the driver to have a drink. When the driver shook his head, Gerhardt drank the rest of the bottle himself and then tossed it over his shoulder into the lagoon.

We slowed down to pass the smaller islands and Gerhardt came back into the cabin and folded his arms across his chest. He smiled from behind his moist sunglasses. His face had reddened from the sea air, and his hair was a tumult above him. Maureen leaned towards him as if she had something to say, and when he leaned forward to find out what it was, she reached up to comb down his hair, but he flinched back with irritation and performed a half-hearted effort himself. The engine picked up again and Gerhardt took Maureen's hand and tried to get her to come outside with him. After tugging on her arm for a moment, he gave up and climbed the stairs again by himself. Maureen turned to me and said, 'He had too much to drink on the plane. He always tends to have too much on planes. I think he's frightened, but won't admit it.' She smiled.

The sun had gone behind a cloud. The water turned darker and with an inconsistent wind became a choppy sea of hungry mouths opening and closing. Gerhardt's trousers wrapped themselves around his pointed shins. He still wore the same proud expression as he looked forward, but I imagined he was colder. I had almost tired of watching him when I saw him turn and, as if he were slyly rejecting a bad piece of meat, neatly vomit into the water. He cleverly positioned himself in the wind so that none of it would get on his clothes. It was very quick and very clean. The driver did not notice, and had I turned away for an instant, I would have missed it as well. He wiped his mouth with a handkerchief and took a packet of mints from his trouser pocket. I presumed it was seasickness. If I had consumed the same amount of cognac at the same rate, on top of whatever he might have had on the plane, I would have also been sick, but I guessed he was a more experienced drinker. I looked over at Maureen. Had she spent the last year with a man who regularly stole bottles of cognac and vomited over the sides of boats? It had never occurred to me that she would not do perfectly well in the world without me, but perhaps she had been surprised by a loneliness that made the likes of Gerhardt acceptable. His money, of course, would have been appealing to her. Money was one of Maureen's needs, although she had no regard for it; it simply made her possible. I cannot believe, however, that wealth alone would have determined her choice of partner. She had never married any of the men who had been so fond of her and who, financially at least, could have given her the life she wanted. In letters she had described her life in Vienna as days spent in the library or at the galleries, evenings in adorable little restaurants on the way home, or the occasional grand affair in a hotel. I could not imagine Maureen spending a year nursing a lush. I could not equate her with the women we had seen in the hotel bars of my youth propping up their drunken men, smiling with embarrassment. No. I decided it was seasickness.

Before long, Gerhardt popped his head inside the cabin again. He grinned as if he had a great surprise for everyone and pointed towards the bow. Through the windows, we had our first view of Venice. Faint on the horizon appeared the tower of San Giorgio Maggiore and the curved, onion shapes of the domes of San Marco. A series of blue, wet-looking clouds had rumbled in behind the city, and with them the water ahead seemed darker still, as if the city had been built on a hill and cast its shadow across the lagoon. A few moist scraps of light were visible on the highest roofs where the sun had slipped through a break in the clouds. The light seemed to be coming from inside the buildings rather than from above: from beneath the flaking paint and cracked teal slate of the tower at San Giorgio, from inside the domes of the palace.

It is a remarkable city to come across in this way. As if a great curtain is spun away, Venice rises from the sea as a reward to those who have found it. Despite the millions who have traipsed though the city – crossed the bridges, floated in the gondolas – it is easy to believe that by merely laying eyes on Venice, one is partly responsible for its perfection. Annie leaned forward and took my hand.

The engine slowed and the boat traffic thickened. The water tapped insistently against the sides of the boat as if the water were suddenly filled with specks of metal, lucky pennies. We passed from the lagoon into the Canale Di San Marco. Several people were enjoying picnics on the steps of the San Giorgio Maggiore. As the boat slowed, we rose and fell more dramatically in the tide. We all sat twisted on the bench gazing through the windows as we passed St Mark's Square into the Grand Canal. Maureen pointed at the mass of tourists traversing the footbridges of the smaller canals that ran perpendicular to us. 'The hordes,' she said and Annie laughed.

Not far beyond the clutter of gondolas around St Mark's Square, the Europa & Regina Hotel appeared. The hotel is comprised of what were once four palaces, then two hotels, the Europa and the Regina, and now one, connected by a central patio and behind it a glassed-in restaurant. Two porters stood on a rickety pier swaying in the canal awaiting our arrival. They wore green trousers and waistcoats, white shirts, black bow ties and very expensive-looking sunglasses. Despite their crisp appearance and the relative distance from which I first caught sight of them, they managed to look bored. They began a conversation with our driver when it seemed we were still much too far away for them possibly to be addressing anyone on board. The city seemed to have only recently turned dark and cloudy. A few defiant hotel guests remained on the patio, their hair askew in the sudden breeze, their dress too light for the chill in the air. Something in their expressions, in the way they held their coasters on the table as the tablecloths flared exposing the rusty white table legs beneath, suggested the breeze had arrived with us.

As we moved broadside on towards the pier, our little vessel rocked with amazing awkwardness. It suddenly seemed possible that we might actually crash into the pier, knocking the porters, who now stood with their arms outstretched towards us, into the water. Just when things seemed to get really dangerous, the two porters reached down and, with a quick exchange of rope with our driver, safely clasped us to the pier and the rise and fall abruptly ceased.

Annie was the first out of the boat. A hand in each of the porters', she positively flew up onto the pier. I remember this image, her flying above me, her legs pressed tightly together as if she were diving into a pool, with great pleasure. One of the porters turned his head and gave her another look as she passed him. I felt great possibilities. As if that glimpse of Annie flying above me reminded me of the purpose of our visit. This was our honeymoon, despite the fact that my mother and Gerhardt had come along. I had not forgotten, but I had, in a sense, forgotten Annie. Love relationships are a series of separations and reunifications. An idle thought can suddenly make the person beside you a total stranger. Half a dozen desertions and triumphant returns can pass in a single car journey. In the amount of time it takes to travel to the country and collect a small dog two people can abandon and betray one another in any number of ways.

At the check-in desk I took my rightful spot next to Gerhardt. I watched Annie and Maureen in a mirror above the desk where they stood amongst the flower pots and electric opening and closing doors of the lobby. They did not speak. They looked tired and road weary. Maureen walked over and plopped herself down in a striped chair that probably had not been sat on in years. At the time, I'm not sure I properly noticed that this was my first experience in a hotel with Maureen when it was not she who was chatting up the attendant while I waited with the bags in the background.

When the attendant turned to us, he addressed us in English and Gerhardt spoke to him in Italian. After we had handed over passports and signed the proper papers Gerhardt gave me one of the bulbous brass knobs that served as key rings. As it turned out, Gerhardt and Maureen's room was in the Regina; ours was in the Europa. This meant we took separate elevators. We agreed to meet for dinner. We said our *ciaos* and Annie and I walked through the lobby and up a few marble stairs and through a sitting room that served as vestibule to the dining room. It was well tailored, but plainly a room to walk through rather than sit in. Large imitation tapestries hung from metal rods on the walls. An extended Japanese family occupied the large sofas in the centre of the room, apparently planning their evening out. Annie paused to inspect one of the elaborate tapestries. In bright reds, it depicted a field dotted with workers bringing in a harvest.

'Remarkable,' said Annie.

'Everything has to be brought in,' I explained. 'Food. Everything.'

We continued through the room, down a few more marble steps and along the hallway, past several glass display boxes filled with clothing and jewellery. We passed a noisy kitchen with swinging, finger-smudged doors and found our elevator, half the size of the grander elevator that had transported Maureen and Gerhardt to their rooms.

Our room looked over a secluded *campiello* and down onto the glass ceiling of one of the kitchens below. The room was quite small and was almost entirely filled by an enormous double bed with a varnished oak headboard. All the furniture was in a similar neoclassical style. A bottle of champagne floated in a bucket of ice on a table near the window. Annie went over and picked up the card.

'It's from Theo,' she said. ' "Happy honeymoon". Isn't that nice?'

'Yes,' I agreed. I had actually picked up a half bottle of Moët from duty free and had been concerned about how to get it properly cold. I no longer needed to worry.

A small blue armchair sat snug in the corner on the other side of the bed. The oak cabinet at the foot of the bed contained a television. Two windows draped with white curtains stood on either side of the chest of drawers. 'Would you mind opening one of the windows?' Annie asked. She sat down on the bed with an exhausted sigh. I opened the window and then wandered into the dark-tiled bathroom. It was roughly half the size of the bedroom. It contained a long, deep tub, a bidet, a proud-looking toilet and piles of fluffy white towels to match the robes and slippers hanging behind the door. 'Come and look at this,' I called.

I had never stayed in a hotel of this calibre before. As time went on, Maureen and I visited increasingly more economic hotels. I had been out to eat in posh hotels with Theo, and occasionally Maureen and I left our inexpensive hotels and had lunch at the more famous hotels. Later, lunch became just tea or drinks when that was what she felt we could afford. By the time I reached my late teens the hotels where we stayed had become almost seedy. Not the sorts of places that rent rooms for the hour, but where deception is worth the cost of a whole night. They were always quite empty, just a few rumpled men smelling of perfume who wouldn't meet your eye in the lobby and then the women who smiled automatically when we passed in the hall. When I was sixteen I quite accidentally visited one of these women in her room when we stayed in a hotel in Madrid. We met in the hall. She had been out getting soda and asked me in and I agreed. I sat where she had urged me, on the edge of her bed holding a small cup of wine. She wore a pair of faded turquoise leggings, pulled up over the small bulge of her stomach. She had removed her make-up and had dark eyes. She looked old and not undesirable. We sat there having a pleasant time together. She spoke a few words of English and I a few words of Spanish. And then suddenly I realized the nature of our interaction, or at least the direction it was going. It was the way she held my hand steady as she refilled my glass. I left abruptly, and probably quite rudely. Sometimes I regret it.

After a moment, Annie appeared at the door to the bathroom. She was barefoot and held one foot curled protectively over the other. She looked around the room and raised her eyes. She seemed mildly annoyed. I don't know what annoyed her. I suppose it's annoying to realize such luxurious bathrooms exist when you don't have one of your own.

The bell rang and our bags arrived. I tipped the blond porter. He looked at me knowingly when Annie came out of the bathroom and rattled the banknote in his open fist. He remained just long enough that it seemed he wasn't going to leave – as if I had forgotten something – and then he turned and departed. Annie unzipped her suitcase where the porter had arranged it on the stand and removed her toiletry kit. I didn't feel like unpacking. I followed her into the bathroom and sat down on the edge of the tub. She began carefully to arrange her belongings along the cold tile shelf. She watched me watch her in the reflection of the mirror.

'What are you staring at?' she asked.

'Your particularities,' I said.

'Have you not memorized my particularities yet?'

'Yes, I have. I'm just enjoying watching you.'

She finally turned and opened her sweater. With a quick yank, she freed her blouse from her skirt. 'I'm going to have a bath,' she said and leaned across me to turn on the taps.

About an hour later, the phone erupted into shrill rapid sounds. How familiar we become with the way our machines talk to us. This machine sounded distinctly foreign. I was lying across the large bed. I must have fallen asleep. The television was on without any sound. I tried to ignore the phone perched just out of reach at the opposite end of the bed. Without twisting my head, I was able to watch it ring. I have always been amazed that phones do nothing as they ring. They sit perfectly still as if they were not responsible for the interruption. I heard Annie pick up the receiver in the bathroom.

She appeared a few moments later flushed and dripping, wrapped in a towel. Her creamy, slightly top-heavy legs were almost completely naked. She frowned at her reflection in the standing mirror beside the curtain. She lifted the heavy rear of her haircut before dropping it again. She did not look at me, but would not have made the gesture had I not been in the room.

She began to work her way through her case, folding things into drawers and slipping dresses onto hangers.

'Who was that?' I asked.

'We are to dress for dinner,' she said in a posh accent.

'Oh yes?'

''Fraid so, old boy.'

She stopped what she was doing and stood up straight. She had been bent over her case. She touched the small T-shirt in her hand to her brow. 'I think my bath was too hot,' she said. She came over and sat beside me on the bed looking woozy. After a moment of consideration, she removed her towel and lay down on top of me. 'Let's stay here,' she said.

'No dinner?' I asked.

'In Venice.' Her voice was muffled. She was talking over my shoulder with her face pressed into the bed cover. 'Let's live in a hotel in Venice forever,' she continued.

'You haven't seen the city yet,' I protested.

'I saw it from the boat.'

I stroked my hand up and down her naked back. 'What time is it?' I asked.

'After six, or something. We're to meet your mum and Gerhardt on the patio at seven. It looks like it's beginning to rain, however.'

I turned and looked out of the window. Just a handful of drops had begun jaggedly to streak the glass. We proceeded to make love – our first and only time while in Venice – with the lights on and the curtains (Annie must have done it while I was asleep) pulled defiantly open.

Fifteen

Annie was still dressing as I paced around the room in my jacket and tie. She was being far more careful about what to wear than usual. I sat down on the bed and flicked on the Italian television. She disappeared into the bathroom again and was gone for some time. Finally, I knocked on the door and told her I'd meet her downstairs.

I took the elevator to the lobby and walked past the kitchen. The buzz of frantic activity inside was palpable, as if a dangerously overwrought machine worked furiously behind those doors. The ante-room now stood empty, but the ashtrays were full of white-filtered cigarette butts. Most of the chairs in the dining room remained unoccupied except for a few large parties that included small children with napkins tucked in at their necks. I walked towards the front desk and tried to orient myself as to the direction of the patio. I retraced my steps the way we had arrived: down the long marble hallway and past the bar where an elderly man played the piano, apparently for his own amusement.

I stepped outside. The rain had stopped. The air had grown colder and I felt my skin stiffen beneath my shirt. A reflection of yellow electric lights bobbed urgently in the water. A man sang an aria from *Turandot* to the passengers of a gondola out in the middle of the canal. He was standing, his arms outstretched, a small hat in his hand. Towards the end he somehow turned it into the gypsy song from *Carmen* and from that into a Whitney Houston song, to the appreciative applause of his audience. A waiter was rubbing down the outdoor chairs and tables while a small group of hotel guests waited for a dry place to sit. Amongst them stood Maureen and Gerhardt. I walked across and touched my hand to her elbow. She was wearing a light dress with folds of fabric that floated down from the shoulders, covering the tops of her cold arms. 'Isn't it good to see you?' she asked.

Gerhardt smiled at us irritatingly and then sprang forward and staked our claim to a newly dry table. Almost simultaneously an enormous cruise ship slowly appeared from behind the buildings on the other side of the canal. The ship moved incredibly slowly. More and more of its dramatically lit pristine white hull and dark rows of windows emerged from behind San Giorgio Maggiore, the last building on the peninsula opposite. It was a startling sight. The gleaming white boat overwhelmed the darkened, weathered buildings from behind which it came, like a snake shedding a skin. I almost expected the buildings to collapse when the ship had fully emerged. There was something quite unnerving about it – a reminder that something as impractical as Venice had been kept around purely for entertainment.

'Look at that,' said Maureen with wonderment. I nodded. We stood there and watched it slide away, as if on well-oiled rails. When the ship got alongside St Mark's Square an explosion of flash bulbs went up from the hundreds of invisible figures standing portside. A few moments later, another soundless series of explosions indicated that the ship had moved past the Doges' Palace and the Basilica. The buildings were instantly lit up, splashed with the simultaneous effect of hundreds of individual flashes. 'Terrifying,' said Maureen.

We sat down around the table Gerhardt had secured near the edge of the patio.

'This is fantastic, isn't it?' He gestured out at the canal and then pushed a hand through his hair. He couldn't seem to get it right, however, and reached into his inside pocket for a comb. 'I'm glad we could share our first *ombreta* together,' he said. 'It's traditional to have a little glass of wine before dinner, but I propose we have champagne.' He turned in his chair and waved down one of the dignified waiters and ordered a bottle. While we waited for it to be delivered, Gerhardt surveyed the guests who had been steadily filling the rest of the tables. Finally, someone caught his eye. 'She was on the boat with us, no?' he asked.

Maureen and I looked around. The woman who had arrived late on the boat stood in the doorway of the hotel. The electric doors jolted at her from either direction and her face was lit from the flame of one of the gas lanterns on the pier. She wore the same black boots she had worn on the boat, but a different sack dress, and carried a hard black handbag.

'We should invite her over,' said Gerhardt.

'Oh, please don't,' said Maureen.

'Why not?' asked Gerhardt with some surprise. I could not believe he knew my mother so little. 'I think she is here alone,' he said and stood up from the table. He gave his hair another flick and walked briskly across the patio towards the woman. When she saw him coming, she made a visor with her hand above her eyes as if there were a glaring sun peeking above the buildings across the canal. Maureen and I watched as they exchanged a few words we could not hear. 'He's always doing this,' said Maureen sadly.

It seemed this woman needed some persuading. Finally, she nodded her agreement and permitted Gerhardt to lead her over towards our table. He pulled out his own chair, which allowed a view of the canal. 'Why don't you sit here? Oh dear, you've just told me your name and I've already forgotten it.'

'June,' she said, with apparent distaste for the word. 'Juniper Reynolds.' She shrugged. She had a pleasant smile, and beneath her weathered skin, a girlish face. She wore a bright shade of vanilla-pink lipstick that is popular with American country club women. She adjusted a red silk scarf around her neck and combed her fingers through her long hair, pulling it down on either side of her face. It was black, streaked with grey, giving it a cool metallic feel.

'This is my fiancée Maureen Garraty and her son, Gordon,' said Gerhardt. I stood and shook her hand. It must have been on shaky legs. *Fiancée*. There it was, I thought. Good God.

Maureen and the woman shook hands delicately. There was a small white diamond on the ring finger of Maureen's left hand. I looked at her for some explanation, but she did not meet my gaze. I had never considered that she would get remarried. Maureen, simply, did not have the space for someone else in that way.

I could not stop staring at her. I suppose I was upset. Gerhardt did not look at me twice. He presumed she had already told me the happy news.

June Reynolds sat down and Gerhardt took the fourth empty chair between Maureen and me. 'This is actually Gordon's honeymoon,' he said, turning to me. 'Where's the bride, by the way?'

'Getting dressed,' I said. 'She'll be down at any moment.'

'How nice,' said June. 'A honeymoon and a *pre*-honeymoon.'

'Yes,' said Gerhardt with pleasure.

'Were you married in Venice?' June asked.

'No. It's a belated honeymoon. We were married a year ago.'

'Oh, how nice.'

We all nodded. It didn't seem at all nice to me at that moment. I had not realized our trip was celebrating two marriages and I might not have agreed to come if I had.

'You are American?' asked Gerhardt.

'That's right,' responded June. There were flashes of gold at either ear when she turned to rummage through her bag and several large rings on her delicate fingers when she removed a packet of Vantages and guiltily put one into her mouth. She did not look comfortable. She held the cigarette between the ring and middle fingers on her right hand and did not properly inhale; she merely opened her lips and let the smoke spill out across her face. The light was dim, but I thought her eyes had begun to water.

'Are you traveling, or just visiting Venice?'

'I'm traveling. I've been in Florence for the last two weeks and I'll go on to Rome when I'm ready.'

'Very good,' said Gerhardt. 'That's just what we like to hear. Most people tend to rush, don't they?'

'Actually, I've been living in America only for the last year. I've been out of the country for the better part of the last twenty.'

'Just like you, Maureen,' said Gerhardt.

'Yes,' said Maureen.

'I'm from Philadelphia originally. What about you?'

'New York,' said Maureen.

'Not far, then,' said Gerhardt proving his knowledge of American geography. 'How long will you be in Venice?'

'I have no idea.'

'Right, right, when you're ready, as you said.'

'What about you?'

'Just a week and then Maureen and I return to Vienna and Gordon and Annie to London.'

'Oh, Vienna,' she said. 'I intend to go there.'

'I'd be happy to advise you on places to stay.'

'That would be wonderful,' she said. She leaned over and retrieved her bag once more and set it on the table in front of her. She removed a small black notebook and pen, unscrewed the top and found a blank page. Gerhardt had not expected to be taken up on his offer so swiftly but quickly got into the swing of it. I got the impression he enjoyed few things as much as advising people on travel. The conversation quickly became a private one between the two of them. They were interrupted only when the waiter came over and poured a glass of champagne for June before topping up the rest of our glasses. Maureen sat silently. I thought she was feeling guilty for not having told me of her engagement, but I could be wrong. I watched the gondolas floating past. They usually came in groups of two or three, enabling one man to sing to all the boats and thus earn double or triple the money.

Annie finally appeared wearing one of the new outfits she had bought for the trip. She wore a purple skirt and matching jacket with a fur collar stained a darker shade of purple. It is one of the great pleasures of married life (one that I miss) to watch your wife slowly cover herself with clothes and then see her appear in public and know what she is wearing underneath.

She approached the table and smiled as if she knew she looked wonderful. I got Annie to take my seat, despite Gerhardt's suggestion that she take his. She sat down and Maureen took her hand. 'I admire a late entrance,' she said.

'June Reynolds . . . Annie Garraty,' said Gerhardt.

'Hello, there,' said Annie. They shook hands. 'From the taxi?'

'The water taxi, that's right. I hear you two have recently been married.'

'Yes,' smiled Annie. 'Well, about a year ago.'

'You waited a year for your honeymoon? That's very disciplined of you.'

The waiter appeared at Annie's side much quicker than he had for the rest of us. 'What are we having?' she looked around the table. 'I suppose I'll have a glass of champagne as well . . . , *perfavore*.' She formed the Italian word very carefully the way she had practised.

'You should,' said June growing more confident by the moment. 'Lots to celebrate.'

'Yes,' said Annie.

Glasses were raised. They were gestured first towards Annie and me and then towards Gerhardt and Maureen. Annie did not look at all surprised by this, as if she were perfectly aware of their engagement. 'And my first visit to Venice,' said Annie.

'Oh, yes, that is something to celebrate,' said June. 'It's my first visit as well.'

'Ah,' said Gerhardt. 'We can fill another page in your book. I have had the good fortune to visit numerous times.'

'I would be very grateful,' smiled June. 'What do you intend to see?'

'Well, Giudecca is probably the most undisturbed part of Venice proper. And of the islands—'

'Torcello,' interrupted Maureen.

'I was going to say, if you want advice on what art to see, you should ask Maureen. She's an historian.' Maureen did not flinch at the word historian. She sat up straighter as if to carry the load that came with such a title. 'She's writing a book,' Gerhardt continued.

'Really?' asked June. 'What sort of book?'

'A guidebook,' said Gerhardt.

'In the nineteenth-century tradition,' added Maureen. 'You should see Torcello. The cathedral of San Maria Assunta is magnificent. It's seventh century originally, rebuilt in the eleventh. They've been working on the mosaics. Some of them date from the eleventh century. The cathedral itself is, without question, one of the best examples of Veneto-Byzantine style you could hope to see. That's really what I'm here for. Henry James said it resembled the "bleached bones of a human skeleton washed ashore . . ." but of course you should do the *Accademia* and some of the churches. Peggy Guggenheim's house is of interest as well. She had the most enormous private gondola; it's worth seeing that at least.'

'How lucky I am to have found you two,' said June. Gerhardt and Maureen remained admirably quiet. 'I've spent a little time in Istanbul, speaking of Byzantium. Have you ever spent any time there?'

'No,' said Maureen. 'My work hasn't taken me there.'

'I suppose the Turks don't take such good care of things.'

'Nor do the Americans,' said Maureen.

'Don't they? I don't know. I think I disagree with that,' said June. 'How exciting to write a book, though. I wish I had done something like that. I could have done something like that with all the places I've been. I think we're quite similar, aren't we? We have had wonderful opportunities. I had my girls, though. I don't regret any of the time I spent with them.'

'You have daughters?' asked Gerhardt.

'Two. They live in the States. I spent last year with them. I have been so far from them since they went away to college I wanted to be near them again.'

'Of course,' said Gerhardt.

'Yes.' June took a large breath of air as if she were about to begin a speech and then let it go without saying anything. Her daughters must be impatient with her, I thought; they tell her she talks too much.

Suddenly, the bottle was empty and Gerhardt waved over another. Maureen continued to make recommendations for what to see and June copied everything down in her book. 'You should of course see the Ducal Palace; it's probably the most lovely building in Venice. But it's so crowded. You used to be able to time it and avoid the tourists at lunch, but now it's a constant running stream.' Annie and I looked into our empty glasses. I wondered if we should have another drink. 'The best thing you can do is find a quiet little church somewhere and have your own private audience with a painting. San Rocco has one of the finest Tintorettos. You can only really find Canaletto in the *Accademia*, unfortunately, but you should do that. He's fun . . . And see the Carpaccio at the San Domenico in Chioggia if you want a day trip. It was his last one.'

'I'm quite hungry,' I said.

'Should we get some peanuts?' asked Annie.

'Let's go for dinner,' said Gerhardt. He looked at his watch. We have a reservation at eight, but perhaps we should head over and have another drink there. We can have a Bellini.

'All these artists named after drink,' said Annie.

'It's drink named after artists, dear,' Maureen corrected.

'I know,' said Annie quietly. 'I was joking.'

'It will give them time to find us a table for five instead of four.' We all looked at June who continued to write in her notebook. The silence intruded on her and she looked up.

'What? Oh, no. I wouldn't want to tag along on a romantic evening. I'm perfectly used to eating alone. I planned just to have a little something in the hotel and then go to sleep early. You don't think I need a reservation in the hotel, do you? No matter. If I do I'll have it in my room.'

'Come with us,' said Gerhardt. I felt that his second favourite thing to do aside from guiding people around foreign cities was to invite strangers to dinner. 'We have a reservation at Harry's.'

'I shouldn't . . . should I?' June looked around at us.

'Of course, you should.' Gerhardt jumped up. 'Let me call and make sure we can be five and that will decide it.' Gerhardt walked purposefully towards the bar.

'Does he speak Italian?' June asked.

'Yes, he does,' I said.

'He's quite a catch,' she told Maureen and Maureen laughed, in that manner she had, with her head tilted back, which could lead you to believe (after it went on for a while) that she was laughing at something quite different from what you had initially thought.

Gerhardt returned a few moments later, holding both hands behind his back. 'Not a problem,' he smiled. 'Let's head over.'

'Well, let me sign for these, at least, to thank you for your hospitality,' said June, gesturing at the empty glasses.

'Already done,' smiled Gerhardt and produced both hands in front of him as if he had made something disappear.

'Oh, you didn't,' pouted June. 'You're too much.'

'Not to worry. Shall we?'

The five of us shuffled off the patio and then through the hotel. We deposited our keys at the desk and wandered single file through the narrow alleys away from the hotel. Walking just in front of me, Annie stopped to stroke a cat moving silently along the wall.

'Oh, don't,' said Gerhardt gruffly. 'You mustn't touch.' Annie looked shocked. 'I'm sorry to snap,' he said. 'They have been known to carry disease.'

'In the nineteenth century,' Maureen laughed.

When we emerged into the wider street, Annie and I walked a few paces behind Maureen, June and Gerhardt. When we crossed over one of the bridges where gondoliers tied up waiting for customers, Gerhardt turned around and smiled at us. He pointed with both index fingers at the gondolas and grinned like a schoolboy who had suggested something rude. I asked Annie if she wanted a ride in a gondola and was a little disappointed to hear that she did. I've always been slightly embarrassed for the passengers in gondolas. They tend to look anxious and apologetic, as if we as a species are no longer capable of travelling so languidly. 'Venice is a walking city,' I told her. 'Maureen rates it the best walking city in Europe in her book.'

The expensive boutiques were closing. Shop girls in stockings bent their knees and dragged metal grates down in front of the windows. We passed a chemist window that displayed tortoiseshell combs in every size and shape imaginable. The streets were well lit and the sky had begun to darken. The pavement became white, the canal water pure green, and the houses, reflected beyond the slick stone steps, perfectly still.

'They're engaged,' I said, incredulously, when I was sure we would not be overheard.

'I know,' said Annie. 'He told me at the airport. I thought you knew.'

'No. Didn't you think I'd tell you if I knew?'

'I thought perhaps you weren't ready.'

'Don't you find it infuriating?' I asked.

She laughed.

'Well I do. I feel hijacked. It's our honeymoon,' I said.

'We're here with your mother and her boyfriend, it's not your typical honeymoon.' She took my arm. 'Don't be annoyed,' she said. 'Don't let it bother you.'

Harry's Bar was crammed with people. We crowded around the bar and each had a Bellini while we waited for our table. Fortunately, the wait was not long, although I imagine longer than it would have been had we been four instead of five. We sat in one of the curved leather banquettes in the corner of the room. Gerhardt chose a bottle of Amarone from a Brunelli vineyard and the waiter nodded his solemn approval. I remember because Gerhardt invited me to taste the wine for him and it was very good.

The bar area became slowly more crowded until it seemed to be ridiculously and dangerously full. Waiters in white coats waded through the crowds balancing impossible numbers of champagne glasses filled with pink Bellinis. Two young English couples stood at the end of the bar furthest into the restaurant.

The men loudly toasted one another. Their wives lowered their heads and clinked their glasses quietly. The men became increasingly loud. Their toasts, again to one another and then to their wives, became clearly audible above the din. A man in a very good Italian suit approached them. He tilted his head and spoke softly and apparently asked them to leave. Several waiters in white coats quickly escorted them to the doorway. One of the young men stood in the doorway a moment, holding onto the door, refusing to be pushed out. He said repeatedly, as if he were speaking to the whole room, that he was not drunk, until finally he disappeared.

At Gerhardt's insistence we all ordered risotto with inkfish, a local specialty, to start.

'It's a glamorous crowd,' said June. 'Look at those two for instance.'

Maureen looked at Annie's hand resting on the table beside her plate. 'Annie, you should take your hand off the table while you eat, but don't keep it in your lap; people will wonder what you're doing down there.' Annie seemed unsure of whether or not she had properly heard Maureen. She jerked forward and then looked at me to confirm whether or not Maureen had said such an extraordinary thing. I stroked her leg under the table. Annie looked at the side of Maureen's face for a long time, but Maureen did not notice, or at least she pretended not to. Finally, Annie seemed to decide that Maureen had made a joke. She smiled and kept her hand where it was.

'Don't they seem to be from a different era?' June continued.

'Where?' asked Gerhardt.

'That couple in the corner.'

'Oh yes,' said Gerhardt.

We all looked around. The couple in question wore very fine clothes. The woman had a stunning head of red hair, professionally maintained. She wore tinted glasses. Her face had begun to slip. A small ridge of gathered flesh ran the length of her jawline. The skin between her glasses and this slight ridge was perfectly smooth and powder white. It was only after a good moment of looking that one realized this woman was at least seventy. She had clearly had some form of plastic surgery and would have to again by the looks of things. Her husband was in worse shape. His eyes had sunk low in their sockets, like a toad's. He had shaved ineffectively and sat slumped in his chair. They were not talking, but they casually held hands as they reviewed the other patrons of the restaurant.

'That's because they *are* from a different era,' said Maureen. 'They must be ninety-five years old, hey, Gordon?' Maureen seemed to be in a better mood since the secret of the engagement was out. It must have been a terrible burden to keep it from me. I resolved not to express any interest. I would not inquire exactly how long they had been engaged or when they intended to seal the arrangement. I did not want to know.

'They're not that old,' said Annie.

'I wonder where they're from?' June said.

'They look French to me,' said Maureen.

'Yes, could be,' said June, obviously not convinced. 'I'll be going to Paris. Perhaps you could suggest somewhere to stay.'

'The George V,' said Gerhardt conclusively.

'It's extortionately expensive,' said Maureen. 'But perhaps that's not an issue for you.'

'They could well be Venetian,' said Gerhardt. 'Harry's is popular with visitors but it's a place for locals too. They could be the last of the old guard.'

We had a second bottle of wine with the main course. I had confit of duck. Annie had a large portion of carpaccio. Maureen had lamb. I don't remember what the others ordered. June talked more than her share throughout the meal. It turned out she had spent the last thirty years in a variety of different locations in the Far and Middle East. She had lived in Japan, Saudi Arabia, the United Arab Emirates and, despite her husband's chivalrous insistence that she remain in Japan, had even accompanied him for a six month stay in Mongolia and spent a few nights in a fur tent. Her husband worked in oil. As she did not volunteer his whereabouts, we did not ask and presumed he was where she had left him minding the family oil wells.

We had desserts and then coffee. When the bill came, there was another small struggle between Gerhardt and June. As she tugged at the bill, June exclaimed, 'I'll put it on my husband's card,' which seemed only to strengthen Gerhardt's resolve. A look surfaced in his eye that seemed to say that he would be damned to be beholden to an oil-slick man he did not know.

The tables were packed snugly in, and when we got up to leave there was some confusion as we each chose different routes to the door. June took this opportunity to slip off and approach the table where the old couple were working, very slowly, through a shared crème brûlée. We only realized she was not with us when we reached the front of the restaurant. We all turned to see what had happened to her. She was leaning into their table. The old man had moved forward and cupped his fingers around his ear. Finally, he sat back. June raised a hand that seemed to be a gesture for them to stay in their seats, though they had shown no signs of moving. They both smiled and nodded their heads. It seemed she had got her point across if, as I imagined she had, she had stopped to pay a compliment.

The woman nodded with an air of distraction, as if she were quite accustomed to being acknowledged in public.

June looked pleased with herself when she joined us at the entrance to the restaurant. 'I told them they were the most glamorous couple here,' she said. 'She's an actress.'

Annie turned back for another look. 'Is she?'

'She certainly is,' said June.

'Who is she?' asked Annie. She was straining for a look. 'Sophia Loren?'

'I don't know, I didn't want to ask, but I'm sure of it. Just look at her.'

We walked back the way we had come. Annie held my arm as I tried to walk slowly enough not to overtake Gerhardt, June and Maureen, who were walking very slowly in front of us. I think June was dictating the pace. The high, bursting sound of her voice ricocheted off the walls lining the narrow streets. Her voice had changed with the drinking. It had gone up in pitch and sounded strained. Annie drew us to a stop in front of a display window of a shop. A sparkling collection of hand-blown wine glasses stood at different levels up and down a little staircase draped in silver silk. The glass looked paper thin, as if it would shatter in any but the gentlest fingers. The delicate lip to each glass was lined with gold, as was the rim of the base. The soft lights concealed around the inside of the window frame reflected off the glasses and glittered out onto the street only to be reflected back by Annie's eyes. She gasped at the sight of them. 'Look!' she said. The others rounded a corner up ahead. 'How much do you think they are?' she asked. 'What time do they open?'

While we concentrated on the display, and Annie imagined,

I suppose, sipping from one of those glasses on our sofa at home, I felt a hand slip itself through my free arm; Maureen had come back to find us. 'These are nice,' she said.

'Aren't they?' responded Annie.

'Yes.' We all looked at them together, envisioning a little drinks party to which we were all invited, and then Maureen changed the subject. 'Are you enjoying yourself?'

'Yes,' said Annie. 'It's wonderful.' We left the window and continued on, the three of us with linked arms.

'I'm glad. I've always been partial to Venice. Did you know that Marcello Maostrianni hid here from the fascists during the war? He had a little secret room above someone's flat.'

'Really?' asked Annie. 'Why was he hiding? Is he Jewish?'

'I don't know now that you mention it, but I've always been partial to the city and I think that's one of the reasons.'

Annie laughed.

'Don't laugh,' I said. 'Maureen loves Marcello.'

'I do too,' said Annie.

'Gordon is making fun of me,' said Maureen.

We crossed over the footbridge and turned into one of the alleys that led to the hotel. Up ahead the figures of Gerhardt and June were waiting for us in the darkness. 'This woman is dreadful, don't you think?' whispered Maureen. 'Gerhardt is always doing this: inviting people along without thinking, before we knew anything about her.'

'She seems harmless enough,' said Annie. 'Maybe a bit mad.'

'Well, the sooner we're rid of her the better, as far as I'm concerned,' said Maureen. 'You'll think I'm mean, but I'm not. Annie, you don't help someone like that by patronizing them. They've got to know they're making themselves a burden.'

Annie nodded, but I think if it hadn't been my mother taking such an instructional tone she would not have been so polite.

When we reached the hotel, June insisted we join her in the bar for a drink. She made Gerhardt promise he would permit her to treat everyone. He agreed reluctantly.

The bar in the hotel was now almost full. The piano player continued to ramble through his collection of old favourites. 'Anything Goes', a slow steamy rendition of 'California Girls', a few numbers from *West Side Story*. The staff seemed harried. The waiter was relieved to deposit us in a corner with a small sofa and a matching set of armchairs. Annie and I sat next to June on the sofa and Maureen and Gerhardt sat opposite us in the armchairs. June was quite animated after all the wine. She kept looking around and finally jumped up and announced that she would go to the bar to get a waiter.

'They'll be here in a just a moment,' Annie said. June ignored her and hurried off. 'She's drunk,' Annie laughed when she had gone. 'She's leaning on me.'

Maureen watched June at the bar and nodded solemnly. 'She's embarrassing herself.'

June returned a moment later holding an irritated waiter by his arm. 'This nice young man will take our order.' We all ordered cognacs. When he returned with the drinks, Maureen apologized for June's behaviour. June looked hurt but did not say anything to let on that she had heard.

When the waiter had gone, June started straight in. 'I'm from Philadelphia and have lived in foreign countries more than I have in my own. And you, Maureen, you're the same. And Gerhardt, you're Swiss, and you said you lived in Paris for ten years and now you live in Vienna. And Gordy, you've lived away from America most of your life. We're all refugees, aren't we? Global nomads. A bunch of gypsies.' She raised her glass.

'I was born in London and I still live in London,' smiled Annie.

'Yes,' said June absently. 'It's strange, isn't it? It gives us a strange look at the world. A bunch of global nomads,' she repeated. She liked the sound of that best. 'Doesn't it, Maureen? An odd perspective?'

'Oh come off it,' said Maureen brusquely. 'That makes us sound slightly more downtrodden than we are, doesn't it?'

June continued to hold her glass up for a toast. I lifted mine as well, but was the only one to do so. June lowered her glass without taking a sip of drink. 'We don't really have a home, do we?'

'It's a privilege to travel,' said Maureen.

'Of course it is,' said June, trying to buck herself up.

'And I think it's slightly poor taste to call us gypsies or refugees considering the state they're in.'

'Well, I certainly felt like a gypsy floating all over the Asian continent making a new set of friends every two years whenever we moved. It was such a strange feeling to run across someone I knew five years before. We had been best friends, looked after one another's children, swapped recipes, secrets . . . and then we vanished from one another's lives. It was exactly like being a gypsy and meeting a fellow gypsy. Did you know that the gypsies started off in Romania? They're all over the world, but they all came from the same place. That's exactly what it was like. Now that I don't have to move around, I can't manage to stay in the same place for more than five minutes. It's just in me.' She was leaning forward. 'You understand that. It's just in my blood.' She clenched her fists. 'And you seem to be the same way,' she was pointing at Maureen. 'You and I are kindred.'

'Oh, for God's sake,' said Maureen.

Annie shifted in her chair. When I looked over at June again, I was shocked to see that she was weeping. 'Oh, I'm sorry. I guess I misjudged you.'

Gerhardt looked terrible. He couldn't think what to say so he said, 'We'll be going out to Torcello early in the morning, perhaps you'd like to join us.'

'I misjudged you,' June said again.

'Yes,' said Maureen, coldly.

'I'm sorry,' said June again. 'It's the wine. Red wine always makes me weepy.'

'The Amarone is a very strong wine,' said Gerhardt.

'It's just . . .' June was ignoring him. She drifted off and then returned. Astonishingly, she punched the seat cushion between us. She strangled the small paper napkin with which her glass of cognac had been presented. 'My husband. We've been married thirty years next summer and last year, out of nowhere . . . he left me. Can you believe it . . .? Someone younger. Can you believe it?' She was looking only at Maureen who glared back defiantly. 'So I went to visit my daughters. They both live in Boston. I thought of buying a place there, but I was getting underfoot.' She startled to sniffle. She had stopped producing new tears and somehow, this was worse. 'They said to me, "Mom, you don't need to sit around being miserable. You can go out and see the world." ' She wore an expression of deep determination. Suddenly, the new boots were explained. 'That's what I've done.' Her face distorted into tears again. 'I've come out to see the world . . . and I'm terribly lonely,' she put her head in her hands and let out a sob.

By now, some of the other guests were looking at us. Annie took June's hand and stroked her arm. 'There, there,' she said. Through sniffles, June thanked her.

'That's no excuse,' said Maureen. 'For God's sake. That's no reason to travel. I'm not travelling because someone threw me out.' She took an uncharacteristically large gulp of cognac.

'No, no. That's not what I meant at all,' said June miserably.

'I travel for some purpose, you understand?'

'Yes,' June sobbed.

Gerhardt put his hand on Maureen's knee. 'No,' she brushed him off. 'I don't like the suggestion that a woman can't make a life of travelling the world, especially, as in my case, when her reasons are academic, without the suggestion that she began, first and foremost, as a failure at home.'

'I don't think anyone's saying that,' said Gerhardt calmly. 'And I don't think you know enough about the situation to call anyone a failure.' He nodded at June as if he thought she might not think he was talking about her.

'I left Gordon's father because he was dull, I'll have you know.'

June began to cry harder. 'My husband was dull,' she managed. 'And I miss him.'

'Of course you do,' said Annie.

'Look, when you've finished whispering into her ear,' said Maureen.

'All right, Maureen . . .' said Annie. 'All right.'

'I wish someone had said something to me when I was young, so you should listen, Annie.'

'Maureen,' I interrupted. 'For God's sake.'

'For God's sake what? I wish someone had explained to me what I'm telling you: one does not have to make the sort of compromises one does. Life can be what you want it to be, if you will it properly.' She turned to June. 'You shouldn't be limping around Europe. Go home and be miserable if you need to be. But you should be out here for entirely different reasons than you are.' She looked into her glass of cognac and put it down. 'Now, I'm exhausted and we have an early start tomorrow.'

I don't know if she expected Gerhardt to follow her or not. He sat frozen in his chair. When she had left the bar and clipped along the marble hallway towards the elevator, he leaned forward and finished his cognac and then took Maureen's glass on his knee. He whistled. 'Well,' he said. 'Your mother can become quite excited, can't she?'

'Yes,' I said.

He did not look amused, however, despite the whistle. 'I've never seen her like that.' He looked genuinely frightened.

'No?' I asked.

'No.'

'That's not what I meant,' said June.

'Of course not,' said Annie.

Gerhardt was thinking something over. He finished what was left in Maureen's glass. 'Perhaps we should all go to bed,' said Gerhardt. 'Are you going to be all right?'

June nodded.

'Would you mind seeing her to her room?' he asked Annie.

'Not at all,' she smiled. She still held June's arm.

'I'm going to take care of these drinks, I won't hear an argument. You can buy us some tomorrow.'

June tried to pull herself together. She sat up straight and wiped her eyes. 'Yes, tomorrow would be nice.'

Gerhardt settled things at the bar and then waved before

disappearing into the hallway. He looked frightened of what awaited him upstairs.

After a minute the three of us walked arm in arm out of the bar and down the hall towards the lobby. June had stopped crying, but she now walked with a slight stoop as if she had been suddenly stricken with age. Annie made the sort of idle chat one makes with the very old. Silence feels worse with an elderly person, although they don't seem to mind it at all. It is the impending eternal silence that makes one talk stupidly, as if to a child, describing the objects in the room, the birds in the trees, the forecasted weather. June was staying in the Europa half of the hotel like us. We rode with her up to the seventh floor. Annie said things like, 'This is a small elevator, isn't it?' and when we reached her room, 'You're not far from the elevator, are you?' as if we were minding a dotty old aunt and June, like a dotty old aunt, answered her questions patiently.

When we had deposited her safely back in her room, Annie and I rode the elevator back to the third floor and found our way back to our own room. As we got ready for bed Annie said, quite absently, 'Poor June.' She had not wanted to say something so patronizing until we were in private.

'Yes,' I agreed. I sat on the bed and switched on the television as Annie removed her jacket and hung it in the closet. She wore a silk camisole underneath. She removed her shoes and inserted her felt-covered shoe trees before arranging them behind the door. She unzipped her skirt and hung it on its own hanger next to the jacket and then carefully removed her stockings and draped them over the back of a chair to air them out.

'Your mother was cruel to her.'

'Yes,' I said. 'She was. I think she's terrified at the prospect of marrying a bore like Gerhardt.'

Annie removed the camisole and pulled a cotton T-shirt over her head. When her head re-emerged through the top of her shirt, she said, 'He's not so bad. He's a good catch, like June said,' she smiled.

'He's not up to her,' I said.

'No, probably not.' She went into the bathroom leaving the door open behind her. She removed her make-up and washed her face. She brushed her teeth furiously for a very short time and then flossed, never losing eye contact with her reflection. When she returned, strands of her damp fringe were stuck to her brow. Her face was red in the places where she had given it a particularly vigorous scrubbing.

'How do you mean, he's not up to her?'

'I find him dull,' I said.

'Yes, yes,' she nodded.

'And Maureen, whatever you can say about her, is not dull.'

'No,' said Annie. 'I think she's great.' She looked out of the window for a moment. 'Can't he be up to her in some other way?' she asked.

'How do you mean?'

'Well, they seem to like to do the same things.'

'I suppose,' I said.

'They like to travel and see art and all of that.'

'Yes.'

'And they like to stay in hotels and eat and wear those funny hats they have.' Her shoulders dropped. She seemed to have failed to convince herself of something. 'You don't think she feels strongly for him? Fondly, or something?'

'What did you think of the meal?' I asked.

'Oh, fantastic, wasn't it?' She brightened up.

'That couple looked awful, though. They looked half dead.'

'They were holding hands,' she said.

'I can't imagine they enjoyed June coming over like that.'

'I'm sure they did.'

'Don't you think they felt patronized?'

She thought about this for a moment. 'No.'

'I think they would have felt patronized.' I couldn't find a way to agree with her, so I said, 'I was disappointed by the desserts.'

Annie crawled under the covers beside me. 'Aren't you going to get ready for bed?' she asked.

While I was in the bathroom, the phone rang once and Annie picked it up immediately. I finished brushing my teeth. When I returned to the room, Annie was sitting up in bed reading. 'Who was that?'

'That was June, thanking us. She called down to the desk and was frightened they would give her Maureen's room instead. She wouldn't even say hello for the first few moments. Your mother's put the fear into her.'

I nodded. 'She's very good at that.'

'I think your mother was unfair, but I must say, I don't disagree with her. June's a bit of a nightmare. Maureen should never have said what she did, but all that global nomad nonsense . . . What rubbish.' She shook her head. 'I sympathize with her. It's not nice to be chucked out, but it must be nice to be able to travel the world to get over your divorce. She needn't make it sound like something it isn't.' She switched out her light and threw two of the three pillows onto the floor. 'It's really sort of pathetic. Poor thing.' She was quiet for a moment. 'Maureen's mad, though.' She chuckled dreamily.

'Yes,' I said. 'I can't believe they're getting married.' I climbed into bed and lay there for a moment. I switched out my light and looked up at the ceiling for several minutes. I was thinking about Maureen and Gerhardt lying down together. There was a movement at the window. The curtain swelled silently with a breeze. It craned daringly all the way into the room and then it slowly deflated, sliding over the table and then outside into the darkness. The sound of Annie's breathing meant that she had already fallen off to sleep.

Sixteen

The following morning, sunlight fell oblong onto one corner of the bed. The sounds of church bells rang dutifully all over Venice. I heard someone in high heels crossing the courtyard outside, but when I went to the window the courtyard was empty except for a few pigeons drinking from a puddle. The courtyard was still in shadow, but the light above the surrounding buildings suggested the sun shone strongly nearby. As a city built on water, Venice does funny things with sound. The scrape of a plate placed on the pavement for a stray cat, a child running, an animated conversation, can sound as if it is next door, when it is, in fact, much further away.

I left Annie sleeping and went downstairs for breakfast. The day seemed warm as it poured through every window, but no tables had been arranged on the shaded patio. Breakfast consisted of a large buffet in the main dining room. The room was warm and muffled with excessive sunlight. The maître d' was too busy pouring coffee to properly supervise the seating and the guests had distributed themselves unevenly, as if they had come in groups of five or ten and had wanted to sit only with the group with which they had arrived.

Maureen and Gerhardt were already seated at a window table looking out over the canal. Gerhardt always got a good table. When he caught sight of me, he stood and waved. I had hoped to have my coffee alone. A friend of Maureen's once put forward the theory that the success of a marriage depends solely on contradictory sleeping patterns. She was leaving her husband because he would not leave her to herself in the morning. By this theory, Annie and I should still be happily married.

Maureen wore dark glasses. She accepted the small kiss I deposited on her cheek with distracted gratitude. 'I have a terrible headache,' she said. 'That wine.'

I sat down next to Gerhardt. 'Cafe American?' he asked and poured me a small cup of coffee from a silver pot. 'How are you feeling?'

'I feel fine. I thought it was a very nice wine.'

'Yes, I feel fine as well. Maureen is convinced that there was something wrong with it. How's Annie?'

'She's still sleeping, but that's not a bad sign.'

'I wonder how poor June is feeling,' Gerhardt smiled. 'She drank far too much.' Despite the coffee, there was a great smell of mouthwash coming from him.

'Apparently, so did I,' said Maureen. 'Gerhardt has just been lecturing me on my bad behaviour.'

'You were quite hard on her.'

'You think so as well, do you? I suppose that's no surprise. You never liked me to get excited.'

Gerhardt laughed. 'That's exactly what she said to me, "You don't like for me to get excited, do you?" I think it's an insult. She's calling us mild.'

Gerhardt beckoned a waiter and spoke to him slowly in English. 'My fiancée has a terrible headache. What I would like, and this may be unusual – ' he lifted two fingers and held them about an inch apart – 'is about that much whisky.'

'I don't think that's a good idea,' said Maureen.

'Whisky?' repeated the waiter.

'Yes, please,' he said. Maureen held the bridge of her nose between two fingers. '*Un whisky, perfavore,*' said Gerhardt.

'Yes, I know,' said the waiter. 'Whisky, I understand.' He looked at his watch and walked away.

'Go have something to eat,' said Maureen. 'Before the Germans eat everything.'

I left Gerhardt looking offended. Gerhardt is Swiss German. I filled my plate with scrambled eggs, prosciutto, melon and bread. I took a glass of juice and promised myself I would come back for more. On my way back to the table, I looked up and saw June, also taking cover behind dark glasses, standing beside Maureen and Gerhardt's table. She was speaking quickly and held a hand on Gerhardt's shoulder. He had gotten halfway out of his chair and was caught awkwardly between sitting and standing. It was as if she held him in place. He seemed unable to decide if he should sit down again, or if he should force his way to his feet. I dawdled for a moment, hoping to avoid embarrassing June any further by being witness to whatever apology she was making. I was sure it would not be dignified. She was taking her time, however; it seemed they were chatting. I decided that if I waited any longer it would become obvious that I was avoiding her. Furthermore, my eggs were getting cold.

When I approached the table June turned and smiled kindly, but formally, without recognition of the intimate fact that I had helped her to her room the night before. 'That looks delicious,' she said.

'Yes,' I said. 'Have you eaten?'

'Not yet.' I walked around her and sat down.

'I wish you would join us,' said Gerhardt.

'Thank you, that's kind, but I don't want to intrude. And besides, I like to read over breakfast.' She indicated the newspaper and several letters she held under her arm. 'I received a letter from my eldest daughter and something from my lawyer.' She laughed. 'My husband feels guilty so he won't cancel my credit cards. He won't do anything without going through my lawyer. We'll see how long that lasts. I'm sure he's going to say something about it here.' She paused and thought for a moment. 'I wish you could meet my daughters,' she said to me. 'The youngest is about your age. Twenty-two?'

'Gordon's twenty,' said Maureen.

'But of course, you're married,' she laughed. She turned to Maureen. 'Your son is charming. He and his wife were very patient with me last night. I am terribly embarrassed all around, but I'm not one to cower in my room.'

The waiter came over and placed a port glass of whisky in front of my mother. He handled it with distaste and walked away without inquiring if there was anything else we needed.

'Is that a whisky?' asked June with surprise.

'Yes. Does wonders for the headache,' said Gerhardt.

'Does it? Maybe I'll try some.'

'Do,' said Maureen coldly.

'Do you get headaches as well, Maureen?'

'Terrible.'

'I'll leave you then.' She took the paper and her mail in both hands and shook them with determination as if she were about to depart on a long journey and they were the sole supplies in which she had entrusted her survival. 'And please, again, accept my apologies for last night. I have managed to get your mother and Gerhardt to agree to join me for another dinner before we all go on our way. I don't want to impose on a family trip, but I would like to make last night up to you. I feel I ruined it for you.'

'Not at all,' said Gerhardt.

'I'd be very happy if you and Annie would agree as well.'

'That's very kind of you.'

'It is, very decent of you,' said Maureen. She seemed to be feeling worse.

'All right,' said June. 'I'm going to try that whisky.' She waved a finger at Maureen and walked determinedly to the furthest end of the dining room before she chose a seat right next to the doors. She sat down with her back to us facing the wallpaper and began to go through her mail.

'Poor thing,' said Gerhardt. He leaned forward and poured the whisky into Maureen's coffee. 'This will improve you.'

Maureen watched the slick brown liquid curl into her coffee with a bitter expression. 'I'm quite impressed actually,' said Maureen. 'I thought she would pretend it hadn't happened.'

'What time did you intend for us to go to Torcello?' I asked.

'I've postponed the boat until tomorrow,' said Maureen. 'I couldn't bear it the way I feel. I get these headaches all the time now.'

'It's not the wine, then,' said Gerhardt with pleasure.

'It doesn't help,' she said. 'I'm afraid I'll be spending the rest of the day in bed, like your clever wife.'

'She'll be up by now. I suppose I should take her something.'

'Do,' she said. She finished her coffee and stood up. 'I'm sorry, but it will be nice for you and Annie to spend the day together wandering around. Gerhardt, I'm going to lie down.' She touched her hand gently to my shoulder, turned and walked through the dining room. She did not stop to say anything to June.

Gerhardt offered me his paper. He reached across the table and took a long sip of Maureen's coffee, of which she had drunk almost none. He seemed anxious and fidgeted with things on the table as I tried to read. He took several more sips from her cup. 'What are you going to take Annie for her breakfast?' he finally asked.

'I don't know.' I pretended to think about it. 'Just some bread and coffee, I think.' I went back to reading. I knew he wanted to talk, but I wasn't in the mood. I think he wanted my thoughts on the events of the previous evening. I had managed to travel successfully with Maureen for some years and he hoped to benefit from my expertise. I wasn't inclined to help him.

After a little while of huffing and puffing and rattling his coffee cup against its saucer he stood up. He shook his room key at me and said, 'I'll leave you and Annie to it today. I may do some wandering myself. If you'd like to have a drink later this afternoon I'll be out on the patio at five. I don't think your mother is going to be much use today.' I found this last comment slightly offensive. I watched him walk slowly down the middle of the dining room. He was an incredibly thin man when you looked at him from behind. In certain men, age first shows in their buttocks and thighs, an erosion of muscle mass that makes their trousers seem empty. This was Gerhardt's condition. He paused and said something charming to June and then turned briskly towards the elevators. I wondered what it was like for Gerhardt and Maureen when they were by themselves in their room together. For someone unused to Maureen's ability to be alone in the company of others, it would have been discomforting. Maureen lying on her bed with a damp towel over her eyes and Gerhardt asking repeatedly if she was all right, offering to massage her feet or run her a bath. He would lurk around folding clothing, opening books, imagining she would feel neglected if he went out when she would be hoping above all that he go away and leave her alone. They were so obviously ill suited.

I have never enjoyed reading the newspaper. My attention drifts from article to article so that I remember the stories quite wrongly and combine facts that have nothing to do with each other. With Gerhardt gone, it was safe to fold the paper away and look out onto the canal. Venice is one of the perfect cities. As Maureen's book suggests, it is a testament to will power, but I understand why some don't care for it. It is a city inhabited almost entirely by tourists and there is something fraudulent to its old-world ways. As I looked out onto the canal that morning the last of the delivery boats were finishing unloading their produce for the hotel kitchen before scurrying out of sight like stagehands. I watched as a police boat floated past, its sirens blaring. What do the Venetian police do? They investigate lost wallets, perhaps; or is there a problem with drunk driving? The only people who own private boats have drivers for them. I suppose there must be tourists who refuse to pay their bills or who refuse to leave their hotels; the management must have someone to call. But if their primary function is to make sure the tourists are happy, this makes the Venetian police more like game-park wardens than police.

I took Annie a plate of assorted breads with a napkin over the top and a coffee I kept warm by using a saucer as a lid. When I entered the room she was sitting up reading. She dropped her book and stretched indulgently. 'What have you brought me?' she asked. I handed her the plate and sat down at the table with the guidebook.

I told her I had seen Maureen and June.

'How did June manage?' she asked.

'She seemed in good spirits,' I said. 'She invited us for dinner to make up for last night.'

'That was brave.' She took a loud bite of toast and crumbs rolled down the slope of her knees.

'It was, I thought.'

'Was Maureen receptive?'

'She was. We're not going to Torcello as planned. Everyone is feeling a bit rough after last night.'

'What do you want to do today, then?' she asked. 'Shall we stay in bed?'

My head was lowered over the guidebook. 'I suggest we walk to the Rialto and then walk over to San Giovanni Crisostomo. And then we can have lunch. Here, have a look.' I held up the picture in the guidebook of the Rialto Bridge. 'I'd say we should go to the *Accademia*, but you should go there with Maureen so she can give you the grand tour.'

'Oh, God, must I?' Annie asked. 'I've never been one for museums. I know I should see it since I'm here, but I'd rather walk around on our own. I'll feel ignorant with Maureen.'

'Nonsense,' I said.

'We can do both, can't we? See what needs to be seen and just walk around. Does your little book say anything about an English-speaking bookstore? I think I'll be finished with this by tomorrow.'

When we got outside we found it warm enough that we did not need our jackets. I suggested we could tie them around our waists, but Annie insisted on taking hers back. I was left alone for a moment in the campiello, empty except for the pigeons pressed against the shadowed nooks of the building. A fountain jutting out from one of the walls made a continual trickling sound against the stone. Annie returned very quickly. 'They took it for me at the desk,' she said, triumphantly. 'They think we're silly for not taking them. They said it's not warm yet.'

We left the courtyard by way of one of the many narrow alleys. We chose a different alley from the night before. There was a small bowl of milk on the pavement. Annie looked around for her cat, but it was nowhere to be seen. We followed the cool shaded alley all the way to the sunlit main street. We stood and watched the crowd, a stream of colourful figures flowing past, and then stepped into it and let ourselves be carried away.

We were swept towards the *Accademia*. The force of the crowd was so strong we were taken over a series of bridges and through a *campo* and past several churches and found ourselves on Pont dell' *Accademia* before we realized what had happened. We stood out of the way and watched people photograph one another and debated whether or not to go into the museum since we were already there. Annie resigned herself and said it was up to me, which meant she'd rather we didn't. She looked down the Grand Canal back towards our hotel. This was, it struck me, almost the exact perspective from where Caneletto had painted one of his more famous paintings. The paintings I have stored in my memory sometimes amaze me. I do not think I have a recollection of them and then they appear in my mind without warning. I remember visiting a chateau in Brugge once, where, just before the chateau's exit, there is a sixteenth-century painting of an empty courtyard. And then one steps outside directly into that courtyard and aside from one single building in the distance nothing is changed. Strangely, it takes a moment to realize why the courtyard is so familiar. Maureen wrote that this is the effect of a great painting: the feeling that you have been there before.

Annie looked wistfully down into the water. I thought of telling her of the importance of where she stood, but didn't think she would be impressed. We had set out from the hotel with enthusiasm and already our spirits were low. I decided the best thing was to have a coffee over which we could collect ourselves. I took Annie by the arm and we stepped back into the flow of tourists. We used the tide of pedestrians to sweep us over the bridge and right past the *Accademia* where the streets instantly quieted – that pleasurable feeling of being one street away from a parade. We found a small cafe and had two espressos and two cigarettes each while standing at the bar. I decided we should stay with our original plan and try to make our way to the Rialto.

At first I tried to keep track of where we were, checking street names and consulting the map, before I gave in and permitted myself to meander the way Annie likes to. As soon as I stopped worrying she seemed to become instantly more fond of me. She walked with her arm through mine. I no longer objected when we stopped and gazed at storefronts. We found a stationery store and debated over whether or not to buy a pair of carved stamps, one with the letter A and one with the letter G. Annie suggested that we seal our letters with them in red wax, but we agreed that neither of us wrote many letters and the letters we did write were not the sort we would want to seal with a stamp. We stopped at a glass store and despite my protests that we return to buy what she wanted at the end of the day (to avoid having to carry something breakable) she insisted. She said, 'Whenever anyone says they'll come back, they never do and they regret it.' She bought a set of clear glass blowfish with bright red lips and black eyes. The largest was four inches tall, the smallest the size of an aspirin.

We got lost several times, but always found our way back on track, usually closer to our destination than we had been before. Venice is smaller than it seems. Places become familiar very quickly and those familiar places are much closer together than one initially thinks. After we had been walking for a time we began to see fewer tourists and more people carrying out chores that looked like the day-to-day rituals of any other city. Mothers and their children shopping; a man slipping from a doorway looking twice in either direction before hurrying off clutching his briefcase; an elderly woman dropping bread in a square for the pigeons.

We had lunch at a small restaurant near the Rialto. As we entered, the proprietress came forward to meet us speaking in Italian. It is the best way to flatter a tourist. Several men sat at the bar looking at Annie and me, laughing to themselves. Annie beamed as the woman addressed her in Italian and pointed at her dress. After she had seated us and gone off to find us menus, I suggested that the old woman could be saying any number of insulting things at our expense. I indicated the men sitting at the bar.

Annie asked, 'How would she have guessed we don't speak Italian?'

'Well, we don't,' I said.

We tried to order, but the proprietress dismissed what we said and told us that she would order for us. The food was average. We each had an inadequately dressed salad and an over-cooked bowl of pasta. Clearly she gave us the food she made for tourists. You can find the same thing in a bad restaurant in London, or anywhere else for that matter. Maureen would not have put up with it, but the proprietress served us with such satisfaction, obviously giving us what she thought we wanted, I could not bring myself to make a fuss. Furthermore, Annie did not like to complain unless someone was being openly rude. The carafe of red wine was quite good and this made up for things slightly. After the meal, the proprietress came over and gave us each a small glass of complimentary grappa and laid a hand on Annie's shoulder. Annie smiled obediently and held perfectly still and looked at me as she drank from the glass as if she were posing for a picture. The proprietress stayed with us smiling for several minutes and then brought the bill.

After lunch, we stood on the famous bridge and took pictures of one another. In the photographs we look as if that was a long time ago and we might have grown into very old people since then. Several groups of teenagers sat around smoking cigarettes and strumming guitars. We watched the boats disappear beneath us. Annie rubbed her shoulder as she looked down into the canal. She said, 'God, she gripped my shoulder so hard. I think she's hurt me. I wonder if she did it on purpose.'

In the market the crowd was intolerable. It became difficult to walk. It was the hottest it had been all day and the smell of the produce and the sticky bodies pressed up against one another became terrible for a few minutes and then, quite suddenly, the crowd began to disperse. We left as quickly as we could, having been much happier on the quieter streets we had occupied before lunch. It is impossible to be in a hurry in Venice. The main streets are too crowded, and the side streets, although you feel as if you are making progress, take such a convoluted route they don't make up any time whatsoever.

By the time we found our way to the San Giovanni Crisostomo we were both fatigued. Like most of the minor churches, it was empty. We sat down in a pew where we had a clear view of Bellini's portrait of St Christopher, St Jerome and Louis of Toulouse. 'Maureen loves this,' I whispered. St Jerome is an old man reading from a book balanced in the branches of a tree. Standing beneath him, the two younger saints are very handsome and gaze confidently out over a landscape. One of them has a small child perched on his shoulder. Annie gazed at the three wistfully. She said, 'There was a time when people used to think that if a sinner was a beautiful sinner the gods would go easier on him, just because of his beauty.' She stood up and straightened her skirt. 'There was a whole movement, led by artists, of course. We should ask Maureen about it.' She turned and walked all the way down the aisle and dropped to her knees in front of the altar. She folded her hands in front of her. It was cool in the church, a relief from outside. As I watched her, I felt profoundly calm and lowered my chin to the top of the pew in front of me. There have been religious experiences over less. However, this feeling of well-being abruptly fell away, as they tend to. Suddenly I was quite unnerved watching her pray. We had spent the day together; we were, after all, on our honeymoon, but it suddenly occurred to me that I did not know what she would be asking for. That's what it's about isn't it? She was making no audible sound. Her shoulders moved as she moved her lips. I had the urge to walk down the aisle and make her stand up. The woman I had married was whispering her most private thoughts, her hopes and desires, to what she earnestly believed to be the maker of all the universe, and I had precisely no idea, not the first one, what the nature of that conversation might be. I caught myself gazing at my young bride with a vague sense of distrust. I watched her until she had finished her prayer and then as she walked back up the aisle towards me. 'Do you have some money so we can light a candle?' she asked.

We lit several. Annie made wishes and asked me to make one. I wished, I think, that Annie and I could remain as happy as we then were, or something like that. I immediately told her what I had wished. She frowned and said you can never say a wish out loud, especially not to the person involved.

When we re-emerged, the sun was still bright but it had fallen lower in the sky and made a clearly recognizable reflection in the water. The hotel felt a great distance away and the prospect of walking when it was almost certain we would get lost no longer seemed appealing. We agreed we would take a gondola if we found a place to hire one. I took her hand. We did not find a place to hire a gondola until we were so near the hotel it didn't seem worth it, so we walked all the way, saying very little as we went.

Seventeen

We decided we would have coffee on the veranda beside the canal. Gerhardt had mentioned he would be out there at five, and it was barely four, so I thought we would have at least some time alone before he joined us. We did not go up to the room or even collect our key. Much to my disappointment we found Gerhardt already seated between Maureen (wearing a hat I hadn't seen before) and June, who sat rigidly as if she were being interviewed for a job.

'How was your first day in Venezia?' Maureen asked. 'What have you got?' She reached for Annie's bag. 'Shopping!' Annie did not surrender it, however. She instead slowly removed each of her new blowfish and arranged them in a row on the table. 'Isn't that wonderful?' asked Maureen. 'Look at them, how sweet.'

'You're feeling better?' I asked.

'Much,' said Maureen. 'I just needed another few hours in bed. Gerhardt is so tough on me. Up at seven, breakfast at eight, so regimented. Aren't you?' Gerhardt did not smile. He was far more subdued than usual. June seemed anxious. She looked down into her coffee. It occurred to me that they had been in the middle of a serious conversation when we arrived.

'I hope we haven't interrupted you,' I said.

'Nonsense,' said Maureen. 'It's your honeymoon, Gordon,

how could you be interrupting us? If anything, we've been interrupting you. At least you get some bedtime hours together. I've just been upsetting poor Gerhardt. I'm afraid he doesn't know what he's gotten himself into with me, do you, Gerhardt? I'm not terribly agreeable, am I? You should have warned the poor man, Gordy, the first time you laid eyes on him.'

'I couldn't,' I said. 'It was at my wedding.'

Maureen was all smiles. She looked only at Annie, patting her hand for emphasis. Annie smiled intermittently and looked away, trying to look busy as she wrapped up her blowfish.

'What have you been up to, Maureen?' I asked.

'Nothing at all. You say that so suspiciously. I've just come down from upstairs and found June and Gerhardt here enjoying a lovely afternoon together. Apparently, June is refusing to drink anything at all after last night; otherwise you would see an empty bottle of wine. Gerhardt has had to order them by the glass, haven't you? He would never order a whole bottle to himself. Certainly not in the middle of the afternoon.' Gerhardt said nothing. He looked redder in the face than when I'd seen him at breakfast. He folded his arms and exhaled with irritation. June was smiling nervously beside him. She seemed unsure of Maureen's tone. 'I've come down from my nap and found the two of them having quite a time together. He's been giving her his expert opinion on Rome, where you'll be going next, won't you?'

'Yes,' said June.

'And then we got into a disagreement.'

'Hardly a disagreement,' said June.

'Oh, come on,' Maureen laughed.

The waiter arrived with coffees for Annie and me and Gerhardt defiantly ordered another glass of white wine.

'Should have had the bottle after all,' said Maureen.

'You are a very bright woman, and I don't know why you are insisting on being unintelligent about this,' Gerhardt said.

'Our disagreement is as follows: we were discussing the Vatican, St Peter's Basilica, where of course you've been, Gordy.' She patted my knee. 'And you, Annie, *should* go. After listening to Gerhardt give what, I might add, I thought was a flawless description of the ride in from the Rome airport and the stray cats at the Coliseum (if that sort of thing interests you) I simply said that the Swiss guards at the Vatican are *castrati*: neutered upon induction to prevent their loyalties being swayed by temptation. And Gerhardt, who is, of course, Swiss, disagrees. I'm not sure whether he disagrees with the idea that they would agree to be snipped or with the idea that a good Swiss man could ever be swayed in the first place. But I'm sure of it, I read it some place: the Swiss were the only ones who'd agree to it. That's why they're the guards.'

'It's totally untrue,' said Gerhardt. He looked deadly serious. He took another large gulp from his glass. 'For someone so concerned about the factual history of art, I find it quite shocking that you have now decided to talk such absolute rubbish.'

'What do you think?' asked Maureen.

'It can't be true,' I said.

Annie laughed. She had finished carefully rewrapping her fish.

'You think this is funny?' asked Maureen.

'Yes,' said Annie. 'You're obviously having a joke. Catholicism is one of the sexiest religions. They'd never approve of that.'

'Obviously,' said Maureen after a moment. 'Why do I treat

you this way?' she asked. 'I am punishing you for getting drunk in the afternoon as I specifically instructed you not to do; with a strange woman as well.' She leaned over and touched Gerhardt's hand, but he did not respond. He looked out over the canal.

'Hardly a strange woman,' said June. 'I humiliated myself in front of you all last night.'

'No, of course, I'm only having a joke, as Annie suggested. I am pleased you could look after my fiancé as I slept, otherwise he might have grown bored and wandered off.'

'I seem to be doing everything wrong for you,' said June. 'I offended you last night and now I've offended you again. I was just coming outside to read, I have my book here, look,' she lifted her paperback novel as proof. 'And Gerhardt was here so I accepted his offer to join him. He looked quite lonely.'

The waiter delivered Gerhardt's glass of wine with great ceremony. Gerhardt snatched it from his hand and took a large gulp.

'I do starve him of entertainment.'

'I don't know why you are insisting on taking it this way; it is not what I mean at all.'

'No,' said Gerhardt, still staring directly ahead of him. 'Maureen is just having fun with us.'

'Isn't it tragic how easy it is to offend people,' continued June. 'I have had a great deal of experience with this over the years. Judging from my behaviour since we met, I'm sure that's no surprise to you but, living in all those strange places, I was forever standing up when I wasn't supposed to, or following my husband when I was supposed to stay with the women or some such thing. I must say I don't like those sorts of restrictions much, and from what you said to me last night, Maureen,

I don't think you like them much either,' and then she broke off and asked, 'Are you cold?' Maureen had retreated to the back of her chair and was shivering slightly. 'You look as if you're freezing.'

'Yes,' said Maureen. 'It's gotten cold all of a sudden. Is anyone else cold?' She looked around at us. 'No? Probably because I was sleeping.'

'Would you like a sweater?' June asked. She looked at Gerhardt who was glaring at the canal. He took up one of June's cigarettes and blackened it with three matches. 'Gordy, why don't you run and get your mother a sweater?' June asked.

I looked at Maureen. She seemed quite uncomfortable. 'Would you like me to?' I asked.

'Yes, do, Gordon,' said June. She pushed Maureen's key across the table in my direction. I rose, but Maureen had still not looked at me, or said anything to suggest she was aware that people were talking about her. She held her arms tightly around herself and I thought for a moment that she would begin to rock maniacally forward in her chair.

'Anything in particular?' I asked.

'I think my headache is coming back,' said Maureen. She put her hands to her head. 'It's crippling.'

'You're just cold after a nap,' said June. 'Go on, Gordon.' I waited another moment for Maureen to tell me whether or not I should go. I didn't like the thought of entering the hotel room she and Gerhardt shared; I could think only of his intimate things spread out across the room, his socks and shorts in a musty heap beneath the curtains. The change Maureen had undergone from one moment to the next seemed incredible. Like an old woman, she had lost her way between what were usually familiar places. I had never seen her let someone take such care of her in the way she now allowed June to do. Then June was laying her hand across Maureen's brow. 'Do you feel you might have a fever?' she asked.

'I never get sick,' said Maureen, weakly.

I rode the grander elevator on the Regina side of the hotel to the sixth floor and found my way to their room. The maid had already been, or else Maureen had become a tidier person than when we lived together. Gerhardt had selected far superior accommodations for himself and Maureen. The suite consisted of several rooms. The first was a sitting room with two chairs, a sofa, and a large glass coffee table. A basket of fruit sat in the centre of the table beside a half-full bottle of champagne adrift in an enormous pool of ice. Maureen's books were piled on a wooden sideboard behind one of the chairs; two pairs of silk Chinese slippers were arranged neatly on the floor underneath. A large pale blue book on the history of modern Egypt, which I suspected to be Gerhardt's, rested on the table under a pair of reading glasses.

Through a pair of French doors I could see the view of the Grand Canal. I pushed them open and went out onto the balcony. Two chairs and a small table were positioned between several potted plants. The patio curved around to the bedroom where another set of French doors stood open. Seagulls curled and called in the air. What a lazy pleasure it must have been, I thought, to lie in bed in the morning and listen to the busy sounds outside. I leaned over the edge and looked down at the boat traffic moving gently back and forth on the canal. A weak motor chop-chopped its way along as the tide tapped against the stone banks of the canal. The air was still and I was sure I could hear snippets of conversation drifting across the water from one of the gondolas. Compared with the antique, creaking sounds of the vessels below, the larger boats floating further out in the lagoon seemed ominous and clumsy. A dark cloud of birds swarmed above one of the barges. It had not occurred to me to wonder what they do with Venice's garbage. They send it to the mainland, of course.

Beneath me I could see the patio where I had been sitting only moments before. I could make out Annie, in her shining red top, and June still leaning slightly towards Maureen, although she seemed to have removed her hand from my mother's brow. Gerhardt was still staring off across the canal. I wondered if Maureen had watched Gerhardt and June from the same spot before going down to join them. I cannot believe Maureen was jealous of June and the attention Gerhardt paid her. June was a cultured and interesting woman, handsome to some I'm sure, but absolutely nothing compared with Maureen. As I turned to go inside, I noticed an empty champagne bottle lodged behind one of the large potted plants. The balcony must have served as the perfect place for Gerhardt to be alone when Maureen was working or when she slept.

I entered the bedroom from the patio. The wallpaper was intricate and old fashioned, the bed, a vast cloud of off-white duvet. The maid had already turned down the sheets and laid out chocolates on the pillows. I briefly contemplated taking one, but thought they would be missed. From across the room, I could see into the bathroom. It was roughly the size of Annie's and my entire room with twin sinks carved out of a marble countertop. From a single glance, I could distinguish her sink from his: the glistening gold bottles of perfume, her make-up brushes and the jewellery box she had carried since I can first remember.

The closets were on the other side of the bed, and as I went round, I almost fell headfirst over a short fold-out cot arranged between the larger bed and the wall. It was such a familiar sight – this wire contraption on rickety wheels – I was almost not surprised to see it there. I had spent years on ones like it. Another pair of chocolates lay on its sad little pillow.

I wondered which one of them slept there, and did this mean that at their home in Vienna they occupied separate rooms? I decided it did, and I decided it must have been Maureen who objected to sharing a bed. Maureen had not shared a bed with any regularity since I had been old enough to occupy my own little cot. Perhaps he suffered night sweats, or perhaps he snored, or perhaps he could not keep his hands off her.

I opened the closet and marvelled at a vast display of sweet-smelling shirts on hangers, their French cuffs turned up and held in place with small plastic cufflinks. There was an enormous variety of colours, each in at least three different shades. On the floor there was, absurdly enough, a pair of men's riding boots, and beside them, a smaller pair that I presumed were Maureen's. Riding boots. What had she got herself into?

When I returned carrying Maureen's sweater over my arm, she did not seem concerned that I might have seen the cot in the room. Perhaps she thought the maid would not have already arranged it there or perhaps she hadn't felt there was anything shameful about it, but I thought there was. It suggested something fraudulent about her and Gerhardt's relationship. I might have felt relieved, but it only made me feel sad for Maureen.

She had perked up slightly and was making conversation with June. June took the sweater and arranged it over Maureen's shoulders. June seemed to be playing her nurse's role slightly too enthusiastically. But Maureen was enjoying being nursed.

'Thank you,' said Maureen to June. 'I am feeling better. That was odd: all of a sudden I just started feeling incredibly cold.'

Gerhardt still looked angry. He had obviously remained silent since I'd left. Annie leaned forward and touched him gently on the arm. He looked around, surprised at such tenderness. 'And what did you do today?' she asked.

Eighteen

June took us all out to supper that evening. An old friend she had known in Tokyo had recommended a restaurant off the tourist track. We walked down a series of narrow alleys and through poorly lit *campos*, which in another city would make the smart traveller afraid for his safety. At one point during the confusion we were definitely walking in circles. Annie whispered to me that we had passed the same yellow dress displayed in a shop window at least three times: she was getting to like it, she said, and if we passed it once more, I would have to buy it for her. Even Gerhardt admitted he was lost. As we walked, June spoke nervously, apologizing and reassuring us we were at last heading in the right direction.

The restaurant we finally found was very good. If I could remember where it was, or its name, I would make note of it here along with detailed directions in deference to Maureen. The crowd was Venetian and we were overdressed. They took no notice of us, despite the fact that we seemed, at least to me, to be intruding on something intimate. After a few more glasses of wine, Gerhardt had returned to his jovial self. He even held Maureen's hand. For a moment, she too looked happy. He told a prolonged story about a school friend of his whose parents lived in Tanzania and had taken him hang gliding with the birds in the rainforests there. He said he'd had a very adventurous youth. He looked down at his knife and fork sadly and said again, 'Very adventurous.'

On the way home, Gerhardt, walking jauntily between June and Annie, sang and showed us the tricks of the echoes. Some of the pedestrians we passed looked at him, which only seemed to encourage him. Maureen and I walked together several paces behind the three of them. I could hear Annie laugh. He even managed to get her to sing with him, and she had always claimed to dislike her voice. June turned back to us often and smiled with satisfaction at having repaired the damage of the night before.

'June's all right,' I told Maureen.

'Yes,' she said. 'She irritated me last night, but she's nice enough. Not the sort of woman I would like to be . . .' She turned and looked at me seriously. 'Human refuse. You'll never let me end up like that, will you?'

'No,' I said.

'I think her daughters probably booted her out – couldn't stand the sight of her after a year. Young people don't like disappointment, do they?' She put her arm through mine. 'Oh, dear,' she said wistfully. 'It's a sad world, isn't it?'

We walked to the end of a dark alley and through a low archway into a wide cobblestone *campo*. I imagined there would have been stalls during the day. A gutter ran through the middle, lined by a series of stone posts: Gerhardt and Annie leapfrogged three in a row. The moon was particularly strong as it lay across the open square. The light had a theatrical quality to it: the sort of moon that up till then I had only ever seen floating derelict in the ponds of the romantic rococo paintings Maureen despised. It had a much better effect in real life. If there is no such thing as a Venetian moon, then there should be. I've never seen the distinctive lavender light any-where else.

Their laughter dwindled as Annie, June and Gerhardt slipped out of the square ahead of us and we were left alone. I could hear only the sound of Maureen's teetering shoes as she walked next to me.

'Look, I'm sorry I didn't say anything about the engage-ment. I meant to before Gerhardt blurted it out. I hope you're not angry.'

'No,' I said. I wanted to ask if she was really going to go through with it. The idea seemed like such a bad one to me. He very obviously did not excite in her an overwhelming passion and I guess I felt that she deserved better. I'm sure I would not have objected as much if he had been a man I admired. But I did not ask her. Some instinct told me not to pry in these matters.

'You know, I got a letter of congratulations from your father,' she said.

'That was nice of Theo.'

'I wrote a letter about six months ago telling him I would not be asking for any further economic assistance. I didn't think it would be right now that you're raised and on your own.' She did not look at me as she spoke. She looked straight ahead at the dark archway through which the others had disappeared. 'I thanked him for his generosity and told him I hoped he was pleased with the way you turned out.'

'How did he respond to that?' I asked.

'Your father was gracious, as he can be on the subject of money. He said he didn't think it was a question of his gen-erosity at all, as much as his duty. He said you had turned out fine and he actually thanked me. "Not just for Gordon," he wrote, "but for everything." '

'Is that right?' I asked.

'Yes,' she said. 'He congratulated me on my engagement and told me if I was ever in any trouble to contact him immediately. He even included the name and number of some assistant in case he was unavailable: I'm one of his children now.'

'That's very decent of him,' I said.

'I would never do that, you understand. I would never go back and ask Theo for more money, once I've told him I wouldn't.'

We left the square and were again by the water. It was suddenly darker without the moon. The boats moored at the side of the canal knocked against the embankment. June and Annie had stopped and appeared to be peering into the water. I could not see Gerhardt and for a moment imagined he had fallen in. And then I caught sight of him. From my perspective, he seemed to be standing up to his waist in the canal. There was a light on in one of the black houses above. It swayed in the water as if a yellow sheet had blown loose from one of the laundry lines. Annie and June were laughing. I could tell by the way Annie hunched over and pressed her knees together.

'Oh, God,' said Maureen. 'What has he done now?'

We walked briskly towards them and looked down to see Gerhardt standing uneasily in a gondola. His back was to us, his arms outstretched towards the sky. The boat was thrashing wildly in the water beneath him. Before I realized he was purposely throwing his weight from foot to foot, I was seriously concerned he would overturn the boat and tumble into the canal. As I looked at him, I could see how he had once been athletic.

He turned towards us. 'Come on,' he said. 'Maureen, you'll join me.'

'I won't,' she said. 'Now come out of there. You're going to get arrested.'

'Maureen's right,' said June. 'It's like getting into someone's car.'

'It's like breaking into someone's house,' said Maureen. 'They're worth more.'

'Oh, God, what the hell is the matter with all of you,' he said. He made the boat make another large splash in the water as he turned away. 'Come in!' he bellowed. The boat lurched as if he had actually stomped his foot in irritation. 'Gordon,' he said quietly. 'Help the ladies in and untie us.'

'No,' said Maureen. 'I'm going home.' She did not move, however. She stood there and looked at him. 'Come out of there, please,' she said finally. Gerhardt lifted his arms into the sky once more, letting out a great howl. Lights flicked on in some of the other windows around us. 'Come on,' she said again. 'You're waking the neighbours. Help me, Gordon,' she said. She lifted her dress and reached for my hand. She was lighter than I expected as I lowered her into the boat. She never let go of her dress as she inched towards him spider-like across the boat, stepping over a coiled rope and the wooden benches from where the cushions had been removed. She spoke quietly. 'If you turn over this boat, I'll murder you,' she said. When she got near enough, she put her hand on his shoulder and he dropped his arms: it seemed to be a great relief for him. He made no sudden movements that would have knocked them both into the canal. 'Now, come on,' she said. He obediently let her take his hand and the two of them began the unsteady walk along the length of the boat towards the shore.

'I just wanted to have a little fun,' he said. His accent seemed to become thicker when he drank. I thought he was going to cry.

'But you get carried away,' she said soothingly.

Nineteen

Early the following morning all of us (except Annie) gathered for breakfast. June was now an official member of our party. It went without saying that she would accompany us on the trip to Torcello; or perhaps it was discussed when I was not present. Maureen was distracted. She claimed more than her share of the breakfast table with her pile of books, each with several colourful bookmarks, and a yellow legal pad covered in notes. She said almost nothing throughout the meal. This was absolutely familiar to me, but appeared to be unsettling for Gerhardt. At one point she almost pushed his coffee cup into his lap with the end of her pad.

Gerhardt looked terrible. His face was the dry colour of chalk and he had failed to remove a dash of shaving cream that had attached itself to his earlobe. He was sheepish and guilty, but confused, much in the same way our dog used to get when we tried to punish her for something she had done too much earlier in the day to remember.

After breakfast we reconvened in the lobby. Annie joined us, having eaten little of the breakfast I brought back to the room for her. Gerhardt had arranged for a taxi to meet us at the pier beside the hotel patio. The driver wore a leather jacket and a Panama hat. He had soft hands with which he helped each of us into the boat, except for Gerhardt who waved him away and leapt onto the deck unassisted. This seemed to brighten his mood. The driver smelled strongly of cigarettes. He had no interest in trying to communicate with us. He spoke to the hotel bellhop and laughed heartily. When we had all found places inside the cabin, he stepped down to have a look, apparently to be sure we were all happily situated. He smiled when it looked as if we were.

It was lovely on the water, warmer than it had been the day before. Gerhardt stood outside beside the driver looking forward in his conqueror's pose. Maureen, June, Annie and I sat turned in our seats watching as the city passed. A good number of eager tourists had risen early to see the monuments in the crisp morning light, when they were best.

The air in the cabin soon became stale and I went outside to join Gerhardt and the driver. The driver smiled and Gerhardt patted me on the shoulder. I sat down on the lowest of three varnished wooden steps that led up and over the side. A warm breeze skipped across the water. I was looking back towards the city over the engine's wake as we moved into the open lagoon. Gerhardt dropped down into a crouch beside me. 'I'm very pleased we could all make this trip together,' he said. The trip to Venice, as a whole, I think he meant. It was the right time to say such a thing.

After I agreed, he didn't say anything at all for a moment. We both looked back at Venice. And then, although his face was turned away and there was that breeze, I think he said, 'I love this city.'

He turned and smiled. 'And I love your mother. I do, Gordon.' He nodded emphatically. 'She is the most intelligent woman I have ever met, and I am not one to take that sort of thing lightly. I have learnt more from her in the year I've known her than . . . Well, do you know I've been married before?'

'I didn't,' I said.

'Yes: three times, all very quickly. No children. No brothers and sisters for you, I'm afraid . . . But I never felt about my other wives as I do about Maureen.'

I think I nodded and said, 'Good.' I had not even thought to dread such an episode; it had not crossed my mind that Gerhardt would want my blessing. I think of it now and it seems obvious he would want to prove his intentions to me. I was, after all, Maureen's only family.

'She is a difficult woman as I think you know, but it is a part of what I love about her,' and then he quickly added, 'I love *every* part of her.' He looked unhappier than he had before he began to speak. From his expression, it seemed what he was saying sounded as unconvincing to him as it did to me.

'I know you do,' I said, reassuringly. He was merely overwhelmed by Maureen, however. I had seen it many times before. She was such a bright light he could see nothing of her, so he presumed it must be love.

My reassurance did not satisfy him. He looked at his shoes. If there had been grass beneath his feet he would have grabbed a handful, and sifted it thoughtfully through his fingers. He seemed to be searching for something to say, something to prove he was surrendering to emotion. After a time, I thought I should say something. He seemed so uncomfortable, I was almost willing to tell him what he wanted to hear: that she loved him too. I am weak in the face of unhappiness; it is a kind of vanity. But he spared me this lie. 'It really is nice to have you and Annie with us . . . All of us together like this. I'm glad we did it.' He nodded.

From over the sounds of the slapping waves, I heard singing. It rose and fell with the quake of the boat, at moments all but disappearing, indecipherable from the repetition of waves at the hull, the ceaseless engine and the breeze. Gerhardt had heard it as well. He lifted his head as if he had caught a pleasant smell. I looked around, but could not see where the sound was coming from. The driver did not seem to have heard anything. And then a boat appeared beside us. It was filled to capacity with young men all wearing the same yellow and blue hats, scarves and jerseys. They passed close beside us and sang louder for our benefit. Some of them waved as best they could. They were crammed in so tightly many of them could not lift their arms. They looked like an ecstatically happy group of refugees. We waved back.

Annie came out from the cabin to have a look. She was holding her book. 'Look at that,' she said.

'Football,' said the driver.

'I wonder where they play?' said Annie.

Gerhardt exchanged a few words with the driver and reported that the yellow and blue team was not the local team. They came from Verona. They would be playing a green team, one of the local sides, in a stadium on the other side of the train station, north of Venice. Had we been going in the opposite direction we might have passed a boatload of green supporters, he said.

'Fun, isn't it?' asked Annie. She turned to go back inside, but Gerhardt had begun to tell a story. The singing had reminded him. His story concerned a Venetian nobleman who fell in love with a woman he had never seen. Every night he heard her singing, which was extraordinarily lovely, from somewhere across the canal. He fell in love with her voice. 'He was so besotted by her, he could not stand the presence of his own wife so he paid one of his servants to take her out into the lagoon at night. The servant was to pretend he was taking the woman to a fancy-dress party where her husband would join her later, but in the middle of the lagoon under the moonlight, the servant was actually meant to hit the poor woman over the head and drown her. As the nobleman watched the gondola float away, he thought he was finally free to find the woman he loved. Suddenly, he heard the singing again. After a moment's confusion, he realized it was coming from his wife. The magic of the canals is such that her singing in another part of the house had sounded as if it were coming from far away. He jumped into the lagoon and swam after her, but when the singing had stopped and he realized he was too late, he gave up, took a mouthful of canal water and sank to the bottom to join her. The singing had stopped, however, not because the servant had carried out his instructions, but because he had also fallen in love with the voice and decided to wager his own life in the form of a great kiss on the mouth of his master's wife. She was not pleased at first, but when he told her of her husband's plan, she became more receptive and the two were married and lived happily together.' He laughed.

We arrived at Torcello, and slowly circled the island until we came across the narrow opening that led into its only canal. The canal was barely wide enough for two boats to pass in either direction. We tied up beside a small restaurant and the driver helped us to shore. Standing up on the cement bank, Gerhardt looked down at the driver and told him firmly what time we expected him to take us back. We would spend a few hours at the cathedral and then have lunch, he explained. The driver smiled and waved. He removed his hat, revealing, to my surprise, a bald head, and waved again. As we walked away, following the canal in the direction of the cathedral, I turned around and saw the driver stepping into the restaurant. A woman met him at the door and kissed him on both cheeks.

As the path took us further from the restaurant, it became more dilapidated, more like a country road, with loose stones and pits of sand. We passed several chicken coops behind the restaurant and then the canal stopped in a small circle with just enough room for boats to turn around.

The place of interest, the reason Maureen had insisted upon our taking the trip, consisted of three dusty structures in varying states of decay. Maureen spoke as we walked. 'The cathedral of the San Maria Assunta was originally built in the seventh century and rebuilt in the eleventh. Next to it, the Church of San Fosca was built in the eleventh century when the cathedral was rebuilt. And the third building you see there, the Mueso dell' Estuario, is relatively modern, although it seems to be crumbling as fast as the other two which is not untypical. They can build things that last thousands of years and half of modern Rome is falling down.' (Out of interest, this line appears in her book verbatim.)

The buildings stood in a garden surrounded by fields of dry earth spotted with rugged bushes. Maureen led the way across the open courtyard holding her shoulder bag tightly behind her. The rest of us hurried to catch up. It was Maureen's excursion, but when she was 'on site', as she liked to call it, she did not like to play the tour guide. June seemed to want to stay close to her, as did Gerhardt, perhaps to supervise the two. Only Annie paused at the crucifix in a glassed case at the entrance to the cathedral. Maureen walked right past and presumably June felt

this was an indication it wasn't worth a stop. I stood beside
Annie and looked up at the sad yellowed figure. It was obviously modern. There was no plaque describing its origin. Some
devoted soul had included flowers, the dried petals of which
now rested at the bottom of the case.

Inside, the central chamber of the cathedral was in darkness
except for the far north-westerly corner where sunlight flooded
the open windows at the top of the domed roof. There were
only two other people inside, whispering to one another as they
contemplated the high altar. It was cold and the air inside was
damp. The grey stones of the floor had been worn away and
dipped at the centre. Maureen stood in the centre of the aisle
gazing around her. We all seemed to wait to see what she would
do. As I looked around, it struck me that Maureen and I had
been there once before when I was very young.

It was a humble structure – not a cathedral as the feudal
lords of other parts of Europe conceived them. The entire
western wall was covered in a green tarpaulin, presumably for
some restoration. There were no signs of any workmen. I
guessed they worked only at night when they would not intrude
upon the tourists. A series of columns ran down the centre of
the room towards the altar. I remembered that beneath the altar
there is said to be a sarcophagus containing the remains of
some saint. This was one of those pieces of information
Maureen used to give me as a child to keep me interested.

Maureen sat down in a pew from where she could study the
mosaic of the apotheosis of Christ and the Last Judgment,
which she had proclaimed to be of greatest interest to her. It
covered the entire north wall and was divided into six panels
depicting, amongst other things, Christ's descent into Limbo
and Satan hungrily awaiting his share of souls as the Archangel

Michael weighs the fate of the dead. The images of judgment are quite terrifying: crude but graphic depictions of eternal suffering which, even to a non-believer like myself, provide an uneasy feeling and can lead to a debilitating degree of intro-spection.

'They're marvellous,' said Maureen with hushed excite-ment. Her eyes widened as if to take in all their beauty at once. 'They've just finished work on them. They're just marvell-ous.' She got up and moved towards the wall. For a moment I thought she wouldn't stop. She wore a look of such conviction, she seemed to believe that she could pass through the space between the tiles and join the figures in the mosaic on either side. 'The identity of the artist is unknown.' She seemed to be addressing all of us, but she could just as easily have been talking to herself. 'It dates from either the twelfth or thirteenth century. Of course, it's a product of faith.' Maureen stood perfectly still gazing up at it for several minutes. She seemed overwhelmed. And then she remembered what she was there for and removed her notepad and jotted something down before staring at the image once again. June sat down behind her and began scribbling in her own notebook. Gerhardt stood off to the side contemplating the image with his chin in his hand – trying to look interested, I thought. Annie and I remained in the centre of the aisle until she turned and wandered further into the darkened interior of the cathedral. I watched her go and then pause to curtsy and make the sign of the cross in front of the altar. I remained in front of the mosaic for a few minutes more and then followed her. I passed the other couple in the aisle as I went. They smiled politely and gave way without letting go of one another's hands. I walked to the far corner of the cathedral where I thought Annie had gone, but she wasn't there. Nor was she in the opposite corner, drenched in dusty sunlight. The altar blocked the centre of the open space. I couldn't see around it, so I walked in a square towards the only corner where I had yet to check for her. She was not there either. Somehow I managed to look up. I was standing beneath the central apse and the mosaic of the Madonna. She rests on a gold background of such vivid colour it seemed to be daylight seeping through the stones. I remembered having seen this as well. Mary was holding baby Jesus in her left hand, gesturing towards him with her right, with a look of placid confidence. The figure of Mary is enormous, there is so much of her, and by comparison, the baby Jesus is small and fragile looking, but she seems to be proud of him, all the same. By comparison, the apostles at her feet are almost forgotten. All this with a collection of coloured stones. I was gazing upwards when Maureen appeared beside me.

'Isn't she lovely,' she said looking up. 'We know they got help from the Greeks, but there's nothing of comparison in all of Greece.'

Sunlight filled an archway at the rear of the cathedral. Annie is particularly susceptible to the cold. I thought she might have gone out to get warm in the sun.

She was sitting on a bench having a cigarette gazing into the neighbouring garden. The bells in the campanile were ringing. They say that on some days they can be heard in Venice. I remember frowning at my watch, as it was only ten of twelve.

'Not impressed?' she asked. She shaded her face with her hand and looked up at me.

'I thought you might want to light a candle.'

'We'll do that in the church next door,' she said. 'Look at

this,' she pointed into the garden. 'I just watched them come out over there,' she said. She indicated the entrance of the church where white confetti littered the ground. 'They started ringing the bells for them. I thought this was just for tourists and then out they came.' About a dozen people, the men dressed in black suits, the women in dresses, toasted a bride and groom. The couple were kissing. Rows of glasses rattled in the wind on two rectangular tables covered with white table-cloths.

'It looks like something out of an advertisement.'

'It's amazing, isn't it?' She pointed at the wedding party. 'They're pretending we're not here. The whole party just walked past and not one of them looked in my direction.'

'I suppose they got married this early so that they wouldn't have too many tourists to contend with.' I looked at Annie as she gazed intently at the wedding party. She wore an expression of troubled curiosity. 'Do you wish we had been married in a place like this?' I asked.

She laughed. 'This is something out of a fairy tale. Look at them . . . It's not real.'

We did not have lunch in the same restaurant where the driver had eaten. Gerhardt said there was somewhere better further along the canal. We ate in a large garden under a lemon tree. Gerhardt ordered two bottles of wine and by the end of the meal we were all quite exhausted. All but Maureen who had not fully participated in the lunchtime conversation and had not finished her first glass of wine. She had been busy reading through her books and her notes. Just when I thought I was prepared to crawl under the table and take a nap, Maureen stood up and announced that she was going back to the cathedral for a second look.

'I'd like to come along,' said Annie. 'I didn't get much of a look this morning.' She glanced around the table, somewhat uncomfortably. Annie does not like to make a spectacle of herself in any way.

'Love to have you,' said Maureen. Annie stood and they walked away, arm in arm.

After they were gone, June turned and put her hand on mine. 'I think it's nice for them to have a little time alone.'

'Yes,' I agreed.

They were gone over an hour. June and I had two coffees each, Gerhardt had a grappa and we shared June's packet of cigarettes. After a time, Gerhardt went inside to pay the bill. When he returned, he walked right past us and stepped over the short stone wall separating the garden restaurant from the small field filled with lemon trees. He walked for a little while and then turned to face us. I thought he was going to say something, but he lay down on his back, balanced one leg on the knee of the other for a time and then was still and, I thought, asleep.

June and I spoke intermittently. She told me more about her daughters. If I hadn't been married, I would have been sure she was offering them to me in that remarkably uncamouflaged way that mothers can. She began by telling me how much I would get along with Sheryl, the eldest, who, it turned out, was also married (perhaps this is what she thought we had in common). When we moved on to discussing my photographic career, she changed her mind and pushed Connie, an art major at Boston College. She had great legs, June said, because she did track. We quickly ran out of things to talk about. She spoke to me the way I imagined she had with her daughters' childhood friends, when she'd never had to carry on conversations with any of them for over an hour.

I did not worry about Annie and Maureen being alone together. Annie was practical when it came to matters of family. I do not believe that she ever thought to ask herself whether or not she liked Maureen. For Annie, it would have been an unimportant consideration. She did not usually withhold judgment – she had definite and often ungenerous opinions about the people she worked with – but family was beyond reproach.

Gerhardt remained motionless in the field with large black flies circling above him. I thought of going over to check his breathing. It would have been quite fitting, I thought, had he died, abruptly, after lunch.

When Maureen and Annie returned, they seemed to have been thoroughly energized. They walked arm in arm and were laughing about something they did not explain when they made it back to the table.

'You were gone a while,' I said.

'Did you commit the mosaic to memory?' asked June.

'Just about,' said Annie.

'We've had a meeting of the minds,' said Maureen. 'Haven't we?' Annie nodded obediently. Maureen had not released her arm. 'Where is Gerhardt?' asked Maureen. June and I pointed to the heap lying under the tree in the field.

'Oh dear,' said Maureen.

'I think it's all the rich food,' said June.

Maureen gazed at him for a few moments and then went back to her earlier thought. She tapped me on the shoulder. 'I've been discussing religion with your wife.'

'She's very religious, my wife.'

'That's right,' said Annie.

'She's articulated something I have had bouncing around in my head. We were looking at the mosaic and I made the flippant remark that I once thought it literal and narrow-minded to believe in organized religion – something for the unimaginative person – and she told me, quick as a flash, it has occurred to her that it might be literal-minded not to believe.'

'Or at least be open to it,' said Annie.

'Oh,' said June. 'That's a nice way of saying it.'

'Isn't it? I think it's articulated something for me exactly.'

Annie smiled. She made a gesture towards the table but was restrained by the fact that Maureen still held tightly, but affectionately, to her arm. 'We're agreed on one particular point, however.' Maureen continued. 'The ascent to heaven is impossible. The apotheosis as it is depicted in the mosaic inside cannot be taken seriously as a literal explanation for what happened. Only as a metaphor,' said Maureen. 'Which would not make you very popular with your pope.' Maureen gave Annie a little squeeze. 'The miracle is essential: it's why they're going out of business.'

'He's not my pope,' said Annie.

'That's right,' said Maureen. 'You pick and choose, don't you?'

Annie laughed at this. 'Yes,' she said.

'I don't know why metaphor should undermine its validity. I am not a believer like you, but if I were I would need no other proof than beautiful pictures. And since so many were made out of worship, perhaps I am a believer.' She shrugged. 'What is amazing to me is that so many beautiful things were created in such wicked times. What greater indication of God can there be but to look at a miserable middle-aged world, plague-ridden, slaves, death in childbirth, and paint something beautiful?'

'I agree with you,' said Annie. 'Or write something, I would add.'

'I can't believe you, Gordon,' she poked me again, 'have never mentioned your wife's interest in literature. Literature and painting are the most closely aligned of all the arts.'

'I'm a reader,' Annie protested. 'I would hardly describe myself as someone with an interest or understanding of literature.'

'Nonsense, don't run yourself down. You are not only a reader: you're a lover of books. If you look at the history of art and literature they go almost hand in hand. A painter like Bellini is essentially painting some of the intricate, racy scenes from the *Decameron*. Look at the slowly merging world of the Impressionists and you have Proust, the drawing rooms of Sargent and James. It goes all the way up: I don't count the abstractionists, except perhaps Stein and Picasso.'

Annie smiled. 'Well, of those, I've read James,' she said. 'And I find him a little dense.'

'Don't bully the girl,' said Gerhardt, rumbling towards us. His hair was ruffled and covered in grass, his shirt tail floated behind him. A large triangle of his face was red from the sun. He looked as if he felt dreadful. He sat down with a crash and took a long drink of water.

'I'm not bullying her,' said Maureen. She turned back to Annie, whom she had yet to release. I don't think I am wrong in remembering Annie actually struggling slightly to step away from her. 'You mustn't let anyone discourage you,' Maureen said to Annie. 'Do you know that this is the first century where it has not been considered an art in and unto itself to be a lover of the arts?'

'Yes,' said Annie.

'Oh, don't just agree with me unless you do. One of my favourite painters is Mary Cassatt because of the paintings she did of members of the audience at the opera. They themselves, the lookers, are worthy of study she seemed to be saying. Don't you agree? Do you know the painting, *In the Loge?*' she asked. 'Do you know they used to fill the opera boxes with mirrors so that the inhabitants could be more clearly seen?'

Annie was now definitely struggling, reaching towards the table. 'No,' said Annie. There was a flash of anger in Annie's face, which she quickly dropped. She turned and looked steadily into Maureen's face. 'Let me just get a *cigarette.*' She pulled herself from Maureen's grip and reached for June's packet of Vantages. 'May I?' she asked.

'Of course,' said June.

'It is also interesting to keep in mind that it was only possible to be a professional looker, as you say, if you were a part of the upper classes,' said Annie.

There was something clearly wrong with Maureen. As she watched Annie lean across the table for a cigarette, she looked as if she might burst into tears. She pointed at Gerhardt. 'How much has he had to drink, anyway?'

'I think he's suffering from over-consumption of food, rather than drink,' said June.

'Yes, you said that, thank you, June.'

Gerhardt looked up from his daze. 'What's that?' he asked.

'Nothing,' snapped Maureen. She turned back to Annie. 'Didn't you think that was marvellous?' she asked. 'Those mosaics are quite extraordinary.' She reached for Annie again and gently gave her arm a little shake. Maureen seemed profoundly unconfident in the gesture and looked at me in such a rushed manner it was as if she didn't know me.

'I did,' said Annie, shortly. 'Marvellous.' She looked at her watch. 'Isn't it time by now? Our driver must be waiting for us,' she said.

'Oh, yes,' said Gerhardt, struggling to his feet. 'Let's go, I think I've paid this.'

'You have,' said June helpfully.

On the way home, Gerhardt insisted we stop at the island of Burano so he could visit the men's room. Maureen elected to remain on board where she busied herself reviewing her notes; she seemed to have calmed down slightly since her semi-hysterical return to the restaurant, but still seemed preoccupied by something.

June, Annie and I accompanied Gerhardt onto shore. The centre of town was busy, the buildings painted in the characteristic vivid yellows, reds and greens. It resembled one of those model miniature cities popular in Holland. June bought us a lace tablecloth as a wedding present. While June went off to pay for our gift (which I had dutifully discouraged her from buying) I asked Annie if she'd had a nice time alone with Maureen. She said she had, but she was distracted by something; she was staring into the half distance with an unfocused look to her eyes. I presumed she was merely enjoying the tablecloth she continually stroked as if it were alive.

Twenty

Annie and I spent the late afternoon napping in our room. The sea air had made us tired. I had a bath and shaved. At one point, a pigeon appeared at the window and gazed in at me. When I returned to the room, Annie was awake. She was reading. I wish I could say she was not; that she could not; that she was only pretending to read. But she was reading. So much so that she had trouble taking her eyes from the page. After a moment, she put down her book. She pulled the sheets further up her chest and looked at her reflection in the television set. I could tell she was about to say something. 'Your mother doesn't think you're good for me,' she said.

I was strangely relieved. I had felt the presence of something all afternoon and was glad to finally know what it was. I stopped wiping the excess shaving cream from my face and sat down at the edge of the bed.

'What makes you think that?' I asked.

'She told me.' She was still looking at herself in the television.

'She told you that?' I asked. 'Did she say it specifically? Sometimes, it's difficult to understand her, especially in the presence of great art. She talks about the figures as if they were alive.'

Annie smiled. 'She said I mustn't be afraid. And then she asked if I was sure that you were good for me.'

'What did you say?'

Annie leaned forward and took the towel and rubbed my face for me. 'I said of course I was.'

'And what did she say?'

'She said she wasn't sure you were.' She studied my face for a moment and something in my expression told her it was safe to go on. 'She said that you do not possess the emotional maturity to be capable of love quite yet. She said it was entirely her fault and that she had tried her best, but that she was probably not the best candidate for motherhood.'

Something now in my expression told Annie she had gone too far. I had never imagined Maureen would be capable of such malice. In love, she once told me, there is constant betrayal, but this was different, this was viciousness.

'Don't get upset,' she said. 'I think your mother might actually be a little mad.'

I walked to the window and looked down into the skylights of the kitchen. A dozen men, all wearing little white hats, were busily preparing dinner. I could feel her watching me from where she sat in bed.

'I tried to make her feel better. I told her I didn't think you had turned out badly,' she said, trying to make light of it.

'What else did she say?' I asked.

'Nothing else.'

'I'm sure she said something else. Maureen is long-winded.'

There was a pause as Annie considered her best course of action.

'Are you sure she didn't say anything about how she tried to raise me on beautiful things, and keep me away from boring, practical things, but that it hadn't worked? They have no effect on me?'

'She might have said something along those lines.'

'And what do you think of that?' I asked.

'I think she might be mad. I think she felt terrible after she said it. That's why she was talking all that rot about literature and art. She was trying to make it all right again. Look, I wasn't going to tell you, but I thought . . . I don't know, I thought I'd be betraying you if I didn't, but now I think maybe I shouldn't have.'

I could feel Annie wondering what I would do. I stood up on the window still and faced the open window. 'Gordon?' she asked. 'What are you doing?'

I opened the towel and urinated on the skylights above the kitchen.

Twenty One

We met for drinks on the patio before dinner. We had to wait for June who was on the phone with one of her daughters. Annie, I noticed, was more attentive to me than usual. She held my hand and patted it gently. Maureen avoided my eye. I caught her glancing at me twice, and both times she looked quickly away like a guilty child. Gerhardt ordered a bottle of champagne and drank most of it himself. June appeared and accepted just a splash with a little orange juice and explained that she had a fear of champagne. 'My mother used to say champagne makes good girls dance and drop their pants.' Maureen said nothing as we sat outside. Gerhardt asked her repeatedly what was wrong and she responded that she was tired.

Gerhardt had booked us a table at a restaurant in another hotel. He said its restaurant was far superior to the one in our hotel. He added, 'I don't know why they don't get that sorted out.' He had stayed there once many years before, perhaps with another wife, and said that the rooms were far below par, but the food and the home-made grappa – in every imaginable flavour – were not to be missed. On our way, we passed through St Mark's Square. The crowd had thinned out significantly since the rush of the afternoon. Tourists and flick-ering glasses of beer filled the outdoor tables along the covered walkway. The square was brightly lit with lanterns. The white pavement was littered with the refuse of the day and crowded with pigeons pecking calmly at packets of crisps and crusts of bread. The sky had darkened to a racy gas-blue behind the respectability of the lanterns. There were at least half a dozen bands playing for different groups of tables around the square. There was a string quartet playing something melancholy not far from a jazz trio and beyond that, bizarrely, a polka band playing a polka. The music mingled and overlapped: the perfect accompaniment to the confusion of languages at the tables.

We walked swiftly through the square, a few paces between Annie and me and the rest. At the end, just before we passed under the arch into one of the narrow streets, a group of six musicians was playing a waltz. Half a dozen couples danced, swooping amongst tables, with varying degrees of grace. Gerhardt could not resist. Without warning, he lunged at Maureen, catching her skillfully by the wrist, his other hand around her waist. For the second time I saw the athleticism in Gerhardt. He had her perfectly in place, moving the first two steps to the left, her hips crushed against his, before the look of horror could surface on her face. He swung her around, forward and to the back, showing us his grinning face one moment, her miserable frown the next, like the spinning sides of a coin. June clapped and then stomped as if she were having trouble keeping herself under control. 'Oh, a waltz,' she cried. 'How lovely!' She began to weep. 'You two should dance as well.'

I watched them dance. There was something frightening about it. Her feet dragged along the pavement, her left arm struggled in his grip while the other hung lifeless at her side – she was resisting passively and aggressively at once. I have never taken dance lessons, I wish I had, but I knew this was not the way the waltz was done. 'Why must you maul me so?' she cried, but he ignored her or else he did not hear her, for his expression did not change from that grinning mask. Perhaps I misunderstood her. Annie and June laughed when she cried out. But I began to imagine the two of them together in the darkness: his stumbling to her bedroom at night, her pretending to be asleep. His clothes hurled in a pile in the corner of the room and his groping forward, extended towards her like the arm of a cuttlefish, his black poisonous fluids, and I almost pitied her, trapped as she was. The next time he turned her towards us, she lifted that lifeless arm and reached out for me. Each time she spun around, she was still reaching for me, but I did not take her hand. Instead, I turned and took Annie's and the two of us engaged in a clumsy waltz of our own, much to June's delight.

Everything in the restaurant was on display. A convoluted table laden with food snaked its way through the room. The famed bottles of grappa occupied the portion of the room nearest to an enormous and unseasonable fireplace, next to an exotic display of fruit that extended into an adjoining room where a mound of ice was covered in shellfish.

We were seated uncomfortably near the fireplace and all immediately shed layers. I sat between June and Maureen. Annie sat on Maureen's left and Gerhardt's right. June said to Maureen, 'Thank you so much for taking us out there.' Annie nodded her agreement. 'And you, you lucky thing, had the opportunity to go back twice,' continued June. 'It really was the most impressive thing I've seen since I've been in Europe. I must say, I think the Madonna is the real star of the show.

The other is far too frightening. It's like the inside of this restaurant.' And we all looked around.

We ordered and we ate. Gerhardt tipped the end of the wine bottle into his glass and immediately flagged one of the red-coated waiters for another. Maureen was silent. She looked shaken after her ordeal. But something had been decided in the square. She did not take her eyes from the tablecloth, as if she were performing furious calculations in the cross-stitching, until she leaned forward at one point and said to Annie, 'You must remove your hand from the table when you eat.' I could not remember then why it sounded familiar. June smiled and said it was good advice, but Annie ignored her. I was not watching. There was a revolving door at the front of the res-taurant, and a lantern outside flashed against the wall when the door turned. There were also several tanks of fish and I might have been watching them, their mouths opening and closing, as they stared at the buffet.

There was a sound – what sounded like a flap of wings from the rafters, a small cry – and I was reminded of the time Maureen and I sat in a restaurant opposite Notre Dame when a pigeon got in and all the waiters chased the poor bird around until it killed itself against the glass. A man at a neighbouring table sprang out of his chair, his napkin dripping from his hand, and his wife's hand on his sleeve. He was staring at our table. When I turned back, everything seemed in order. Everyone was seated where they had been a moment ago, except for Gerhardt who had fallen to his knees beside Maureen. Everything else seemed fine except for the fork standing erect between the tendons of Annie's left hand for just an instant before it slowly fell, with a clang, onto her plate.

The waiters kept their distance. Conversation had ceased

throughout the restaurant. I could clearly hear the stretching of the burning wood in the fireplace. Annie's hand began to bleed. I looked at Maureen. I wish I could say she appeared, at that moment, savage, that there was a flame in her eye, but there was not. She seemed quite calm. She may even have popped some morsel of food into her mouth. Annie slowly stood, cradling her injured hand against her chest, and she looked at me. It was a look I recognized: as if she were giving me a moment longer to react more appropriately. I had been subject to that look many times before – when we were alone together or with friends – whenever I failed to do something she expected. I remember that look as it appeared at what turned out to be the final dinner of our honeymoon, and I know I let her down.

I said nothing. I did not know what to say.

'I only touched her,' said Maureen testily.

'Let's all sit down,' I said.

'Yes, let's,' said June. You could almost hear the phone lines buzzing back home to Boston with the news. Gerhardt had begun dutifully to do what I had told him, clambering back onto his chair, when Maureen looked up at Annie and pointed at me: 'Do you see what you're in for?' she asked. And Annie, slowly realizing that I expected us to sit down and order dessert, raised her right hand as if she was going to strike Maureen. She instantly changed her mind and turned and walked across the room towards the ladies' room.

The rest of us sat there in silence, the looks of the rest of the customers in the restaurant bearing down on us. Finally June said, 'Perhaps you should go and see if she's all right.'

'Yes, do,' said Maureen.

'I think you should keep quiet,' said Gerhardt. Maureen did

not even look at him. I thought that perhaps this was some-thing she had already told herself.

I stood outside the ladies' room and listened. I heard the water running. 'Annie,' I called. 'Are you all right?' There was no answer. I knocked on the door, but there was still no answer. The water kept running and then a toilet flushed. There was some muffled conversation and then the door opened and a woman, not Annie, emerged. She looked at me as if she knew what I had done and went back into the restaurant.

'Is she all right?' asked Gerhardt. I turned to see him holding a glass of brandy (his remedy for everything) and a fresh white napkin.

'I don't know,' I said.

'Annie?' he asked in a commanding, manly voice. 'I'm coming in, all right?'

'Yes,' she said very casually.

I walked in behind Gerhardt. The room was brightly lit, but the walls were red, the unifying theme of the restaurant. Annie was running her hand under the cold water.

'Let me have a look at that,' said Gerhardt.

She dutifully lifted her hand. It looked unnaturally white from the cold water and it shook slightly. There were four little holes between the tendons of her middle and index fingers. She did not look at me.

'This doesn't look so bad,' said Gerhardt in a jolly voice. He became very grave and lifted the glass of brandy. 'This will hurt,' he said.

Annie nodded and looked away. He poured the glass of brandy over her hand and I saw her face flinch in the mirror. He patted her hand dry with a paper towel before tying the napkin tightly around her hand. It seemed he had done this before, perhaps in the Swiss Boy Scouts. Annie lifted her hand and looked at it and then looked at its reflection. She looked like a featherweight boxer preparing for a fight.

'Thank you,' she said.

'No trouble,' smiled Gerhardt. 'I don't think she intended to hurt you, Annie,' he said. 'I think it was a mistake.'

'Would you two mind excusing me?' she asked. 'I now need to use the toilet.'

'Of course,' said Gerhardt. 'Gordon . . .' He put his hand on my shoulder and guided me from the room.

Outside he said, 'Why don't you wait here and I'll take Maureen and June back to the hotel. I think what we need is a few hours for everyone to calm down.' He patted me on the shoulder and went back into the restaurant. I was amazed how sober he was in a crisis. I waited. Finally, the toilet flushed and the taps ran and then she stepped from the door.

'I'm ready to go,' she said.

We walked through the restaurant together. Everyone turned to look at us. She held her hand in front of her as if it was a torch on fire and at the sight of it people began to whisper. We walked home almost in silence. I said only one thing as we crossed over a little footbridge where happy couples were climbing into their rented gondolas. 'I'm sorry,' I said. And then, 'I think Gerhardt's right. I don't think she meant it really.'

'Your mother stabbed me in the hand with a fork.' Her calm was frightening.

'I think she didn't mean to do it that hard. She just meant to touch you.'

'Well she didn't seem very apologetic.'

'She can't, she's like a child in that way. What are you going to do?' I asked.

She turned and looked at me with what I now realize was disgust. 'Do?' she asked. 'I haven't decided. Perhaps I'll have her arrested.'

As we passed through the hotel lobby, Annie held her hand in the same obvious manner she had in the restaurant and people looked at her and commented. In the room she sat down in a chair by the window and put a cigarette in her mouth. 'Can you light it for me, please?' she asked, indicating her hand. I lit it and sat down on the bed. I was suddenly incredibly exhausted by the whole episode. A strange, sickly exhaustion, as if my health would be in danger if I did not lie flat on my back. I closed my eyes and quite unwillingly drifted off to sleep.

I slept deeply, but when I awoke, it was with a start. I was instantly sorry I had fallen asleep. It was early. I had the feeling that there were very few people awake in the world. Annie was sitting in the same chair, but she had not been there all night. I could tell from what she wore, from her hair, mussed at the back of her head, and from the rumpled outline in the sheets beside me. She sat looking out of the open window, doused in a thin layer of early morning light. She had been crying. Her make-up had run and her face was swollen.

'Come lie down,' I said.

'There's a flight at eleven. I've booked myself on it. That means taking a boat at eight-thirty or so. I went downstairs and did it after you were asleep. You can come if you like, there's room, or else you can stay here.'

'Of course I'll come.'

'There's something very wrong with you and Maureen,' she said.

'What do you mean?' I asked.

'I don't know,' she said, 'but I had no idea it went this deep.'

'What went this deep?'

'Your affections for one another.'

'Don't be silly.'

'I won't compete with her.' She shook her head hopelessly. 'I don't think I can. You should just stay.'

I got out of bed and began to pack. I had not even removed my shoes before I'd fallen asleep. It was an odd sensation. 'Let's just go,' I said. I stopped when my bag was half full and walked over to her. I put my hands on either armrest so that I had her trapped within the chair. 'Let's just go home,' I said. 'We won't have anything more to do with her.' She looked up at me as if she did not believe me, but before she could speak, I said, 'Nothing. Do you hear?'

Part Three

Twenty Two

In the darkness of the Heath, we were man and wife again. The dog wandered between us, twisting her head back and forth between loyalties. Annie looked unhappy. Her hands and feet were cold. 'You can have a nice warm bath when you get home,' I told her.

'Read a prayer at Maureen's funeral,' she said. 'Even if she didn't believe in it.'

When we returned to the top of the hill we saw the whole grey city and its flashing lights. We stood side by side and looked down. The empty bathing lake with nothing to reflect was a pure and oily black.

'I'm not going to the Algarve with my father,' she said.

'No?' I asked.

'No . . . I'm going with Heathcliff.'

'Heathcliff?'

She shook her head. 'Graham. You remember him. I'm going back to him. He's been around these last few weeks. We were in love, Gordy, and what we've realized is that we still are.' She wouldn't look at me. 'I didn't want to say anything. All afternoon I've been thinking I shouldn't say anything, not now, but no one likes a liar. I'm sorry about Maureen, but I thought lying would be . . . Well it wouldn't be any help, as hard as it is to tell you.' She glanced around either for the dog, or to check if there was anyone nearby.

'But I never went to see her,' I said. It was her turn to look confused.

'What are you talking about?' she asked. 'I never asked you not to see her.'

I stared at her silently. She reached out and touched the upper part of my arm. She squeezed it gently as if she were checking that there really was something in the sleeve.

'Don't pretend this is such a surprise,' she said. 'Come on, Gordy. We didn't last very long. It's not the end of the world. There was something not right and we found that out pretty quickly.' She turned her head to an angle and smiled. 'It's better this way, that we found out now,' she continued. 'I don't think you can make decisions the way we did.'

'Have a lovely time. Get some sun and things. I wish you luck . . .' As I spoke, I moved backwards away from her. I had to stop, as I felt the hill falling away behind me and I had the sudden sensation I would fall and roll down backwards into the bathing pond.

'Gordon,' she said pleadingly. She stepped forward.

'Please don't come any closer,' I said. I held out my hands to keep her away.

'Well, come and sit down, for God's sake,' she said, still coming towards me.

'How could you?' was all I could muster. She stood back, looking at me with horror. This is not, usually, the way I behave. I am ashamed to admit that I said it at all, but once it was out, I could not reclaim it. 'I wish you the best of luck.' I nodded finally and turned away. If someone had been watching from across the park, they might have thought I had finally convinced this persistent stranger she had the wrong person.

'How could *I*?' I heard her say as I walked away. After a moment, she called after me, but she didn't follow. I walked straight down the hill. The grass looked blue in the darkness – a quiet sea for me to cross.

She didn't call after me again. She stood still and watched me go and resisted shouting my name. She resisted the selfish temptation to try to make herself feel better by calling me back. I suppose I am grateful for that.

I had walked for several minutes before I finally turned and looked back in the direction I had come. There was no sign of her. The top of the hill was empty. My feet were wet again. They made a squelching sound with each step. I had not decided on the direction that I would go when I went. I headed for some trees and when I got there realizcd I did not recognize where I was. I found myself in an unfamiliar part of the Heath. It used to be what I liked most about the Heath; one does not have to be a stranger to get pleasantly, temporarily lost. But at that moment, I took no pleasure in being lost. I turned several times in a circle looking for a bearing and then decided there was nothing to do but go back the way I had come.

Twenty Three

Theo arrived on the Cape the day before yesterday. We met for dinner the night he arrived. He is staying in one of the larger hotels, one of the few that has not yet closed for the season. The windows have been winterized, the canopies have been taken in, leaving the cement patio and steel canopy poles exposed to the wind. He's not very fond of it, but has not, as far as I know, eaten anywhere else since he got here.

From across the dining room, Theo looked worried as he sipped from his martini, the twist of lemon bobbing face down. There was a time when I wanted to be just like Theo. And then there came a time when I hated the idea. As I watched him dip his little finger into the drink, and then into his mouth, I merely admired the fact that he had survived relatively unscathed.

As I came across the room, he looked up at me. He wiped the sad expression from his face with his napkin and stood, his hand extended. A long time seemed to pass as I slipped across the luxurious carpet before I surrendered my hand into his.

'Hey, there, Gordy,' he said. 'How are you?'

'I'm all right.' We shook hands for a moment longer, looking sincerely at one another. 'Let's sit,' I said finally. He released my hand and fell ungracefully back into his booth.

'What can we get you to drink?' he asked. He waved over a waiter and ordered me a martini. He waited until it arrived and then we raised our glasses. 'To your poor mother,' he said with finality.

'Yes,' I said.

'A wonderful woman. She was troubled, but that doesn't take anything away from her. I was crazy about her.'

'That's what Annie said.'

'What's that?'

'That you were always crazy about Maureen . . . Annie said you were always in love with her. That's why you bought her the house.'

Theo frowned. 'There are things a man has to do despite the failure of a marriage. She had run out of money . . . It doesn't mean I was in love with her.' He frowned with more emphasis.

'I didn't say it. Annie did.'

Theo shrugged and took a large sip of his martini. He held the long cardboard menu at arms' length and gazed down his nose through the top part of his bifocals. I am sure he already knew what he wanted, but he scrutinized every item. Perhaps he wanted a moment of silence. As he held the menu, he extended it a little too closely over the flame of the candle, and it slowly began to blacken. I watched smoke curl up the backside of the menu, leaving a blue-black stain along the white cardboard, and thought for a thrilling moment that it might go up in flames. Just in time, he retrieved the menu, never knowing how close he had come to setting it alight, and rested it on the table in front of him.

After the waiter took our order, and disappeared with the singed menu, I contemplated the black stain on the white table-cloth with the end of my finger.

'Annie has left me,' I told him.

He nodded, as if to suggest it was something he always knew would happen. 'Do you think it's for good?'

'I do.'

'She's never coming back?' he said into his glass.

'No.'

He has never told me that I made a mistake. Maureen thought that I made a mistake with Annie. Theo never took me aside and asked: Don't you remember? Never marry young. And we were very young. Perhaps he does not remember giving me that advice. Never marry again, Theo. I might return the favour.

'Gordon,' he said. 'You'll be all right. Look at me. I've lived through it more than once. I want you to know that you can come to Florida any time you want. You can come and stay. I think we should see more of one another. It's very sad about your mother, and now that we're both unmarried men . . .'

After dinner we walked from the restaurant into the lobby. Theo put his arm around my shoulder and walked me towards the exit. 'You sure you're all right staying at your mother's?' he asked.

'I'm fine,' I said.

Music came from a party in one of the ballrooms. The sound was muffled and then a door opened and the inviting music poured out of the room, interrupting the ringing phones and politely modulated conversation at the concierge's desk. Theo guided us towards the open door and we looked in. A group of people crowded around the door, shaking hands. A party was coming to its end. Behind the goodbyes, couples were still dancing. The men wore dark suits, the women heavy winter dresses. An older couple danced in the middle of the room. They had been drinking; their skin glowed from the alcohol. They were still in love, still sexually appealing to one another. But it was easier after drinking. They danced slowly. He whispered in her ear and made her laugh.

'Look at that,' said Theo. He shook his head sadly. 'It's a wedding,' he said.

'How do you know?'

'They invited all the guests who are staying at the hotel. There's only three of us.'

'That was kind of them.'

'You mustn't give up,' he said.

'Give up what?' I asked.

'Trying to be happy,' he said.

I don't think that I have ever consciously tried to be happy. I had always presumed that I was, but perhaps I wasn't.

'Your mother never gave up.'

Twenty Four

I don't think I have clearly explained what happened to Maureen. She did not react well to our leaving Venice. Perhaps, left behind with June and Gerhardt, she realized what she had done: the purgatory to which she had relegated herself. To what I imagine would have been his great relief, she released Gerhardt from the engagement. She did not call me. I sometimes wonder what might have been different if she had – if she had called and begged forgiveness. She called Theo. She confessed everything to him as if he were a parent who could magically improve everything. She said she had committed a crime, a violent crime, and his solution was to buy her this house where I have spent the past week. She agreed to end her travels and stay in one place. She might have changed her mind once she arrived, but, by then, it was too late. She had made an agreement with Theo.

This morning was the funeral. Theo and I decided on a plot in the graveyard near the sea. Unfortunately, it was very close to the neighbouring golf course. As we pulled the coffin from the hearse, there was a group of golfers looking for a ball in the rough beside the fence. They kindly removed their hats in a gesture of respect before playing through.

I assumed it was just going to be Theo and me until a small white taxi trundled up the dirt road. For a moment, I thought I was going to meet whatever friend Maureen had made in her months of exile, but when the door opened, June Reynolds got out.

She struggled up the yellow hill with her skirt in one hand; the other hand out-stretched to balance herself. When she arrived she seemed very happy to see me. She gave me a kiss on my cheek. I introduced her to Theo. She told him she had heard a lot about him. I wondered from whom. She said that she was in Boston visiting her daughters and read the announcement in the paper. The announcement had been Theo's idea. 'I was in regular touch with her,' she said. 'I used her book, as she worked on it, as a guide and was able to be of some assistance in confirming factual information when she needed it. I was her eyes and ears on the ground when she needed them. Of course, she didn't . . . Well, rarely, anyway. She had a mind like a steel trap, didn't she?'

Theo and I nodded.

Our party walked towards the open grave. 'Gerhardt's distraught,' June whispered to me. 'We've seen something of one another since she broke off the engagement. I've stayed with him in Vienna. He's really devastated . . . I don't think there was anyone she could really tolerate as a companion . . . Well, except you.' She patted me on the shoulder.

'Are you two getting married?' I asked.

'Oh . . . Well,' said June with her hand on her chest. She looked so much better than when I'd last seen her, I could think of no other explanation. 'We haven't gotten that far, Gordy.' She looked at the ground and her spine seemed to shrink by at least one vertebra.

'I wish you happiness,' I said.

'Thank you, Gordon.' She looked up at me with wind-tears in her eyes.

The priest was standing by politely, waiting for June to be quiet. I had taken Annie's advice and decided on a few prayers. I don't think Maureen would have minded. The priest began to read. I had chosen the passages from a Bible Maureen had on her shelf amongst her art books in her reference section. The St James' had belonged to her mother and had my grandmother's maiden name written in the cover. The passages I chose were underlined and Maureen's notes filled the margins for reasons (having read her book) I can't tell. I could not concentrate on what the priest was saying. Instead, I thought of the final pages of Maureen's book and realized I had decided wrongly. I should have had the priest read from those pages instead. The effect would have been far less depressing. To hear her words in someone else's voice would have done me good. Her voice lives in my mind. Her impression of what is beautiful and what is not, what will last and what will be forgotten, floating above the grass, the chop of the golf game and then over the waves into the sea, would have made her happy. Perhaps I will print up a small selection of these pages and send it to everyone we've known as a Christmas card. Christmas is a few weeks away. It could be waiting for Annie and Heathcliff in the pile of mail behind their door when they return from Portugal:

> ... One final glimpse from the portal window, from the gangplank, or the railing. The separation always feels like forever. And the protest is always the same, 'But I haven't seen enough. I am not full up! I would like to have seen a little more of Paris. One more afternoon coffee on the St Andre des Arts. One more morning in the Musée Rodin.'

Or, 'Another day in London is all I ask. If I were to get up early and have just a sandwich for lunch I could do two museums in a day ... One more afternoon in Madrid amidst the Goyas and Picassos, if you please. One more lazy afternoon in Rome. One more gondola ride in Venice ... It is here that I have felt most alive, most in love. Here where my eyes are open.' And it feels that life is not possible, it cannot go on at home in normal circumstances and indeed it cannot! ... I pity you ... The only solace is that the door is not shut behind you. There is no rush. No haste required. For no matter the crowd that beats you back there, Europe will look fresh and new to the proper viewer. To friendly eyes, she will part the curtains and reveal ... the same quality that has attracted visitors and the greatest artists since these cities began: inspiration.

Twenty Five

One spring afternoon, almost a year after Annie and I had returned from our honeymoon, we were sitting in the garden when the phone began to ring. I mistook it for the neighbour's. There was a breeze. The clouds drifted by at incredible heights as the remnants of lunch slowly hardened in the sun. Annie sat at the top of the garden stairs. Her legs extended down the stone steps towards the living room's open French doors. She sat twisted sideways over a portion of the newspaper, defiantly reading even when it reared up against the small stone she had placed on its spine. At the sound of the phone, she did not move. When the far-away ringing finally went quiet I guessed I had been right: the ringing phone belonged to next door or upstairs. It was impossible to tell which. Windows everywhere stood open.

A moment later, the ringing began again. Something in the wind changed and this time I was certain it was ours. I leapt from my chair and dashed inside. At that time, I was not the sort of person who could let the phone ring unanswered. I have always envied Annie's capacity to remain, in this way, unreachable. I paused in the living room, my hand on the receiver, and looked back at Annie, a ray of sun bearing down on her. She looked extraordinarily beautiful at that moment, brightly lit, and I was struck by the comparative darkness of the room. I remember everything precisely, though I took no note of it at the time. In truth, I picked up the phone immediately, no moment to catch my breath, or notice my surroundings. These details came slowly, creeping in from the periphery: Annie on the steps, my beating heart, the shadows of the room. As I remember it, however, I'd rather let the phone ring a moment . . .

'Gordy?' Maureen asked urgently. 'That's you, isn't it?' Maureen never called on the weekend. It had been agreed: we spoke on Tuesday evenings when Annie went directly from work to her book group, from where she returned, rosy-cheeked and slightly drunk, after nine. Annie tolerated the Tuesday night arrangement. A year had passed since I last saw Maureen: a year since Annie and I limped home from our botched honeymoon.

I lifted the phone and carried it to the middle of the room from where I could keep an eye on Annie stroking Clara's head. She took a moment away from her reading to talk quietly to the dog. Maureen apologized for interrupting our Sunday. I took her apology sincerely. She spoke with a strange formality. I assured her she shouldn't worry, but noticed the tightness with which I held the phone to my ear as if I feared letting her voice into the room. 'You know I wouldn't call if I didn't need to,' she said.

'Of course.'

'Are you alone?'

'For the moment.'

'Right. I see what you mean . . . I've had extremely high levels of hormones,' Maureen said.

'Oh?' I asked. I did not know what she meant. A self-conscious, declarative statement of this kind was hardly out of character.

'High hormonal level,' Maureen said. 'Body trying to heal itself and all that . . . I've been very low on energy as well. For about a year now.'

She was shy about her symptoms. I imagined little black hairs sprouting from her chin and upper lip. The effect of sudden ugliness on a woman like Maureen would have been terrible.

'They gave me a blood test which confirmed the abnormal hormone level. So they decided on a scan,' she explained. This was when the conversation changed, when the day turned over on itself. 'Right between the eyes,' she paused and swallowed. 'These headaches,' Maureen continued and I imagined her elegant, well-tended fingers running up and down the bridge of her nose. 'They saw what they hypothesize to be a malignant tumour, Gordy. In *my* brain,' she added, as if she still had to remind herself something so banal could take root in her beautiful mind.

I found it difficult to grasp the reality of what she had said. The technical terminology is, of course, designed for this purpose. And through Maureen, I found it even more difficult to comprehend. Maureen's speech had always been infused with what she poached from more informed sources. Throughout my life, she freely quoted the observations of art historians as if they were her own. If someone were to publish her book, it could be a plagiarism nightmare. I only realized how much she had borrowed from the work of certain scholars when I was at art college and read some of those texts myself.

She was still talking, recounting, apparently, everything her doctor had said to her. The room felt suddenly still. A cloud darkened the garden again and I realized my mind was drifting off. How inappropriate, I thought, to drift off then. But, inappropriate or not, that's the way it was. I felt just as I used to when she went on about a sculptor who had made innovative use of jacaranda wood, or the revolutionary effects of a readily available safe lacquer solvent.

'Gordy?' she asked again.

'I'm here.' I could hear her breathing.

'It makes sense,' she said with a small laugh. 'Haven't exactly been myself, lately, have I?' She was here in her home in Cape Cod that Theo had bought her. I had not seen the house then so I couldn't picture her. She was trying to sound jolly but was unconvincing.

'What do you mean?' I asked.

'Well. It makes sense there's something wrong with my head, considering . . . Well, considering my moods.'

I said nothing. Maureen and I listened to one another breathe. She sounded so alive. I could hear her smoking.

'They said it's an easy thing,' she said finally.

Maureen used to say that if she got sick she'd never have any of their operations. She'd prefer to be left alone, she claimed, and die at her own pace. Shoot me, she used to say, if it comes to that. But in the end, she was too afraid.

'They said it's an easy thing,' she said again. She sounded almost ashamed, as if it was some damage she herself had inflicted.

A particularly strong breeze raised the skirt of the tablecloth outside, rattling the silverware against the plates. The sound startled me. I thought it had been Annie entering the room. But when I turned to meet her, to perhaps make up some lie as to who was on the other end of the phone, I found her still reading peacefully where I had left her.

Maureen finished an extra long drag on her cigarette. They would not have to split her open, she explained. They would go up her nose guided by a miniature, deep-sea camera. They would lance the tumour and suck it out of her nostril like a large, hard, bloody piece of snot. 'I'm lucky, they said, to get it so early.' I imagined she had been shown diagrams or videos explaining the procedure. They would cut open her belly and remove a small piece of fat to use as spackling to close up the hole at the top of her nasal passage. The process, they had explained, is similar to the way ancient Egyptians preserved their pharaohs. They pulled their entire brains through their nostrils. I thought the comparison was in poor taste. 'Your mum is being mummified,' Maureen exclaimed with a brave, hollow chuckle.

'It'll be all right,' I told her.

'Well, of course it will,' she said with some irritation. 'Of course it will.'

'When are they planning the operation?' I asked.

'End of the week, supposedly. Doctor Auddi is a dream.'

'Would you like me to come and see you?' I asked hesitantly.

'Sorry?'

'I said, would you like me to come and see you?'

'No . . . no, no,' she said with more authority than I had heard in her voice for some time. 'Stay with Annie.'

'They say it's an easy procedure?' I found myself nodding reassuringly.

'Yes, you stay with Annie.' It was an act of real gallantry on her part. Perhaps she felt an act of such bravery might redeem her.

'Are you working a lot?' she asked just before we hung up.

'Yes,' I said. I was surprised at her question.

'Oh, good.' She took a breath as if she had something more to say, but kept quiet.

'I'll call you tomorrow,' I said.

She seemed pleased by that. 'Tomorrow,' she said and hung up.

I wish the conversation had been more eventful, but it wasn't. I passed a few moments alone in the living room watching Annie before I stepped outside onto the stone patio. The breeze slipped glassily under my arms. I can't remember what I was thinking. Except for a vague, overwhelming dread, my memory of the afternoon is quite without emotion. She didn't look away from the paper at first. She wore the oversize sunglasses she had kept in her hair throughout lunch. Clara lay next to her on her back with her legs in the air. The steam on Annie's tea curled like blue wax when the air was still.

'Who was that?' she asked. At the sound of her voice, Clara flipped around onto her side and looked at me as if I had performed a ventriloquist's trick.

I was silent long enough that Annie looked up at me, although I could not see her eyes through her glasses.

'That was Maureen,' I said, still watching the dog.

I could feel Annie give a slight start.

'She's ill,' I said.

Annie made a light scoffing sound, a sound that meant, *I'll say.* The wind once again raised a corner of the paper and she pushed it down with her hand. I could see the reflection of the print in her glasses.

'Is it serious?' she asked coldly.

'Oh,' I said. 'I shouldn't think so.'

'I'll pray for her,' said Annie. She looked at me defiantly. 'I really will,' she added, and looked back at the paper. I knew she wasn't reading, but she was pretending she could. It was just what Annie had said when we had last seen Maureen in Venice. 'I'll pray for her,' as if it was the lowest relegation; only a higher power could now wish her well.

Annie and I had sat together in our hotel room until it was light enough to go downstairs: about seven. The lobby was already surprisingly busy. While I checked out, Annie sat with the luggage in one of those striped silk chairs where Maureen had sat the day we arrived. They already had Gerhardt's credit card. The concierge told me that Mr Schontz (I had not thought to ask his last name) was having breakfast.

'They're inside having breakfast,' I told Annie. 'Would you like to say goodbye?'

'No, thank you,' she said coldly. So I went alone.

I walked the length of the enormous dining room. Only a few people were scattered around its edges. There was a design in the carpet that I had not noticed before, diamond shapes in which each foot fit perfectly; it was like crossing a red stream on neatly cut stepping stones.

June, Gerhardt and Maureen sat at a long table in the window. They did not see me coming until I had almost reached the table and then Maureen looked up and smiled, as if nothing strange had happened the night before. 'Good morning!' she called so that half the dining room could hear.

I told them we were leaving. June and Gerhardt protested, but I said it was decided. Maureen made no comment. She pretended to be distracted by something she had jotted down. Even when I addressed her directly – 'Goodbye, Maureen,' I said – she looked up and said, 'Goodbye, Gordy,' with a smile and lightness of tone that suggested we would be meeting for lunch.

As the boat floated from the pier, Annie stayed inside. She did not want a last look at Venice. I stood outside alone beside the driver, studying the hotel. I tried to decide where the separate palaces had been united. I looked for Maureen's balcony where I had stood and I looked at the windows in the restaurant to see if I could see Maureen and what she was doing. I did not immediately notice the figure standing on the edge of the pier. Her skirt flared in the wind and she was waving. There is a painting – I cannot remember which – that depicts a woman in a similar pose standing on a lone slick rock as the waves of an angry green sea crash around her. It was a painting Maureen liked. I think she may have been consciously or unconsciously imitating that pose, dramatic as it was; but somehow, I believed it. She was trying to say what she had failed to say before. Goodbye. She was sorry. If I had not known her as well as I did, I would have thought she was contemplating diving into the canal and swimming after us. I waved back until we lost sight of one another.

I looked up at the trees in our garden. The larger ones had only just started to bud, while a magnolia tree in the neighbouring garden had erupted a few days earlier into stunning pink flowers. The petals had already begun to leap dramatically over our wall. A small pile had accumulated on the tops of the high, green grass.

When I turned back towards Annie I caught her staring at me. She was holding down the paper with her right hand.

I think she looked frightened. She gazed at me through those large glasses for a long time. The steam from her tea had cooled and disappeared or else had been swept away by the breeze.